Emily Harvale lives in E
although she would prefer to live in the ~~~~
Alps…or Canada…or anywhere that has several
months of snow. Emily loves snow almost as much
as she loves Christmas.

Having worked in the City (London) for several
years, Emily returned to her home town of
Hastings where she spends her days writing. And
wondering if it will snow.

You can contact her via her website, Twitter,
Facebook or Instagram.

There is also a Facebook group where fans can
chat with Emily about her books, her writing day
and life in general. Details are on the 'For You'
page of Emily's website.

Author contacts:
www.emilyharvale.com
www.twitter.com/emilyharvale
www.facebook.com/emilyharvalewriter
www.instagram.com/emilyharvale

***

Scan the code above to see all Emily's books on Amazon

Also by this author:

Highland Fling
Lizzie Marshall's Wedding
The Golf Widows' Club
Sailing Solo
Carole Singer's Christmas
Christmas Wishes – Two short stories
A Slippery Slope
The Perfect Christmas Plan – A novella
Be Mine – A novella
...

The Goldebury Bay series:
Book One – Ninety Days of Summer
Book Two – Ninety Steps to Summerhill
Book Three – Ninety Days to Christmas
...

The Hideaway Down series:
Book One – A Christmas Hideaway
Book Two – Catch A Falling Star
Book Three – Walking on Sunshine
Book Four – Dancing in the Rain
...

Hall's Cross series
Deck the Halls
The Starlight Ball
...

Michaelmas Bay series
Christmas Secrets in Snowflake Cove
Blame it on the Moonlight
...

Lily Pond Lane series
The Cottage on Lily Pond Lane – Book One
The Cottage on Lily Pond Lane – Book Two

The Cottage

on

Lily Pond Lane

Book Two

Emily Harvale

ISBN 978-1-909917-35-4

Published by Crescent Gate Publishing

Print edition published worldwide 2018
E-edition published worldwide 2018

Editor Christina Harkness

Cover design by JR, Luke Brabants and Emily Harvale

This book is dedicated to David Cleworth.
Thank you for always being there.

Acknowledgements

My grateful thanks go to the following:

Christina Harkness for her patience and care in editing this book.

My webmaster, David Cleworth who does so much more than website stuff.

My cover design team, JR.

Luke Brabants. Luke is a talented artist and can be found at: www.lukebrabants.com

My wonderful friends for their friendship and love. You know I love you all.

All the fabulous members of my Readers' Club. You help and support me in so many ways and I am truly grateful for your ongoing friendship. I wouldn't be where I am today without you.

My Twitter and Facebook friends, and fans of my Facebook author page. It's great to chat with you. You help to keep me (relatively) sane!

Thank you for buying this book.

The Cottage on Lily Pond Lane

Part Three:

Autumn leaves

Chapter One

'Why do you keep looking at me like that?' Mia returned the kettle to its stand and handed a mug of tea to Ella who had been casting furtive glances at her since the moment Jet Cross had walked away from their group at the Summer Fête. That was more than an hour ago. An hour and sixteen minutes to be precise. Not that Mia had been constantly checking her watch, or anything. And checking the time had nothing to do with Jet Cross. Well, not entirely. She was waiting for her mum to come back, after Franklin had virtually dragged her off at the Fête. And what Garrick had been doing for the last hour and a quarter was a complete mystery. He had acted oddly at the Fête. But then, hadn't they all? That damned fortune-teller had a lot to answer for.

'You tell me.' Ella sat at the kitchen table and took the mug of tea.

'How would I know?' Mia dropped onto a chair opposite and fiddled nervously with the handle of her mug. 'Has it got something to do with that stupid fortune-teller?'

Ella leant forward. 'Partly, yes. I'd like to know exactly what she told you because you've been very secretive about the whole thing. But then so has everybody else.' She shrugged. 'It was supposed to be fun but everyone came out of that tent in turn, looking as if they'd been told something they'd rather not have heard. Everyone apart from me, that is. And Tiffany. Ah ha!' Ella pointed a finger at Mia. 'There it is. That look!'

Mia fidgeted in her seat. 'What look?'

'That look of guilt mixed with anger and sadness.'

'Really? That must be one hell of a weird expression.' Mia pulled a face and stuck out her tongue in an attempt to make light of it as Ella grinned at her. 'I think the searing, August sun has gone to your head, Ella Swann.' She picked up her mug and sipped her tea. She needed to keep her emotions in check. She couldn't tell Ella what she was feeling because she wasn't entirely sure herself. No. That wasn't true. She knew precisely what she was feeling, she simply didn't understand why she was feeling it. And she definitely couldn't discuss it with the sister of her boyfriend, even if Ella was her best friend. What could she say? She was in love with Garrick, yet she also yearned for someone else? And she did yearn for Jet Cross. There was no doubt about that. Merely talking to the man, made something inside her come alive.

'Oh yeah? Well it's definitely gone to yours too then. Tell me, because I'm more than a little curious. Why did you look so upset when Jet walked off? Bearing in mind you're dating my brother and you're supposed to be in love.'

Mia choked on her drink. 'I am in love,' she said, once she was able to stop coughing.

'Yes.' Ella looked her directly in the eye. 'But are you in love with Garrick? I really hope the answer's yes. And is there anything else you want to tell me? Anything at all?'

Luckily for Mia, before she had a chance to respond with anything more than the huge gasp of surprise that escaped her, Lori came racing into the kitchen. She flopped onto a chair and grinned like the cat that got the cream – and high on drugs at the same time. She was red-faced, wide-eyed and breathless, looking more like a teenager in love than a sixty-year-old, widowed mother.

'Whatever that fortune-teller told you,' she said, 'you'd better be prepared. The woman's a genius! No. That's not the right word, is it? A paragon? That's it. The woman's a paragon. She was spot on with what she told me and now that Franklin's told me what she said to him, it seems she was right on the nail with that too! Isn't it wonderful?'

'She was?' Mia heard the croak in her own voice and coughed to clear her throat. 'What did she say then?'

3

Lori glanced excitedly at Mia and Ella in turn before reaching out and taking one of Mia's hands in hers. 'Now I don't want you to get upset, darling because I know how you worry about me. Well, we worry about each other, don't we? And that's only natural. But I can't remember the last time I was this happy. Well I can, of course. It was spending those twenty-six years with your darling father. But since then, I mean. I can't recall ever having been this happy since darling Ernest passed away. But nothing's definite yet. Franklin's going to have a word with Jet and we'll have to see how that goes before we make any plans. Plus, of course, he'll still have to return to the States to sort everything out. And then there's the visa business and we all know what a stick-in-the mud the Government can be, don't we? So as I say, nothing's definite. You are happy for me, aren't you, darling? It's so exciting, isn't it?' She squeezed Mia's hand and gave a little scream of delight.

'I'm happy, if you're happy, Mum, but what are we happy about?'

'What's exciting, Lori?' Ella asked, before Mia could continue. 'You haven't told us what she said yet.'

'Haven't I?' Lori laughed. 'Oh dear me. I'm getting more and more like Hettie Burnstall every day, aren't I? But Franklin and I can't believe it. It's just so wonderful. Is there tea in the pot? I could murder a cup of tea.'

'I'll get you a cup.' Ella nodded and got to her feet. 'Franklin looked as white as a sheet when he came out of the tent. And for a Texan with a tan like his, that's saying something. Are you telling us that's what he looks like when he gets good news?'

Lori laughed again. 'It was a shock, I think. It was a shock to me, too, and I'm not sure I handled it any better than he did.'

Mia cast her mind back to earlier that afternoon. She knew she hadn't been the only one upset about the fortune-teller's predictions and now that she thought about it, Ella was the only one who had seemed pleased when she exited the crimson tent. And Tiffany of course. But Mia would rather not think about her. Then Jet had made that ludicrous comment when Mia had joked that she definitely wouldn't be getting engaged. After that, the bloody man had walked away. And if the fortune-teller's predictions were right, Jet Cross had walked out of Mia's life, forever. That thought had upset her far more than it should have.

Ella had gone in next, saying they should wait until all of them had been inside before divulging what they had each been told.

'Bloody Nora,' she had said, beaming at Justin the minute she stepped out of the tent but giving both Mia and Garrick rather odd looks. 'That was the best fifteen quid I've ever spent.'

When Justin had come out he had taken Ella's hand and said, 'I need time to think about that.'

5

Lori had smiled nervously after her turn. 'It's all nonsense. I'm sure it is.' But the surreptitious glances she gave Franklin indicated she wasn't sure at all.

Franklin had looked stunned when his turn was over. He had scratched his head, repositioned his Stetson and kicked a tuft of parched grass with his boot. 'I surely hope it's true,' he had said, seemingly unable to drag his gaze away from Lori.

Garrick was the only one who didn't say a word when he stepped back outside, but he had grabbed Mia's hand so tight it actually hurt.

'Everything okay?' Mia had asked, and added, when he hadn't replied: 'You're crushing my fingers, Garrick.'

He had looked down at their entwined hands, swallowed hard, relaxed his hold a little, and nodded. 'Sorry. Everything's fine,' he had said, sounding as if he were chewing sandpaper. 'She's not genuine, after all. As Lori said it's all a lot of nonsense, isn't it? Don't you think? I mean, how could she really know what's going to happen in the future?' He had cast a frantic look at everyone in the group and each one shook their head, if only just a fraction in Ella's case. 'She can't, can she? It's impossible.'

'She made a lot of sense to me,' Ella said, staring lovingly at Justin before giving Garrick a questioning look. 'I hear what you're saying, Garrick, but I sort of hope at least some of what she predicted for me comes true. Did she tell you something important? Something life-changing, perhaps?'

Garrick shook his head and studied the grass.

Ella sighed and glanced around. 'So are we going to tell each other what she said, or not?'

Mia tutted. 'She didn't make any sense to me. None whatsoever. So I wouldn't know where to start.'

'Same here,' said Garrick, swallowing hard again and coughing to clear his throat.

'I'm not repeating it in case that tempts Fate,' Lori said, laughing nervously. 'Not that I believe it. But just in case.'

Franklin shook his head but didn't say a word.

'I've just remembered,' Justin said, letting go of Ella's hand and turning to walk away. 'I need to have a word with Jet.'

Ella was clearly disappointed. 'Basically no one wants to open up, right? Fine. But if mine starts coming true, I'll tell you and then you may want to rethink because it seems pretty clear to me that the woman told us all one or two things we're not sure we wanted to hear.'

Franklin removed his Stetson, scratched his head and kicked at the dry grass again, before grabbing Lori by the hand, saying, 'Honey. I think we need to talk.' Without waiting for a response, he had marched her off in the direction of The Frog and Lily.

Garrick had looked as if he were about to be sick. 'I need to have a word with someone too,' he had said, and dashed off after Lori and Franklin.

Ella had given Mia a very odd look. 'Well, that leaves us then, doesn't it? What did the fortune-teller have to say to you? Is there something you want to tell me?'

Mia had thought for a second before forcing a smile. 'The only thing I want to tell you, is that I'm feeling a bit light-headed and I need a cup of tea and to get out of this heat. I'm going back to the cottage. If Garrick comes back, will you tell him where I've gone?' She had turned to walk away but Ella had fallen into step beside her.

'I'm coming with you,' she had said. 'I could do with a cup of tea myself and I wouldn't wash windows with the stuff they're selling here and calling tea.'

Now Mia watched Ella hand Lori a porcelain cup, and the happiness on Lori's face was unmistakeable. And that had nothing to do with the tea. Clearly something important must have happened after Franklin had marched her away.

'Start at the beginning, Mum,' Mia said, somewhat hesitantly. 'What did the fortune-teller say and what's happened since to make you so euphoric?'

'At the beginning?' Lori took a gulp of tea and beamed at Mia. 'Well, I suppose that would be the moment I laid eyes on Franklin Grant, wouldn't it? The last time I had a feeling like that was when I met your father. I knew at once that I was going to marry Ernest, and I was right. The minute I saw Franklin, I had that feeling.'

Mia gasped. 'That you'll marry him?'

'No. Well, yes. Um. Not exactly. What I meant was that I knew right away that Franklin was going to be important in my life, and yes, I suppose that we had a future together. Now before you mention the age difference, darling, we're both well aware of that. But does age really matter? What's that saying? Age is only a number.'

Ella went from looking astonished to amused. 'You're only as old as the man you're feeling. Which makes you about thirty-seven or something, doesn't it?'

Mia shot her a disapproving look. 'It's not funny, Ella.'

Ella returned it. 'I didn't say it was.' She smiled at Lori. 'I think it's brilliant. Good for you, Lori. That's what I say. Do you love him? I assume Franklin feels the same? And the fortune-teller predicted you'll have a future together?'

Lori nodded maniacally. 'Yes, yes, and yes!' She reached out and squeezed Mia's hand again. 'Oh please say you're happy for me, darling.'

Mia frowned. 'I am. If this is what you want. I'm just a bit worried, that's all. You've only known him a few weeks. Isn't it a bit too soon to be talking about Love and spending your future together? Even forgetting the age difference.' But as she said it, she realised that was a little hypocritical. She hadn't known Jet for much longer than Lori had known Franklin, so why was it hard to accept that Lori had fallen for Franklin? Mia definitely felt something for Jet, as she had finally accepted today. Whether she wanted to or not.

Lori's expression grew serious. 'You can spend a lifetime with a person and then discover you hardly know them at all, and you can spend a week with someone and know them inside out, upside down and backwards. There's no set timeframe for falling in love, darling. None of us has any control over that. Sometimes Love blossoms slowly from a bud into a flower and grows into something beautiful and serene. Other times, Love sweeps us up like a tornado, spins us round and round and dumps us somewhere that doesn't look anything like Kansas. And sometimes Love takes us by surprise. We don't see it coming until we're in so deep we can't get out, even if we wanted to.'

'And which one is you and Franklin?' Ella asked, grinning.

Lori pulled a silly face and gave a girlish giggle. 'A mixture of all three. It hit me like a tornado, blossomed into something beautiful and now I'm in so deep I'll never get out. Not that I want to. After Ernest passed, I never thought I'd feel this way again. I still have my darling Mia, of course, but it took me a long time to start living without Ernest. Once I did, I began to love life again. I love my book club and my friends. I love the cruises, the days out, meeting friends for coffee. I love it all. But I never expected to fall in love again. That was before I came here. Now, if you gave me a choice of having that comfortable life and getting into bed with a book each night, or getting into bed with Franklin each night but wondering what the future holds, I'll take uncertainty and disorientation any day of the week.' She giggled again. 'And twice on Sundays.'

'Eww!' Mia said. 'If that's a reference to you and Franklin having sex, I'm not sure I want that image in my head, thank you very much.'

'Oh don't be such a prude,' Ella said, laughing with Lori.

'I'm not a prude. I just ...' Mia suddenly remembered what Jet had said, about wishing his mum were still alive and that he wouldn't care what she did as long as she was happy. Lori definitely looked happy. She also looked years younger, somehow. Whether Mia wanted to or not, she had to admit that Franklin was the reason there was a huge smile on Lori's face and a twinkle in her eyes that Mia hadn't seen for years. 'I'm happy for you, Mum.' She leant forward and gave Lori a big hug. 'I'm truly happy for you.'

'So am I,' Ella said, coming round to their side of the table and joining in with the hug. 'But you still haven't told us what the fortune-teller said.'

Mia released Lori from her embrace. 'Or what Franklin said, for that matter.'

'Haven't I?' Lori looked genuinely surprised. 'Well, I think we'll need more tea for that.'

'I'll make it,' Ella said, walking back towards the kettle and grabbing a packet of biscuits as she passed the cupboard. 'Here. Have a chocolate digestive.'

Lori laughed as she took the packet before shaking her head and becoming more serious. 'I really didn't believe in people being able to tell the future. Until today. The moment I sat down, the woman told me I'd lost the man I loved but that I had built a happy life for myself and for my daughter. Can you believe that, darling? She knew all that within seconds.'

Mia thought about it for a moment. 'Perhaps someone in the village had given her information on everyone. I watched a documentary once, about a medium who performed at village halls. She had a researcher who mingled with the audience over tea and biscuits and asked people who they were hoping would 'get in touch'. She then went backstage and told the medium, and voila!'

'Don't be such a cynic,' Ella said, biting into a biscuit as she waited for the kettle to boil.

Lori frowned. 'It's possible, I suppose. Someone could've told her. Everyone in the village seems to know everyone else's business. But they couldn't possibly know what would happen between me and Franklin, could they? I mean, most people would assume we're just having a fling and that Franklin would return to the States as planned and that I would go home. So that's what the woman would've told me, wouldn't she?'

'And she didn't?' Mia asked.

Lori shook her head and smiled. 'Quite the opposite. She told me that she could see me riding a horse, wearing a Stetson. I'll be wearing the Stetson, not the horse.' She giggled and helped herself to another biscuit.

'You … you're going to Texas?' Mia was horrified. 'You can't! I mean, of course you can. It's your life. But Texas? Mum! That's the other side of the world.'

Lori reached out and grabbed Mia's hand once more. 'No, darling. Don't panic. I'm only going for a holiday. And it's hardly the other side of the world. It's a ten-hour plane journey. Franklin has to go back to Dallas at the end of this month and … well, I'll get to that.' She leant forward and kissed Mia on the cheek. 'I'd never leave you, darling, you know that. If all goes to plan, we'll be gone a month, possibly two.'

'We?' Ella put a pot of tea on the table. 'Does that mean Franklin's planning to come back?'

Lori beamed at her and nodded. 'But we're getting ahead of ourselves. I'm telling you about the fortune-teller. The next thing the woman said was that Love had taken me by surprise.' She giggled again. 'That's certainly true. She said that I

13

was right to trust it. That even though others may have doubts, this Love would last a lifetime. That my life was about to change. That by this time next year I would be living in a home filled with sunshine. And that was it.'

'What did she tell Franklin?' Ella asked, refilling their mugs and Lori's cup.

Lori added milk, stirred her drink and smiled dreamily. 'She told him that all his plans were about to change. That he'd found what he'd been searching for. That England would be his home. That he'd struck gold even though some may call him a fool. I'm not sure I like that bit, but I suppose it's true. People will say he's a fool. Why is it okay when older men date younger women, but it's frowned on when young men date older women? I hate those double standards. The only thing that worried me, when Franklin told me how he feels, was children.'

'Children?' Mia asked. 'Oh. You mean, if he wants children, because clearly you can't have them.'

Lori nodded, perhaps a little sadly.

'I read about a woman in her sixties giving birth,' Ella said. 'So never say never, Lori.'

'Dear Lord!' Lori laughed. 'Could you imagine that? But it's okay. Franklin says he's always preferred animals to children so providing I'll agree to us adopting a dog or two, and possibly a cat, he'll be a happy man. And besides...' She winked. '... As Franklin said, "When Mia has kids, we can watch over them." Oh Goodness, darling. Don't choke on your tea!'

'Did the fortune-teller tell you Mia would be having kids?' Ella asked excitedly, slapping Mia on her back.

'No,' Lori said. 'Franklin was merely assuming. Are you all right, darling?'

'I'm fine,' Mia mumbled, before taking another gulp of tea. 'What's the plan then? Is Franklin going back to the States and then returning here once his papers are sorted out?'

Lori nodded. 'He's leaving next week, as planned, but he's asking Jet right now if he can come back and work at Little Pond Farm. He seemed fairly certain Jet will say yes. At the moment, he's living in one of the farm cottages, and he's also sure Jet will agree to that arrangement continuing. Assuming that's all okay, I'll be going with Franklin for a month or so to sort things out at his home. We'll either return together, or, if things take longer, I'll come back before him. He's got dual citizenship because he was actually born in England and his dad's American, so that shouldn't be a problem, but you never know.'

Mia couldn't get her head around this. 'Next week? You're leaving with Franklin next week? So soon?'

'Yes, darling. I'd only intended to stay with you for a couple of weeks, but it's been almost eight already. I'll be popping home to check on everything, although Deirdre, next door's been keeping an eye on the place. I'll come back here after that and then I'll fly out with Franklin on Sunday.'

'Bloody Nora,' Ella said. 'You've made a lot of plans in one afternoon. And all because of a woman in a crimson tent.'

Lori shrugged. 'We'd been skirting around the issue of him leaving since the moment we both realised things were getting serious. I knew he was leaving and I didn't want him to go. He didn't want to go either. The fortune-teller merely brought things to a head and made us discuss the future. If it hadn't been for today, I think I would've been like one of those women in the Romcoms on TV. You know. Pleading with everyone at the airport to stop Franklin's plane, then clambering over the barriers when they won't, and racing along the tarmac. And for a sixty-year-old, that's not a good look.'

'So you're leaving?' Mia said. And the fortune-teller's words popped into her head. "Someone you love will soon walk out of your life. You can't hold them back. Some things are meant to be and some are not." Mia assumed the woman had meant Jet. Perhaps she hadn't. Perhaps the woman had meant Lori.

'Yes, darling, I'm leaving. But whatever happens, I'll be coming back.'

Ella laughed. 'You wouldn't need to chase his plane, Lori. He'd be causing chaos on board, realising he couldn't leave you, and the Captain would have him thrown off. It's almost a pity that isn't going to happen. I'd give anything to see that scene in real life.'

'What did the woman tell you?' Lori asked. 'You looked very happy after your turn but Justin looked a little sheepish. I may be wrong, but did she give you good news about your future too? Men never know quite how to deal with the fact that they're in love. It terrifies many of them to death.'

Ella nodded enthusiastically. 'She said I'd meet the man I'll marry, whilst solving a mystery with my best friend. But that a man I cared for seemed to be leading me a bit of a dance. Well, the first bit's obviously Mia and the mystery of Mattie, and I've met Justin. I didn't get that bit about him leading me a dance, at first and thought she meant he was two-timing me. But we're together every day and frankly, the poor guy wouldn't have the time.' She grinned. 'Or the energy. I make sure of that. But then I realised, Justin's a dancer, isn't he? So that's the dance bit. And she kept going on about dancing. She said she saw a ballet. A famous ballet about a swan. And then I got it. That's Swan Lake, obviously. My surname's Swann and his is Lake. Swann Lake, get it? We're clearly going to get married and I'm going to have one of those arty-farty double-barrelled surnames. I'm going to be Mrs Ella Swann-Lake! I love it! Don't you?' She nudged Mia in the arm. 'Are you listening to any of this, Mia? You seem miles away.'

'Sorry, what? Yes, yes. I'm listening. Yeah. That's great. I'm really pleased for you.'

Ella tutted and gave Mia an odd look. 'Yeah. You sound it. Anyway, Lori, it's weird that you mentioned Mia having kids, because the other thing the fortune-teller told me, was that I'll soon have news which will both thrill me and upset me. I'll soon hear that I'm to be an aunt!' She turned to face Mia. 'So as I said earlier, Mia. Is there anything you want to tell me? Because I've only got one brother and he's in love with you. Are a kid and marriage imminent?'

Mia's mug slipped from her hand, hit the table, soaked her with tea and smashed into pieces on the floor.

Chapter Two

Three things dawned on Mia. The first was that Ella had picked up on the fact that Mia might have feelings for someone other than Garrick, and that the person might be Jet. The second, was that the fortune-teller had been right about the things she had told Lori and Franklin. Was the woman also right about Ella soon becoming an aunt? Because if she was, that could only mean one thing. Mia would soon be pregnant.

She darted a look at her mum, who appeared to be about to explode with happiness. Then at Ella, whose expression was a mixture of excitement and uncertainty. Then another thing dawned on her. The fortune-teller hadn't said anything to her about a baby. Surely if she was pregnant, or would soon be, the woman would have said that. Wouldn't she?

'I'm not pregnant,' Mia said. 'I can't be. And my prediction said nothing about a baby.'

'Oh?' Lori's euphoria faded a fraction. 'Are you sure, darling?'

'Yes, of course I am. She said lots of weird things, but definitely, no baby.'

'I meant, are you sure you're not pregnant? But what exactly did she tell you, now we're on the subject?'

Mia sighed. 'I'm sure I'm not pregnant. As to what she said, well, that she saw great fortune, plus great sadness. Something about the weather. Though I've got no idea what that was about. Wind or something.'

'Pregnant women often get wind,' Ella said.

'Yeah right. How would you know that?' Mia asked.

'I read it somewhere. And I've watched *Call the Midwife*. That'll come in useful if we get snowed in and you can't get to the hospital.' She grinned.

'Thanks. I'll bear that in mind.' Mia grinned despite a feeling of dread welling up inside her. Or maybe that was wind, too.

'What else?' Lori asked.

'Er. Something about Love that's black and white and surprising too. A man I can't forget, and a woman I want to remember. She saw water and fear and overcoming things that've held me back. Oh, and someone I think I can trust, but can't, because their feelings may not be genuine. That Love may not be where I'm looking for it. The bit she did get right was about someone I love walking out of my life very soon and that I couldn't hold them back. Some things are meant to be and some are not. I thought she meant someone else, but that must be you, Mum.'

'Goodness! But as I said darling. I'll be back. What else?'

'Um. Oh! A bell. She heard a bell tolling.'

'Bloody Nora. That means death, doesn't it?'

'Thanks, Ella. But no. She said it was a beautiful sound although it brought a warning but I needn't fear because an angel is on my shoulder. And a powerful spirit is watching over me. Oh. She also said I should choose Love wisely. That I could easily make a mistake. That Autumn will bring changes and opportunities. Oh yes. And that she saw happiness and joy beyond my wildest dreams. That was it, I think.'

'Gosh, darling. She told you rather a lot, didn't she? But let's see. The fear of water is clear. I'm leaving, but coming back. I don't follow the black and white bit at all, or choosing Love wisely. You've chosen Garrick. Pregnancy brings changes, so that could be the Autumn part and the happiness and joy beyond your wildest dreams could be the part about a baby. Don't you think so?'

'No. I don't.' Something else popped into Mia's head. 'Oh God. How long have we been here, Ella?' She grabbed her phone and frantically swiped the screen to get to her calendar while Ella tried to count the weeks on her fingers and Lori said she didn't understand.

'What is it, darling? Have you missed your period?'

'She doesn't get proper periods anymore,' Ella said. 'Neither do I. We're on the contraceptive injection. It affects some people like that. I had my repeat one when I went to London to visit my uncle. Mia must've had hers before we came down here.'

Mia shook her head and stared at the screen. 'I didn't,' she mumbled. 'I meant to, but I didn't. After losing my job and being dumped and then with all the excitement of Mattie's will, I completely forgot. My last injection was in March.'

'March! Bloody Nora.' Ella stared at her in disbelief. 'It only lasts for eighteen weeks.'

'I know. I know. Oh dear God. This is all I need. But it doesn't mean I'm pregnant, does it?' She checked her watch.

'That's not going to tell you anything,' Ella said. 'Aren't you excited?'

'No! I mean. I don't know. And I was checking the time to see if I could get to a pharmacy. I'll have to take one of those tests. But I can't get one today. It's gone six already and it's Sunday, anyway. And the nearest one is miles away.'

'You could ask Bear,' Ella said, beaming at her.

'Bear?' Lori queried. 'Isn't he a vet? Are you suggesting my daughter takes a pregnancy test meant for animals?'

Ella laughed and shook her head. 'He's also a community first responder. You know, one of those first aid slash paramedic people. He might have a pregnancy test in his kit.'

Mia tutted. 'Don't be daft. He won't have one. Being pregnant isn't classed as an emergency. Although in my case, it is. Oh God, this can't be happening.' She leant forward and rested her head on the table top.

'What can't be happening?'

It was Garrick's voice but by the time Mia looked up and saw that he had Justin with him, Ella had already blurted it out.

'Mia may be pregnant. And if the fortune-teller's right. There's no doubt about it.'

'Thank you, Ella,' Mia hissed at her.

'What? He'll be over the moon once it sinks in what I said. Look. He is.'

Garrick's expression changed from one of concern to one of ecstasy and he rushed to Mia's side, pulled her to her feet and threw his arms around her. 'Oh Mia, Mia. You don't know how happy I am to hear this. We're going to have a baby. You and me. Us. Oh God, Mia. I'm the luckiest man in the world.'

'Er. Congratulations,' Justin said, barely audible above Garrick's hoots of joy.

'Wait!' Mia managed to free herself from Garrick's embrace. Her heart was thumping and her throat was tightening as if a noose had been wrapped around her neck. 'We don't know that yet. We don't know anything for sure. It's just a possibility. And a very vague one at that. The only things we have to go on are a fortune-teller's prediction and my stupid memory. Ella shouldn't have said anything. It's probably a false alarm.'

Garrick beamed at her and then at Justin. 'Well, this is perfect. And it doesn't matter if you are or not. I was going to do this anyway, so I may as well do it now.' He fiddled in his pocket, bent down on one knee and held out a box, covered in bright red velvet. 'I love you, Mia Ward. Would you make me not just the luckiest but also the happiest man in the world and say you'll marry me?'

Mia stared at him as beads of perspiration popped up across her forehead and her palms were clammy when she reached out to grip the back of a chair.

How had things suddenly got so crazy?

The room spun. Her head hurt and her body felt as if it was on fire. She may have said yes. She may have said no. But she didn't think she said anything, apart from, 'Oh dear God.'

And she drifted towards the floor.

Chapter Three

Mia opened her eyes and quickly closed them. Bear was hovering over her and she was on her bed. Her mum was sitting beside her, and Garrick, Ella and Justin were talking at the foot of it.

'I think she opened her eyes,' Lori said. 'Mia? Can you hear me, darling? She's not in a coma, is she?'

'No, she'll wake up soon,' Bear said. 'I guarantee it. And her heart rate and blood pressure are normal. Mia? Are you awake?'

She would speak in a second. She just needed one more moment to herself to think.

'Women often faint when they're pregnant,' Ella said. 'There's nothing to worry about, Garrick.'

'But she has been overdoing things. What with the daily walks on the beach trying to overcome her fear, spending days learning to fly that kite, training for the Frog Hill Run, not to mention all the stress of someone putting those warnings on the doorstep. Then there were the bets, and trying to find out about Mattie. She needs to take things easy.'

'She'll be fine,' Justin said. 'She's in good hands.'

'Are you sure?' Lori asked. 'Sure she'll be fine, I mean? Shouldn't we have called an ambulance, just in case?'

Mia couldn't put her mum through this. 'Mum. I'm fine.' She opened her eyes and smiled.

'Oh darling! You gave us all such a fright. How do you feel? Does anything hurt?'

'No. But I do have a bit of a headache. Is there any chance I could have a little sleep?'

Bear nodded. 'Let me just check your pupils then we'll leave you in peace. I believe congratulations are in order.'

Mia sighed. She wasn't in the mood to discuss it. 'Thanks. But it may be a bit premature.'

He grinned. 'The baby, or the congratulations. And you're now engaged, I hear.'

'Am I?'

'Don't you remember Garrick proposing?' Ella asked, stepping closer. 'Is she suffering from amnesia, Bear?'

'I'm not suffering from anything. I simply don't remember saying yes. Sorry. I didn't mean to snap. I'm hot, confused and tired. Please can we talk about this another time?'

'Everyone out,' Bear said. 'She needs to rest.'

'I want Mum to stay.' Mia clasped Lori's hand.

'That's fine.' Bear smiled down at her. 'You take things easy, Mia. Call me if the headache gets worse or if there's any other pain. I don't think there will be, but call me if in doubt. I'm fairly certain it's this heat that caused it. You need to drink more water. Okay?'

She nodded. 'Okay. Thanks, Bear. And … would you mind keeping all this to yourself for a while, please?'

'My lips are sealed.'

Garrick came and stood beside her. 'Are you sure you're okay? Would you like me to stay too?'

'I'm fine. And no. I just want to be with my mum. You understand, don't you?'

'Of course.' He bent down and gently kissed her on her forehead but he was clearly reluctant to leave. Ella had to virtually drag him out.

'Yell if you need us,' she said, smiling at Mia.

The moment they had left the room, Mia swung her legs off the bed and sat up. 'Dear God, Mum. What the hell is happening?'

'Darling? What are you doing? You need to rest.'

Mia stood up and stomped around the room. 'What I need is to get out of this madhouse for five minutes. I don't know how any of this happened. One minute we were sitting drinking tea, the next I'm pregnant and engaged. Did I say yes? Because I don't remember doing so.'

Lori looked flustered. 'Are you saying you don't want to be?'

'Yes. No. I don't know. What I want is to start this day all over again and not go near that bloody fortune-teller, that's what I want. And for Garrick not to have proposed. And for me to have remembered to get that damn injection. And for Jet to not be engaged and for you to not be going to Texas and ... Sorry. I didn't mean that.' She went back to the bed and flopped onto the edge. 'I just feel as if I've boarded what I thought was a carousel only to find out that it's one of those terror rides from hell. I want to get off and get on something slower. Like the kiddies' train or something. I'm not making any sense, am I?'

'You're making perfect sense. The last few months have been a roller coaster. Your job, your ex, the will, moving here, dating Garrick. I've added to that by falling in love, so now you're worried about me. And I know you're concerned about Ella too, even though Justin seems wonderful. I know you love Garrick, darling, but perhaps you weren't ready for the next step. And now, if you are pregnant. Well. That's a real life-changer.'

Mia sighed. 'I'm not, Mum. I'm sure I'm not. People say you know when you are. Did you?'

Lori nodded. 'Yes. But it's not the same for everyone. I had to have a test to be sure. There's nothing we can do this evening, but first thing in the morning, we'll find a pharmacy and get one.

Then we'll at least have an answer to one question. After that, you need to find a doctor. Whether you're pregnant or not. But what about the engagement? Don't you want to be engaged?'

Mia shook her head. 'I honestly don't know. Does that make sense? I love Garrick. I love being with him. I'm just not ready for all this, I don't think. If I was, I'd be ecstatic, wouldn't I? And I'm not. But perhaps it's this pregnancy scare. Perhaps if he'd asked me before this happened, things might've been different. I might've said yes.'

Lori squeezed her hand. 'Perhaps. But the problem, my darling, is that Garrick seems to think you did. And how we tell him you didn't, and yet still convince him you love him, may be a bit of an issue. Let's not worry about that right now. Let's snuggle up and I'll read to you. Then I'll tell everyone you don't want to be disturbed. You get a good night's rest and things may look a lot better in the morning.'

Mia wasn't convinced they would but lying beside her mum and listening to Lori's soothing voice, made her feel much more relaxed. She closed her eyes and let her mind drift back to her time at university then further back, to school, and weekends with her mum and dad. Then further still, to childhood and Christmases and birthdays and her dad teaching her to ride a bike. She'd had an idyllic childhood. She saw herself with Ella and Garrick, playing hide and seek in the garden at one of her birthday parties. The party when Garrick had kissed her on the lips. When she had first fallen in love with Garrick Swann. The year that she was six. The summer she nearly drowned.

She awoke with such a start; she didn't know where she was. The room was in darkness but a silver arrow of moonlight shot in above the top of the curtains. She must have fallen asleep. A fox called out in the distance but other than that, there was silence. Glancing at the clock beside her bed, she saw that it was midnight. She threw back the covers to get some air; the room was stifling. She felt like a caged bird. Not that she knew what one of those felt like. She went to the window and pulled back the curtains. The full moon seemed to be at eye level and it was huge. It cast a wide path of light across the sea and over the dunes and into the garden of Sunbeam Cottage. A path that appeared to lead right to her kitchen door.

She hesitated for an instant before throwing on her jeans, a T-shirt and a cardigan. The room may be warm but there might be a cool breeze on the sand. She tiptoed downstairs and hurried to the kitchen, opening the door as quietly as she could and only putting her sandals on once she was on the decking. Creeping down the wooden steps just as silently and running stealthily towards the wooden gate, instead of opening it, she jumped it like a hurdle and laughed quietly as she cheered herself for having cleared it without touching. Then she ran across the dunes and on to the dark brown sand. Closing her eyes, she spun like a whirling dervish until she toppled over. Laughing, she stood upright and held her head in her hands until she was certain it had stopped spinning. One of her dad's favourite songs popped into her mind and she tried to remember the words as she hummed the tune. It was something about dancing in the moonlight but it had been so long since she'd heard it. She stretched her arms out and swayed to the rhythm until the words came back to her. Every single one of them. And she danced and sang and sang and danced and laughed out loud. Then she stopped. Standing very still, she stared at the moon. And then she howled at it. And howled and howled until she cried. Then she walked towards the sea.

She heard the dog bark several seconds before she saw the man. The man she knew was Jet. The last man on earth she wanted to see right now. And yet the one man on earth she was glad was there.

'Going for a midnight swim?' His voice held a hint of concern even though he'd clearly tried to sound sarcastic.

'Fishing, actually. You?'

'Looking for mermaids. Legend has it they come ashore on the last full moon in August and dance on the sand and howl at the moon. I thought I saw one but I must've been mistaken.'

'You were watching!' She glared at him as he came closer.

He pointed to the beam of light cast by the moon across the sand. 'Couldn't help but notice.

I'm sure you weren't, but I need to check. You weren't going into the sea, were you? Only when someone is afraid of water, taking the plunge when she's clearly upset, isn't the wisest move she could make.'

'*She* isn't upset, for your information. *She* was simply getting rid of some emotions she's been holding in for far too long. And yes. I was thinking of going in. I know you'll think this sounds stupid but the moonlight and singing my dad's favourite song made me feel stronger somehow. More confident. More determined. And if you hadn't turned up and interrupted me, I think I might have actually done it. Paddled, I mean. Not swum. I'm not confident enough to start swimming again yet, especially not in the dark. What are you doing here anyway? It's a bit late to be taking Mattie for a walk, isn't it?'

'It's been a busy day and a particularly strange evening. I couldn't sleep, and nor could Mattie so we came down here instead. Is that honestly what you were going to do? Paddle?'

'Yes. Why? What did you think I was going to do?'

He shrugged. 'I wasn't exactly sure. You looked as if you were enjoying yourself. Until you started crying.'

'I was enjoying myself. And I was crying because Dad and I used to howl at the moon. The memory made me sad. But it also made me happy.

Oh my God! Did you think I was going to drown myself or something? I'm not mad, you know.'

'You don't have to be mad to drown yourself. People drown when they're drunk. And from where I was standing, you looked as if you could be drunk. That's what I thought. That you'd been celebrating and had far too much to drink. Although in your condition you shouldn't be drinking really.'

'My condition?'

'Yes. That's why I thought you probably weren't intentionally trying to drown yourself. Someone who's just got engaged and found out that they're pregnant is hardly likely to throw themselves in the sea, are they? Not when they're in love with someone as *fabulous* as Garrick.'

Mia's mouth fell open and she snapped it shut. Mattie ran into the sea but Jet's gaze remained on Mia.

'Don't be sarcastic about Garrick,' she finally said. 'But who told you that? Who said I'm pregnant and engaged?'

'Are you denying it? Are you saying it isn't true?'

'Yes. I mean. I don't know. About the pregnant bit, at least. I'm taking the test tomorrow. Not that it's any of your business. God. I don't know why I'm even telling you that.'

'Because I asked.' He glanced away briefly and whistled to Mattie who raced from the water to his side, shaking herself a few inches from him.

Not that he seemed bothered. 'And the engagement? Is that true? Or does that depend on the result of the test?'

'What? Are you suggesting that Garrick would only propose because I may be pregnant? Bloody cheek! I'll have you know he already had the ring and he was going to propose before he even had a hint that there might be a baby.'

He shook his head. 'Did I mention Garrick? It takes two people to get engaged. If the result is negative, will you still be engaged? Or is it too late to break it off? Now that everyone knows, I mean?'

'What are you going on about? Being engaged has nothing whatsoever to do with the result. And how does everyone know? I haven't said yes yet. Not for definite.'

He raised his brows. 'I heard you fainted because you were so surprised and thrilled. Is that not the case?'

'No, it isn't. I fainted because. Well. I don't actually know why. From the heat, I think. But it had nothing to do with being proposed to.'

'Well. Congratulations. It all seems a bit of a rush to me, but whatever. Let me know if you change your mind.' He turned and walked away and Mattie followed him.

'If I what?' Mia ran after him and walked backwards in front of him. 'Why would I change my mind and what do you care either way? You can hardly talk about things being rushed.' She poked him in the chest. 'I should be congratulating you. You've just got engaged to someone I didn't even know existed.'

He stopped in his tracks and stared at her. 'I've just what?'

'You heard me. I was there, remember? Or did you only have eyes for Tiffany? She came bouncing out of that tent like a bunny with too many batteries stuffed up her backside and suddenly you're engaged and—'

'Tiffany?' He seemed shocked. Then he burst out laughing. 'You thought … Oh good God, Mia. Although I must admit, that's a fairly apt description of her.' He shook his head. 'Tiffany isn't my girlfriend and she wasn't referring to me. She was merely telling me that the fortune-teller said she was going to get engaged. She's been dating her boyfriend for twelve years, and she's just given him an ultimatum along the lines of 'marry me or lose me forever'.'

'Then who is she? Garrick saw her at your house really early this morning. Well, yesterday morning now, I suppose. And he said she was adjusting your shirt or something.'

'Oh did he? Yes. She stayed the night.'

Mia gasped. 'Even though you know she's with someone else, you still slept with her? Or was she doing that to make her boyfriend jealous? Eww!'

'No! Why do you always think the worst of me? Tiff's my sister, Mia. Stepsister to be precise.

She's the daughter of my dad and the woman he ran off with. She's two years younger than me and I didn't know she existed until about nine months ago. I haven't seen or heard from Dad since he left and it was Mattie who told me about her, though how she found out I'll never know. All she said was that she knew someone who knew Tiff's mum. Anyway, Mattie arranged for us to meet and we've been getting to know each other ever since. She came to stay for the weekend to give her boyfriend time to think. And it worked. He's been texting her all weekend and he arrived on my doorstep this evening. Tiffany and Jeff are now engaged.'

'Engaged? So the fortune-teller was right?'

'Apparently so. As astonishing as that seems.'

'But … but I don't understand. How? When? Your sister? Honestly? She looks nothing like you.'

'There's a lot you don't understand. And a lot I don't either. Tiffany takes after her mum, although she's got black hair from Dad's side, and before you say she's a blonde, I know. But it's dyed.'

'Your sister?' Mia shook her head. 'So you're not engaged?'

'No, I'm not.' He laughed, but it wasn't a happy sound.

'Are you dating anyone?'

He cocked his head to one side. 'Excuse me? What's that got to do with anything?'

'Oh no. It hasn't. Nothing. I was just curious.'

He grinned at her. 'Oh were you? No, Mia. I'm not dating anyone. If I was, you'd be the first to know.'

'Would I? Why? I don't understand you. Sometimes I think you like me. Sometimes I think you're flirting with me. And sometimes you definitely are.'

He looked deep into her eyes and as she stared into his, she was sure she saw something she hadn't seen before. Something akin to passion. Perhaps even, to Love. Or was it merely the glint of moonlight in his eyes?

Suddenly he shrugged. 'Sometimes I do, I'll admit that. I suppose I can't help myself. I take after my dad. Everyone will tell you that. But don't get any ideas. There's something you should know about me. Some of the rumours are true. I don't consider myself a heartbreaker, or a womaniser, or some of the other things I expect I've been called. But I don't do relationships, that much is true. I don't lead women on, other than a little harmless flirting from time to time, I suppose, but I don't lie to them. I tell them the truth.'

'And what's the truth?'

'That I'm not the type to settle down. Marriage doesn't interest me. I've no intention of getting engaged. I'm not going to let a woman move in with me. I'm not interested in a long-term romance. For me, it's all about having fun with someone, then going our separate ways before anyone gets hurt. I'm as different from Garrick as it's possible to be. I don't want kids. I don't want a wife, a fiancée, or a permanent girlfriend. That's not going to change. I'm not going to change. One or two women in the past may have thought I might. But I won't. This is who I am. This is all any woman will ever get from me. Be grateful you've got Garrick.'

His voice, which was usually warm and caring, with a touch of amusement in his tone, now sounded cold and hard as granite. His mouth was a solid line with not the slightest hint of a twitch and the light went out of his eyes as he looked at her for a moment longer before walking past her without another word.

And this time, as Mattie ran after him, Mia walked the other way.

And this time, she didn't look back.

Chapter Four

The test was negative. And Mia had never been so relieved about a test result in her entire life. Garrick, on the other hand, was clearly disappointed. More than disappointed. He looked miserable, confused and anxious, all rolled into one.

'I know you're disappointed,' Mia said, taking his hand in hers after tossing the test in the bin in her en-suite bathroom. 'But it was far too soon for us to have a baby. There's plenty of time for that. And while we're on the subject, we'll have to take precautions. I need to register with a doctor and get another injection but until then, we need to take care.'

'What? Sorry, I didn't hear a word you said.'

Mia sighed. 'It doesn't matter, Garrick. I'll deal with it. Let's go downstairs and tell the others.'

He followed her out of the bedroom, looking like a lost puppy. 'Perhaps we should've got two tests. Just to be sure.'

Mia glanced at him over her shoulder. 'Those things are pretty accurate these days. You heard what the pharmacist said. And besides. I know this may sound strange but I don't feel pregnant.'

'It may be too soon for you to tell. And you hear about people who have no idea they're pregnant until the moment they're about to give birth.'

'That's true, I suppose. But the result was negative and I'm absolutely sure I'm not.' She stopped at the foot of the stairs and turned to face him. 'Why is this so important? I know you said you want a family and how much that all means to you, but don't you think it's better if we build our relationship first?'

'Yes.' He looked down at his feet. 'It's just …'

'Just what, Garrick?'

'Well?' Ella shrieked from the kitchen doorway. 'Is it yes or no? We're dying in here.'

'Garrick?' Mia pressed, but he shook his head, took her hand in his and headed towards the kitchen.

'It's no,' he said, sounding as if he might start sobbing at any moment.

Ella was almost as sad about it as Garrick.

'But if you're not pregnant,' she said. 'That means the fortune-teller got it wrong. And if she got that bit wrong, she may not be right about some of the other stuff.'

'The Swann-Lake bit you mean?' Mia sat down beside her mum and linked her arm through hers. 'But she was right about Mum and Franklin. Just because she was wrong about you being an aunt soon, doesn't mean she got everything wrong.'

Ella brightened at that but gave Lori a quizzical look. 'Everything's still okay with you and Franklin, isn't it?'

Lori smiled at Mia and then at Ella. 'Everything is fine with us. Better than fine, in fact. Franklin spoke to Jet last night and Jet said yes, he can come back and work at the farm and he, sorry, we, can live in the cottage for as long as we want.'

'Oh Mum.' Mia kissed her on the cheek. 'That's wonderful news. But what are you doing about the house?'

Lori shook her head. 'I don't know, darling. It's been our family home for years and I couldn't bring myself to sell it even after you moved out and I was rattling around there on my own. What do you think? Perhaps the time is right?'

'I'm happy with whatever you decide. Dad's been gone for such a long time and despite what Hettie says, I don't believe in ghosts.' Mia tapped her hand on her heart. 'Dad's here in my heart and he's in yours. We don't need our family home to keep him with us. Sell it, if you want, or rent it out and see. You may not like living on a farm. I know I definitely wouldn't. But of course, you can always move in here with me.'

'With you and Garrick,' Lori pointed out. 'Let's see how things go when we get back from Dallas. There's no rush to decide about the house right now. Deidre will keep an eye on it. That's the beauty of having good neighbours.'

'Speaking of neighbours,' Ella said, pouring them all coffees from the coffee pot on the table. 'Hettie wanted to hang around after she did her cleaning today, but I lied and told her you were having the test in town, so she eventually went home. But she knows all about it and she'll be back the moment she realises the van's outside and you're home. It seems everyone in the village knows.'

'I know,' Mia said, with a sigh. 'Jet knew last night. It must've been Bear.'

'Actually, I think it may have been Justin.' Ella put the coffee pot back on a cast iron trivet and slunk down on a chair. 'Don't glare at me. You only told Bear not to say anything, not Justin. I nipped out to get some fresh bread while you were out and I heard him telling one of his customers, and it was someone I've never even seen before. But wait a minute! Did you just say Jet knew last night?'

'When did you see Jet?' Garrick, who had been silent for the last couple of minutes, was suddenly back in the land of the living.

42

Mia took a deep breath. 'I couldn't sleep so I went for a walk in the moonlight. I bumped into Jet on the beach and he congratulated me. Us. On the engagement and the pregnancy.'

'You're always bumping into Jet on the beach,' Garrick said, his brows knit close together.

'We both like walking on the beach. It's just a coincidence.'

'At night?' Ella queried.

'Yes, at night. At any time. What? Do you think we've been sending each other messages or something? You know as well as I do that isn't possible. For one thing, there's no signal in this village and for another, I don't even know his phone number. Or his email. Not that I'd use them if I did.'

'Does it matter?' Lori asked, in a calming tone. 'I think we're all feeling a little fraught this morning. So much happened yesterday, perhaps we all need to take a step back and give one another some space.'

'That sounds good to me,' Mia said, getting to her feet. 'I'm going to go into the attic room and have another poke around. I'm determined to find something that will shed some light on who Mattie was, even if it kills me.'

'I've got work to do,' Ella said, but she didn't get up.

'Me too,' said Garrick, who also stayed where he was.

Lori got up. 'I'd better think about going home to let Deidre know what's happening and to get some more clothes. Oh. That's the doorbell. I'll get it.

'I can't face anyone this morning.' Mia gave Lori a pleading look.

'I'll deal with it.' Lori headed towards the door. 'Don't worry, whoever it is I'll send them away.

But less than two minutes later, she was back and Clive Dale, the solicitor was following behind her.

'Mr Dale!' Mia was surprised to see him. 'Were we expecting you? I'm sorry. Things have been a bit ... hectic lately. It's nice to see you. Would you like some coffee?'

Clive smiled and nodded his head. 'I apologise for arriving unannounced. I considered calling to make an appointment, Miss Ward, but the thing is, you see, I thought you'd want to know. I discussed it with my partners, and my son in particular, was of the opinion that you had a right to know without further delay. So here I am and I hope that it's not inconvenient. Coffee would be most appreciated, if it's no trouble.'

'I'll make some fresh,' Ella said, clearly forgetting she had work to do.

'Is anything wrong?' Garrick asked. 'That sounded rather serious. You said that Mia had a right to know something.'

'Yes, yes. I did.' He glanced around the kitchen. 'Miss Ward, is there somewhere we can discuss this in private?'

'Please Mr Dale, it's Mia, remember? And if it's all the same to you, I'd rather not discuss anything in private. The last time we did that, I missed more than half of what you said. My friends, Ella and Garrick know all about the inheritance and this is my mum, Lori Ward. I'm happy for them to hear what you have to say, if that's all right with you.'

He shook hands with each of them in turn and smiled. 'I'm pleased to meet you all. You, especially, Mrs Ward.'

'Please call me Lori and please sit down. You don't mind sitting in the kitchen, do you?'

He glanced around and sat on an empty chair. 'Not at all. The kitchen is the heart of any home. And the table will prove useful.'

He reached down into a large briefcase and pulled out a notepad, several pens, and a laptop that Mia recognised instantly as Mattie's. The one his son had taken just a few days after they arrived.

'I thought I wouldn't see that again,' she said. 'Have you finished with it? Am I allowed to look at it now?'

'That's what I'm here to discuss with you, Miss Ward. Mia. I apologise. Perhaps it's time you called me Clive. Yes, Mia. We have finished with the laptop, and whether or not you should look at it is the very thing my partners and I have been agonising over for the better part of two days at the end of last week. I was tempted to call on you this weekend, but family commitments prevented it. I came as soon as I could.'

'That does sound ominous,' Mia said, forcing a smile. She had had enough surprises over the weekend. She didn't relish the prospect of another. She waited for him to speak but he adjusted the position of the pens on the table so that they formed a straight line before moving his pad several times by just a fraction of an inch. 'Mr Dale? Clive? What do you want to tell me about the laptop?'

'Ah yes. The laptop. It's difficult to know how to say this, or precisely where to begin. I suppose the first thing I should mention is that, since the day my son gave the laptop to me, it's been with our IT department, which is small by any standards, but we're lucky to have one or two of the brightest brains as far as technology is concerned.'

'That's nice. Please go on.'

'Yes. Let me also add that this has been a difficult decision. Strictly speaking, Miss Matilda Ward is our client and as her executors, we are administering her estate. We feel, however, that as this matter involves you so specifically, we must divulge the details to you. Particularly, as my son has pointed out, with the new GDPR requirements.'

'GDPR?' Mia queried.

'General Data Protection Regulation.'

'Oh.' Mia glanced at Lori and shrugged, none the wiser.

'You will no doubt recall, the laptop was password protected. We've had situations in the past where it has proved necessary for us to gain access to a person's computer files. All legal and above board, of course, but these things happen. It has never taken our little team more than a day or two to 'crack the code'. On this occasion, it has taken them much longer.'

'Is that why you're returning it now? It's taken all this time to gain access to it?' Mia glanced from him to her mum and then to Garrick and Ella.

Clive nodded and licked his lips before adjusting his tie as though it were strangling him. He almost sighed when Ella handed him a cup of coffee. He took several sips and closed his eyes for a second then took a deep breath.

'It has, Miss Ward. Mia. It took them until last Wednesday, in fact. To use their exact words, or as close as I can without causing offence. "This was one mother-something-or-other to crack." Not just one password, but two, together with firewalls and the like. It seems they had never seen anything like it. Except for on one occasion when an associate of one of them had apparently attempted to 'hack' into MI6's computers.'

'MI6?' Mia burst out laughing. 'Sorry, Clive, but you're joking, aren't you?'

He raised his brows and his mouth turned down at the edges. 'No, Miss Ward. I am not.'

'Bloody Nora!' Ella laughed too.

Garrick shook his head. 'You mean to say that Mattie, a ninety-nine-year-old living in a sleepy village in the middle of nowhere had a laptop with military intelligence grade passwords and firewalls? I know everyone around here may be busy-bodies and gossips, but isn't that taking online security a little too far? Why would Mattie need that?'

Lori laughed along with Mia and Ella. 'Next you'll be telling us that great-aunt Matilda was a spy.'

'I can't confirm or deny that. But my partners and I are of the opinion that Miss Matilda Ward may well have worked in the Intelligence Service at some stage during her life.'

'You're serious, aren't you?' Garrick asked.

'Deadly.' Clive gave the tiniest hint of a smile. 'Perhaps that wasn't the most appropriate word to use. Yes. I am completely serious. And what I am about to tell you, I believe, confirms that.'

Mia, Ella and Lori stopped laughing and stared at one another and then at Garrick.

'You mean, there's more?' Mia queried. 'It's not just that the laptop was super-secure?'

'There's more. It will undoubtedly come as quite a shock so may I suggest you prepare yourself?'

Mia grabbed Lori's hand and took a deep breath. 'I'm ready.' Although what he could say that would shock her any more than he had, was beyond her.

Clive also breathed in deeply before linking his fingers and placing his hands on the table. 'Not only were there firewalls on Miss Matilda Ward's laptop, there was also some extremely sophisticated Spyware. Far more so than the usual Spyware used by hackers, or by criminals, intent on gaining access to someone's personal information and accounts.'

'You mean Mattie's laptop had a virus or something?' Ella asked.

'No. Miss Ward's laptop did not have the virus. This was the problem. We have a duty to our client but we also have a duty and responsibility to comply with and uphold the law.'

'Now you're worrying me,' Mia said. 'That sounds as if my great-aunt may have done something illegal.'

'I told you,' Ella jumped in. 'I knew she got her dosh from criminal activities!'

'She did not.' Clive said, glaring at Ella over his glasses. 'But she has taken a certain course of action which is, we feel, even considering the extenuating circumstances and your relationship, both illegal and immoral. Please let me explain.'

'Illegal and immoral?' Mia repeated.

'She was a high-class prostitute!' Ella declared. 'That was my second choice. Is this a good time for a vicar and tart joke?'

'No!' Clive and Mia exclaimed in unison.

'Miss Matilda Ward was not in that profession, I assure you. The action she has taken is related directly to Mia. As I said, the laptop contained extremely sophisticated Spyware. This is a particular type of program that is loaded by someone to gain unauthorised access to another person's computer. Sometimes it merely monitors keystrokes. Sometimes it accesses all a person's accounts and detailed information. Occasionally, it can watch a person's every move. It is, of course, illegal and immoral, as I stated, and I'm sure you can appreciate the difficulty we faced once this Spyware was discovered. The IT team made me aware of it immediately and no one else has seen the laptop or the information on it, but I have discussed it, of necessity, with my partners. Given the situation, we do not feel there would be any benefit in contacting the authorities. Miss Matilda Ward is deceased. The Spyware has been deactivated. It was only used to 'watch' not to carry out any other illegal activities. And, of course, you are related and are now the beneficiary of her estate.'

'Sorry.' Mia held up one hand to stop him. 'I don't understand. Watch? What has this got to do with me?'

Clive sighed deeply, straightened his back, removed his glasses and held them in his fingers. 'Miss Matilda Ward's laptop was running the Spyware. In this case, Mia, Miss Matilda Ward uploaded Spyware onto your computer without your knowledge, no doubt via an email or a link. To put it bluntly, your great-aunt was spying on you, monitoring everything you did online and watching your every move via your webcam. It seems she has been doing so for some considerable time.'

Chapter Five

It had taken at least another half an hour for Mia to fully comprehend what Clive Dale had told her and even then, neither she, nor anyone else in the room could totally believe it. But of course, it must be true. Mr Dale would not have said so if it wasn't.

'It does explain how Mattie knew so much about me,' Mia said, once Clive had finally left. 'To think that all this time, Mattie has been sitting in this cottage, watching me.' She shivered just thinking about it.

Ella grabbed a bottle of wine. 'I know it's not yet midday, but I think we could all do with a drink. Bloody Nora. What a deceitful old bag. And we all thought she was so nice and kind and understanding.'

'She may still have been those things,' Mia said. 'But she was also clearly one hell of a determined woman. She wanted to know about me, and she made sure she did that. I know it sounds strange, but I sort of admire her for that.'

'For being a voyeur?' Ella shrieked. 'She was watching you via your webcam. You know what that means, don't you? She could see you having sex!'

Mia gasped. 'What?'

'Only if you left your laptop open and in your bedroom,' Garrick said. 'Which you haven't done since we've been here so I assume you didn't at home. Besides, I can't really see her watching her great-niece's sexual exploits, can you?'

Ella frowned. 'Hettie Burnstall and all the others in the W.I. get great pleasure out of watching Justin and The Frog Hill Hounds.'

'That's a male stripper slash dance troupe,' Lori said. 'Who wouldn't want to watch those? But watching a relative having sex is a completely different matter. I can't see anyone wanting to do that. But I'm having difficulty in taking this in.'

Mia shrugged. 'Actually, with the state of my sex life before I came here, even when I was with the ex, she wouldn't have seen much anyway. I'm more concerned that she was monitoring me on social media and reading my emails. Even everything I ordered online, she could see. I know she wanted to get to know me but surely she could've just written me a letter or sent me an email asking to meet up, couldn't she? That's what I don't understand.'

'She was ostracized from the family, don't forget,' Lori said. 'Perhaps she felt you wouldn't want to meet her.'

'Well, she could've bloody well asked.'

'I agree,' Garrick said. 'But what interests me is how she got the Spyware and installed it. She either knew people who could do stuff like that, or she was a woman with very particular skills. I know I've always laughed at Ella when she's said she thought Mattie was a spy, but now that I've heard this, I'm wondering if there may be something in that, after all. Clive said he believed she may have worked in the Intelligence Service at some point.'

'A spy?' Mia said, laughing. 'My great-aunt Matilda was a spy? I don't think so.'

'I'm not saying she was a spy. She could've been a secretary who picked up some additional skills or had a friend who had access to this stuff. But then again, spies are often ordinary people, hidden under the cover of an ordinary life. That's what makes them so successful.'

'Yeah,' Ella said, handing Mia a glass of red wine. 'You've seen those TV shows where the family have no idea their dad works for the CIA and they all get kidnapped and he has to come and rescue them, killing all the bad guys in the process.'

'Er. This is England,' Garrick pointed out. 'And I can't see Mattie as a female James Bond, somehow either.'

'Why not?' Ella asked, giving Garrick a glass.

'Because it takes a particular type of person to do that sort of work,' Garrick said. 'But she may have been support staff or been involved in a less active way.'

'I don't know,' Lori said, taking the glass Ella passed to her. 'MI6 is full of people who, on the face of it, live ordinary lives, as you said yourself, Garrick. When you think of it like that, why not Mattie?'

'Because she was ninety-nine,' Mia said. 'Jumping out of planes and killing people with her bare hands might have proved a little taxing.'

'But she wasn't always ninety-nine,' Lori said, after taking a large sip of wine. 'She was young once. And to install that Spyware and watch you, darling, proves she was an extremely resourceful and determined woman. Think about it.'

Mia did think about it, and so did the others as they sat in silence drinking their wine for a couple of minutes, clearly trying to let it all sink in.

'Okay,' Mia said. 'Perhaps Mattie did work for MI6 at one time in her life. Even if it was as a secretary. But, you know, now that I'm thinking about it, this may not be so far-fetched after all and I'm wondering if she was more than that. We've all been astonished at how secretive she was. How there aren't any photos of her. How no one really knows anything about her and yet she knows everything about them. How all her important belongings were hidden away. Even her clothes were in hidden wardrobes, for heaven's sake. The woman was obsessed with secrecy. What if that was why? She would've been in her early twenties during the Second World War. I watched a documentary once about ordinary, everyday women who were recruited to go undercover during the war. What if she did that? What if Matilda Ward was far more than my spinster, great-aunt? And what if this had something to do with the reason why she was ostracized from the family?'

'And what if,' Ella added, 'she wasn't an English spy? What if she worked for the other side? What if she was a traitor? That would piss the family off enough to chuck her out, wouldn't it?'

'Yes' Garrick said. 'And it would've also got her hanged for treason.'

Ella sneered at him. 'Only if she got caught.'

'This is ridiculous, isn't it?' Mia said, suddenly laughing. 'And yet. It's not. We don't know half the things that went on during the war, or even after. Okay, perhaps the idea of Mattie being a spy is a stretch too far, but then again, perhaps it's not. And perhaps it had nothing to do with the war. Perhaps she got involved much later. Oh I don't know. Why did she have to be so secretive? But there must be records, mustn't there? There must be a way to find out.'

Garrick nodded. 'The Imperial War Museum has records, I believe, but spies would've been bound by the Official Secrets Act, so I don't know when those records were released. As for MI6, I have no idea if they keep records or not. And if she was simply support staff, I doubt they'd keep records of that.'

'I wonder if she was licensed to kill?' Ella asked. 'Especially if she was a spy during the war.'

Garrick shook his head. 'Women weren't in combat positions during the war.'

'Some were,' Mia said. 'That documentary I watched mentioned that. They were part of some special force or something set up by Winston Churchill in 1940 or thereabouts. They were taught how to kill with their bare hands and how to make bombs and all sorts of stuff like that. I wish I could remember more about it but I was only half-watching it at the time.'

'You could Google it,' Ella suggested. 'And you could even use Mattie's laptop to do so. There's something ironic about that. The code's been cracked and now we're going to find out all her little secrets.'

Mia grinned. 'Good thinking.' She opened the laptop again, using the new password Clive had written down for her, and typed in 'British women spies during World War Two'. Pages of search results appeared. At the very top, one item caught her attention. 'This is it. Women in the SOE. Which stands for Special Operations Executive.' She scanned the article. 'It says here that several women underwent military intelligence training including sabotage, espionage and silent killing.'

'Bloody Nora. Let me see.'

Mia turned the laptop around so that they could all see the articles and the more they read, the more Mia became convinced that Mattie did this, or something like it.

'It says there were female spies before SOE and some became mistresses of high-ranking enemy officers, risking their lives to obtain secrets and send them back to their British handlers. And look.' Mia pointed at a photo of one of the women. 'It says that many of the women went back to their ordinary lives after the war, never telling a soul what they did for their country. Isn't this amazing?' She slumped back in her chair. 'Mattie may have done this. And look at me. I can't even paddle because I'm terrified of water.'

'You can't compare yourself to these women, darling' Lori said. 'That was a different time. None of us know what we might be able to do if a situation demanded it. We all have hidden strengths. And remember. Only a few women were that heroic. As Garrick said, it takes a certain type to be able to kill with their bare hands.'

Ella burst out laughing. 'Hettie Burnstall has no idea how lucky she was. Mattie could've killed her anytime she wanted.'

'That's assuming Mattie actually was one of these women,' Garrick pointed out. 'And even if she was. That was years ago. What's she been doing since the end of the war? Are we all seriously saying we think she's been working for MI6?'

Mia nodded. 'I think perhaps she was, Garrick. I know I didn't believe it at first, but that's because it seems so bizarre to think that a relative of mine could've done something like this. But as you and Mum said, spies are ordinary people doing extraordinary things. I'm going to find out. I'm going to go through this laptop and see if it sheds any light on it. Clive showed us a couple of the folders with photos of me, but he also said there were photos of Mattie, didn't he? Or did I get that wrong? And did he really say that two of the files deleted themselves the moment his IT team managed to gain access to the file folders? Or was I imagining that?'

'You didn't imagine it. That's what he said. Her email account was re-routed and deleted and a couple of other folders too.'

'Which makes it seem even more likely, don't you think?'

'Possibly.' Garrick nodded. 'But it all seems so incredible, even though I'd like to believe it.'

Mia clicked on a folder called Sunbeam. Masses of photos appeared on the screen. Photos of everyone in the village. Some clearly taken without the person's knowledge and some clearly taken with it. There were photos of all of them, at various ages in their lives, from shortly after Mattie had moved in right up to shortly before she died. It was really rather creepy. Lori, Ella and Garrick peered at the screen as Mia scrolled through the photos. She tried not to linger on the

59

photos of Jet. But she did take a few extra moments to look at the photos of Jet with his mum, and the way he looked at her, made it clear how much he loved her. Mia caught herself wishing he would look at her like that. Even though she knew he never would.

When they found the folder with the photos of Mattie, none of them said a word. Mia scrolled through every one of them, although there weren't that many. They were all photos of Mattie long before she came to Little Pondale. And the more Mia looked at them, the more certain she was that there was far more to Mattie than she could ever have imagined. Which made her all the more determined to find out all she could.

None of them realised that hours had drifted away. Ella opened more wine and they ate the bread she'd bought earlier, with thick slices of the cheese Garrick had purchased from Little Pond Farm. They rarely spoke, except to say 'Bloody Nora' once or twice and to all agree that Mia definitely did resemble Mattie. There were several folders on the laptop and they wanted to get through as many as possible. It wasn't until the doorbell rang that Mia noticed it was five o'clock.

'I'll get it,' Garrick said, getting to his feet, and a few moments later, Mia heard Hettie's distinctive, 'Coo-ey! I hear congratulations are in order, you gorgeous young man.'

'Look.' Ella pointed at a photo of the attic room in Sunbeam Cottage. 'Mattie may've been a super-spy but she still managed to put a photo in the wrong folder. Unless the IT guys at the solicitors moved them.'

'No,' Mia said, hoping that Garrick would keep Hettie at bay. 'Clive told us they didn't touch them, once they realised what they were. But I see what you mean. These are all photos of Mattie, except this one.' She peered at the photo. 'And this was taken fairly recently. Look. Everything in the photo is exactly as it was the day we went up there, remember? Even the book on the desk. Wait a minute though.' She enlarged the photo on the screen and pointed to a pile of extremely slim books heaped on top of one another on the floor in front of the window seat; the spines, some of which looked pristine and some which were decidedly tatty, each one blurred by the enlargement, but still just about legible. 'Are those what I think they are?' She exchanged glances with Lori and Ella.

'Bloody Nora,' Ella said.

Lori nodded. 'I second that.'

Mia shook her head and sighed. 'Didn't Mattie ever do things the easy way?'

'I managed to put Hettie off,' Garrick said, striding back along the hall. 'I told her you're not pregnant and had fainted from exhaustion and the heat, so you need some time to rest. I hope that's okay. What's happened? Have I missed something?' He cast an anxious look at Mia, Ella and Lori.

Mia nodded. 'Yes. We all have. It seems that somewhere in this cottage, there's a pile of Mattie's diaries. I wonder where on earth she's hidden those.'

Chapter Six

Mia knew she had to face everyone sooner or later. The whole village would be buzzing about her 'news'. At least they all knew she wasn't pregnant. Hettie had clearly made sure of that. But after two days of supposed rest, during which time Lori had gone home to get more clothes and check everything was okay, and Mia, Ella and Garrick had searched high and low for Mattie's diaries – and come up empty-handed, it was time she told the villagers 'officially' that she and Garrick were engaged. They should have some sort of celebration. Now that she had finally decided that they were. Garrick, of course, along with everyone else, it seemed, assumed they were, regardless of the fact that she fainted and had not actually said yes. Congratulatory cards, together with cards with Get Well wishes had been arriving almost hourly and as another envelope plopped onto the floor as Mia was making her way downstairs, she smiled and went to pick it up.

But this card contained no congratulations or Get Well wish. This card said 'Bon Voyage'. It was obviously for her mum. She flipped the envelope over and frowned. It was her name scrawled across the front. She shrugged and walked towards the kitchen, opening the card as she went. What it said inside made her stop. The printed words said: 'Sorry you're leaving but have a wonderful trip' but under that, tiny scraps cut from either newspapers, or magazines and glued in place warned: 'If you stay, you'll wish you hadn't.'

For a moment she felt dizzy but she pulled herself together and dashed to the front door, yanking it open and racing outside. She scanned the lane but there was no one in sight. Ducks quacked on the pond and flapped their wings. A squirrel ran across the green, carrying a nut it had no doubt stolen from a nearby bird table, and a cool early morning breeze rustled the hedges and caught some falling leaves. Whoever had delivered the card was either invisible, or a very fast runner. And for some reason, she thought of Jet.

'Mia?' Ella said. 'Why are you standing on the doorstep in your nightdress?'

Mia turned, went back inside and closed the door. 'Because of this.'

She handed Ella the card and envelope and Ella read it.

'Bloody Nora! This arrived just now?'

Mia nodded. 'And whoever brought it should be in the Olympics because there's not a sign of them and I opened the door less than twenty seconds after that dropped through the letterbox.'

'I thought all this nasty stuff had ended. There's been nothing since the toy frog and the dead flowers and that was weeks ago.'

'Perhaps news of my engagement has made them think I need a reminder I'm not welcome here.'

'I think it's probably got more to do with news of Franklin and your mum. Let's face it, you being engaged to Garrick provides no reason for you to stay here. Your mum planning to move into a cottage on Little Pond Farm however. Well. That's called putting down roots. If Lori's staying, you're even more likely to, aren't you?'

'I hadn't thought of that. You're right. Please don't tell Mum about this, Ella. She's off to Texas in a couple of days and if she sees this, she'll worry about me and may not go. I'm not bothered by this and I don't want this nonsense to spoil her chance of happiness.'

Ella linked her arm through Mia's and led her towards the kitchen. 'I won't say a word. But whether she goes to Texas or not, won't affect her chance of happiness. You've seen the way Franklin looks at her. I would stake my life on that man loving your mum, come hell or high water. Sorry. Forget the high water. But you know what I mean. He'll love her whether they're together or apart. He'll move mountains to be with her. And as he's the size of a mountain, that'll be a piece of cake to him.'

Mia grinned. 'You're right again. And mentioning high water isn't going to be a problem for much longer. I was already pretty determined to beat this stupid fear, but finding out all that stuff about Mattie, or at least, believing we know what she did, has made me even more determined. I've been reading up about the SOE and female spies, over the last two nights. I seem to have more time now that Garrick and I have to be more careful having sex.'

'Too much information, thank you. But I get what you mean. And I've been reading up on them too. Not that you seem to have noticed, but Justin and I haven't seen much of each other over the last two days.'

'I had noticed.' Mia laid the card on the table and filled the kettle whilst Ella got the mugs out of the dishwasher. 'But that was because we've been searching for the diaries and Justin's been working, isn't it?'

Ella shook her head and got the milk from the fridge. 'Nope. It's because he's been acting really weird ever since he left that fortune-teller's tent. On Monday, when I went to get bread when you and Garrick were in town, he said he's got a lot on his plate at the moment and that he'll call me.' She slumped on a chair and frowned. 'On Tuesday, I popped over and he said the same. When I said that choir practice was off so we could get together on Tuesday night, he said he had to meet Jet. On Wednesday he said that he doesn't think he'll be free till Friday. And when I asked if he fancied a quick romp behind the flour sacks because we haven't had sex since Saturday, he looked as if I'd suggested burning the place down.'

'Bloody hell. Justin said no to sex? The guy's been all over you for weeks. He couldn't keep his hands off you.'

Ella nodded. 'I know. Perhaps it's possible to have too much of a good thing. Perhaps he's bored. Do you think he is?'

'No.'

'That wasn't very convincing. I asked him if something was wrong and he said no, that he was simply really busy. But I don't know. I thought he was a decent guy. Alexia said he was. But perhaps he's just like all the others. Apart from Franklin, that is. One minute they can't get enough of you, the next, they can't get away from you fast enough. Why can't men just be honest? If all they want is a few weeks of fun and sex, no strings attached, why can't they simply bloody well say so.'

'Jet does. Say it, I mean. He told me that the other night. Sunday night, when we met on the beach.'

'Jet Cross told you he'd like to have a few weeks of fun and sex with you? Bloody Nora. Does Garrick know?'

'What? No. Not with me. He merely told me that's the kind of guy he is.' The kettle boiled and Mia made them coffee.

Ella took the mug Mia handed her and looked thoughtful. 'So when you met on the beach he said, "Hi Mia. I'm the kind of guy who just wants sex and fun and nothing else." Just like that.'

Mia cleared her throat. 'No. He congratulated me on the engagement. And the pregnancy, as I've already told you. Then he said he was the opposite of Garrick and that he will never settle down with a woman. Ever. No matter what. And he told me that I was lucky to have someone as fabulous as Garrick.'

'Bloody Nora. The guy's not gay, is he? It sounds like he's got a bit of a crush on Garrick himself.'

'No! Sorry. I didn't mean to shriek. Of course he's not gay. You've heard of his reputation with women. And he was actually being sarcastic about Garrick. I told Jet Garrick was fabulous and Jet's being throwing that back at me ever since.'

'That's weird. And yes, I've heard the stories of Jet and women, but the odd thing is, have you ever seen him with one? A woman, I mean. Since we've been here, he hasn't shown any interest in a woman. Apart from you. I actually thought he had his sights set on you, you know. But he didn't do anything about it and then you started dating Garrick. Do you like him?'

'Jet? Yes of course.'

'I mean, really like him. Do you fancy him?'

Mia coughed and fiddled with the handle of her mug. 'Honestly? I thought I did. For a brief moment, I thought I may be falling in love with him. I don't know what it is about him but I seem to be able to talk to him about anything. Well almost anything. And …'

'And what?'

Mia shook her head. 'I don't know. I can't explain it. You know when you meet someone and you instantly feel they're going to be a part of your life?'

'Like your mum and Franklin, you mean?'

'No. Not quite. That's about Love. I'm talking about something else. A connection. Like when you know you're going to be friends for life? Like you and me and Garrick.'

Ella nodded. 'You felt that about Jet? That you'd be friends for life?'

Mia shrugged. 'Something like that, yes. As I said, I can't explain it. But it doesn't matter now.'

'Why? Don't you feel that anymore?'

Mia looked at Ella. 'I don't know, Ella. I honestly don't know what I feel. But something's changed. And not for the better.'

'Like with me and Justin. Why does life have to be so bloody complicated?'

'Another card?' Garrick's voice made Mia and Ella jump.

'Yes,' Mia said, clasping one hand to her heart to regain her composure. 'But not a nice one.'

Garrick kissed her on the cheek and picked up the card. His face grew red with rage.

'If I ever find out who's doing this, I'll kill them. Do you think it's time we contacted the police?'

'The police? No way. It's just a stupid prank. Don't tell Mum about it. I'm going to ignore it.'

'But this one actually contains a threat. "If you stay, you'll wish you hadn't." That isn't a prank.'

Mia grabbed it from him. 'It is, Garrick. What can anyone do? I was upset, and perhaps a little frightened when the frog and the flowers arrived. Now I'm simply cross. How dare someone try to scare me off. It won't work.' She straightened her back. 'I'm the great-niece of a possible spy and maybe even a heroine of the Second World War. Things like this don't bother me.' She grinned. 'Did that sound convincing? I'm working on the basis that if I tell myself that enough times, I'll believe it and feel as if I can do anything. I may not come close to *Wonder Woman,* or even to Mattie, for that matter, but I'm telling you now, people had better watch out. I'm now … Mighty Mia.'

Ella giggled. 'Yay! Although we'll have to come up with a better name than that. Mighty could mean you're just fat. What about, Mia the Magnificent?'

'Oh! I like the sound of that. Or Mia the Marvellous.'

'Nah. That makes you sound like you're about to pull a rabbit from a hat. What about Mega Mia? Nope. Forget that. Big woman connotations again.'

'What about you two behaving like grown ups for a change?' Garrick snapped. 'This is serious.'

'What is serious?' Lori asked, approaching from the garden. 'Did something happen when I was away? And why the raised voice, Garrick?'

Mia hid the card beneath her legs. 'No. We're simply talking about having an engagement party in The Frog and Lily, and Ella and I were suggesting fancy dress. Garrick says we should be serious, that's all.' Quite where that had come from, Mia had no idea but Ella quickly got on board.

'I think a fancy dress party would be fab. The theme could be famous couples in history or fiction.'

'But what would single people come as?' Lori asked, relief evident in both her tone and expression as she came inside and took a seat beside Mia.

'Good point,' Mia said, instantly and rather annoyingly, thinking of Jet. 'But he could come as Casanova.'

'Who?' Ella asked.

Oh bugger! Had Mia said that out loud. 'Er. Any single male. And any single females could come as … Um.'

'Medusa,' Garrick said, glaring at Mia as if he knew she'd been thinking about Jet. 'The woman with snakes on her head and anyone who looked at her turned to stone.'

'That's romantic. Not!' Ella said, giggling. 'Go away, Garrick and leave us women to organise your engagement party.'

'And mine!' Mia said, slapping Ella on the arm. 'It's my party too, don't forget.'

'So we're really having a party?' Garrick hesitated and then smiled at Mia. 'Does this mean you're actually going to start wearing the ring I bought you, now? I didn't mention it before because, well, because I wondered if you were having second thoughts.'

Everyone in the room fell silent. Mia pushed back her chair and went to him, stretching up to kiss him on the lips. 'Yes, Garrick. It does. But we won't have fancy dress. And we'll have to have another party when your mum and dad get back from holiday because I know they're away for three weeks. I'm going to go upstairs right now and get my ring.' Until that moment even she had had some doubt.

He wrapped his arms around her and kissed her tenderly whilst Ella made choking sounds and giggled and Lori clapped and cheered.

When he relaxed his hold, Mia turned and smiled at her mum, but Lori was no longer looking at her.

'What's this?' Lori asked, reaching forward.

Oh hell. In her haste to reassure Garrick, Mia had forgotten about it. Now Lori had spotted the 'Bon Voyage' card on Mia's chair.

Chapter Seven

Mia had to do a lot of persuading to convince her mum that there was nothing to worry about and that she should still get on the plane to Texas on Sunday.

'I'm a big girl, Mum. I can take care of myself. Besides, Garrick won't let any harm come to me. And let's not forget, Ella's here too. And not much gets past Hettie.'

'All three warnings got past Hettie,' Lori said.

Mia frowned. She wished she hadn't told her mum about the other two either. 'Fine. Don't go. Stay here and make me feel guilty for ruining your life. That'll make organising my engagement party a really happy experience.'

'Well, I want to be here for that anyway.'

'You will be. We'll have it this Saturday. Then, if you really, really love me, on Sunday you'll get on that plane.' Mia smiled. 'Honestly, Mum. I'm not in the least bit bothered about the silly card. But I'll make you a promise. If you go,

I'll be extra, extra careful. I'll make sure I'm never alone in the cottage and when I go out, I'll always have Garrick or Ella by my side. Okay?'

'That's not fair,' Lori said. But Mia could tell she was relaxing a little.

'Let's make a list of what we'll need at the party,' Mia said, kissing Lori on the cheek and taking the card from her. 'We're going to forget this and enjoy ourselves. Garrick, you go and ask Freda and Alec if we can have our party at the pub. If not, we could always have it here. Oh. But I was going upstairs to get my ring, wasn't I? Mum? Will you and Ella start making a list while I do that?'

Lori sighed. 'I'm still not happy about this, darling, but I suppose you're right. Garrick and Ella will look after you.'

'I won't let her out of my sight,' Garrick said, giving his most reassuring smile, before Mia slipped her arm through his and walked with him along the hall.

'You're sure about this, aren't you?' he asked when they reached the foot of the stairs. 'The engagement, I mean.'

He looked deeply into her eyes and for one moment it seemed that he was the one now having doubts. There was a hint of sadness, anxiety perhaps, about him and she wondered if *he'd* changed his mind.

'I'm sure, Garrick. Are you?'

He nodded. 'Yes. And I don't think we should have a long engagement. In fact, why don't we talk to Tom about setting a date? Wouldn't it be good to get married in the church?'

'This church? St Michael and All Angels you mean?'

He grinned. 'Is there another church in the village?'

She smiled up at him. 'Er. When were you thinking?'

'As soon as possible, Mia. What's the point in waiting? Besides, I'd like to get our sex life back to normal, wouldn't you?'

She couldn't see why getting married would do that and said so adding: 'Besides. Don't couples say they have less sex once they're married?'

'All I meant was that once we're married, we needn't worry about contraception. We'll want to start a family right away.'

'Er. Will we?'

'Of course,' he said. 'Remember the fortune-teller told Ella that she'd very soon be an aunt. We need to get working on that without delay.' He kissed her passionately and when he let her go, he winked. 'Maybe as soon as I get back from the pub. I'll pop into Tom's on the way and check for dates.'

That bloody fortune-teller. Why was he still harping on about her?

'Garrick?' She stopped him as he was striding through the doorway. 'What did the fortune-teller say to you? You didn't tell me.'

He paled visibly but quickly smiled. 'That I've met the woman of my dreams and that we'll have a long and happy life together with a large family.' He went to turn away.

'Hold on. Was that it?'

He swallowed and she watched his Adam's Apple rise and fall.

'Er. I think so. She may have said one or two other little things, but I can't recall. I love you, Mia. I really do. See you later.'

He turned away again and this time she didn't stop him. She still may not know what he heard in that tent but she had the answer to one question. Garrick was harping on about the fortune-teller because the woman had told him something he didn't want to hear. Something that clearly worried him. And it obviously had something to do with his relationship with Mia.

Was he in such a haste to get married because he thought that he might lose her? Had the woman told him his girlfriend might also be in love with someone else?

Because the fortune-teller had told her: "I see a man you can't forget." And as much as Mia was trying to, she simply couldn't forget Jet Cross.

His hair the colour of midnight and those eyes: the promise of dawn. The twitch of his lips that suggested kisses hot enough to melt her and those arms that made her feel so safe every time they wrapped around her. Or those hands that felt like perfectly fitting gloves, just made for her to slip her own hands into.

No. She definitely couldn't forget about Jet.

And despite loving Garrick and despite now being engaged, she had a feeling that she never would.

Chapter Eight

There was no going back now. Today was the engagement party in The Frog and Lily and everyone in the village had been invited. Even the few residents Mia and Garrick had yet to meet.

It was also the first of September, and in Little Pondale, that meant the first day of Autumn. "Autumn will bring many changes and many opportunities," the fortune-teller had told Mia, and the woman had definitely got that part right. Not only was Mia now officially engaged, but a date had been set for the wedding.

'We've got a date!' Garrick had said when he had returned on Thursday morning.

Mia, Ella and Lori were writing a list of things they needed to go to town to buy, and Hettie, who had come to do the cleaning as usual on a Thursday, was sitting with them, adding her two pence worth.

'Saturday's fine then?' Mia asked, assuming Garrick meant he'd asked Freda and Alec to arrange the party.

'What? Oh yes. For the party. Saturday's fine. Freda said she'll organise a buffet menu if you want to pop in to discuss it later. And Alec said we can have the party in the back room. The one they use for such occasions.' He dashed to Mia's side and lifted her up in his arms, spinning her around. 'But what I meant, my darling fiancée, is that we've got a date for our wedding. And Lori, you need to tell Franklin, because we'll want you back here in plenty of time and I'm sure Mia will want you to help her choose her dress.'

'A date?' Mia croaked. 'You mean you've set the date without discussing it with me?'

Garrick stopped spinning and his face fell just a fraction. 'We did discuss it, Mia. I told you I'd pop in to see Tom about available dates.'

'Available dates, yes. Not to actually set one. Please put me down.'

He did as Mia requested, and Hettie poked him in the ribs.

'Silly boy,' she said, shaking her head.

He frowned at Hettie and gave Mia a pitiful look. 'I thought you'd be pleased. I was over the moon when Tom said there'd been a cancellation, although he looked as if we were discussing a funeral, not a wedding. I suppose he's still upset about his gran. Anyway, a couple had second thoughts and called their wedding off, meaning that day was now free. It was either that or to wait for another six months. Call me an idiot, but I was under the impression that we would both rather get married sooner than later.'

'You're an idiot, Garrick,' Ella said, but she was grinning.

'Shouldn't choose a date when it's a cancelled wedding,' Hettie said. 'Oh deary me, no. A cancelled funeral's fine. But cancelled weddings. No. Not a good omen, dear.'

'How can any funeral be cancelled?' Ella asked. 'Do they suddenly discover the person's not dead after all?'

Hettie shrugged. 'It happens, deary. The Victorians put bells on their coffins for that very reason, with a cord inside for the person to ring if they woke up.'

'Can we please stop talking about funerals!' Mia dropped onto a chair. 'This is about my wedding day.' She could imagine how Tom must have felt. It was only a short time ago that he himself had told her he loved her.

'Sorry,' Hettie and Ella said in unison.

'When is it?' Lori asked, shaking her head at Ella and Hettie.

'Oh yes,' Mia said, sighing. 'When am I going to get married?'

'When are *we* going to get married?' Garrick corrected, moving as far away from Hettie as he could. 'October the 27th 2018, to be exact.'

'Next month?' Mia nearly fainted for a second time that week.

'Oh deary me,' Hettie said. 'Just a few days before All Hallows Eve. Not a time I'd choose for a wedding, deary.'

'That doesn't give us much time,' Lori said, ignoring Hettie and looking questioningly at Mia.

'How long can it take to arrange a wedding?' Garrick asked.

Ella thumped him on the arm. 'This time I'm serious. Garrick Swann, you are an idiot.'

'Oh dear God,' Mia said. 'Oh well. I suppose we'd better add wedding dress to this list.'

'Er. You could sound a little more excited, Mia,' Garrick said, mournfully. 'I honestly thought you'd be pleased.'

Mia looked at him and it was clear that her reaction had taken the wind out of his sails. She went to him and slid her arms around his waist. 'I am pleased, Garrick. Honestly I am. It's just that a wedding is a Big Day in any woman's life and we always want it to be absolutely perfect. The church is beautiful so that's one thing ticked off the dream list, but there's so much more to do and what with Mum going away and everything else. Well, the time will be gone before we know it.'

'I'm definitely not going to Dallas,' Lori said.

'Yes you are,' Mia insisted, turning to her and smiling. 'We've got two and a half days before you leave. We were going to the shops anyway. Now we'll simply make a longer list and get everything we need for the wedding too. I'm sure I can find a dress and Ella, you'll be my bridesmaid won't you?'

'Try and stop me.'

'Good. Then we can get your dress today too. Mum? Will you walk me down the aisle?'

Lori beamed. 'Of course, darling.'

'It's a pity we can't get Prince Charles,' Ella said. 'He was fab at the Royal Wedding. Not that you won't be fab too, Lori.'

'Prince Gustav could do it, deary,' Hettie said. 'But he's got very short legs and you'd have to promise not to step on him.'

Despite the ridiculousness of the situation, everyone laughed and suddenly, planning the wedding became the fun, if slightly stressful event it should be. Not only did Mia manage to get everything she needed for her engagement party, at the shops, she also got nearly everything she needed for her wedding. On that afternoon they found the perfect bridesmaid dress for Ella, Lori's outfit, and a going away dress for Mia. Not that she and Garrick were planning to go away, but perhaps they would.

On the Friday they found Mia's wedding dress. Perhaps not quite what she may have chosen given more time and a longer trip to London, but one that she was more than happy with, given that she wanted her mum to be there when she chose it. Any hesitation on her part would mean Lori might feel she had to stay, and Mia wanted her mum to have the time of her life in Texas. As it was, Lori had already said she would only stay one month, and nothing Mia could say or do would change her mind about that. They could've left the dress shopping until her return, but Mia saw the dress and loved it and as Ella said, 'No point in putting it off.'

By the Saturday of the engagement party, the wedding was well on the way to being sorted and when Mia, Ella and Lori popped back into town that morning for manicures, pedicures and to have their hair done, Mia even had time for a couple of small additional purchases. She saw a toy shop with various dolls in the window dressed up as Princes and Princesses. One of the Princes wore a stunning purple jacket embroidered with gold and Mia knew at once it was perfect. And later, as they were leaving town, she spotted a pet shop with an ornate, almost Cinderella-carriage-like little cage in the window. It was made for a bird, but it would work a treat. The jacket would fit Prince Gustav perfectly and, instead of a bouquet of flowers, she would carry him in the little cage. Because once the image had planted itself in Mia's head, she decided it might be fun to walk down the aisle with a rat, and at the end, to pass the cage to Ella, and marry her own Prince Charming.

'Are you ready yet?' Ella shouted, from downstairs. 'We've got an engagement party to get to.'

'I'm coming' Mia shouted back. 'And no vicar and tart jokes, thank you very much!'

Mia rushed along the hall and stopped, to walk elegantly down the stairs. The dress she wore fitted her like a second-skin and she felt like a Hollywood star. For the first time in forever, her hair was swept up into a fancy top-knot style with a few wisps down each side, her make-up was perfect, her nails were a sparkly red to match the dress and high-heeled sandals and her clutch bag also matched. But the main thing that made her feel divine was the set of complementary jewellery. It had been Ella's suggestion.

'Clive said everything in the cottage was yours to use or wear, and that included Mattie's jewellery.'

They'd been excited sifting through the jewellery to find the perfect pieces and when Mia had seen the heart-shaped, ruby drop earrings, the heart-shaped ruby in the centre of a single row of pearls and the matching bracelet, she knew she had to wear them. All a bit much for a party in a tiny, country pub, perhaps, but it wasn't every day that a girl got engaged. And she'd insisted that Lori and Ella should wear some of the jewellery too.

'Bloody Nora!' Ella said, as Mia sashayed down the stairs. 'Have you seen my best friend, Mia?'

Mia laughed. 'I don't look that different.' But she knew she did. Ella did too. And so did Lori, but not quite as much because Lori always looked glamorous, no matter what she wore. Mia and Ella both wore tight, low cut, off the shoulder numbers, whereas Lori's was a rounded neck, long sleeved, slightly looser fitting dress. Even so, she looked equally as sexy, as Franklin's long, loud whistle proved when he had seen her coming downstairs a few moments before Mia.

'I am such a lucky man,' Garrick said, watching Mia walk towards him and he swept her into his arms and kissed her until Ella slapped him on the back.

'You can do that later. I need a drink'

'Where's Justin?' Mia asked, her face burning when Garrick released her.

Ella shrugged. 'He's got a show tonight but he promised to join us later. And I think he will. When I told him on Thursday that I couldn't see him until tonight because now I 'had things to do', his attitude improved a bit. When I was chasing after him, he was backing off, but when I suddenly said I was busy, he seemed keener to see me. Isn't it always the way?'

'You're a real beauty, Mia,' Franklin said, as they went into the living room and he opened a bottle of champagne and poured them all a glass. 'Just like your gorgeous, mom.'

'Thanks,' Mia replied.

Lori laughed. 'Oh, stop it!'

'Coo-ey' Hettie called out. 'The door was open. Can we come in, deary? We've got you a little present. We wanted you to have it before you went to the pub in case it got lost in all the crush tonight. Oh deary! You look like a film star. And you deary,' she said to Ella. And those jewels!' She poked Garrick in the chest. 'You're a very lucky young man and don't you forget it, deary. You make sure you take good care of her or you'll have me to answer to.'

'I know I am. And I intend to, don't worry.' Garrick smiled but took a few steps away from Hettie.

Hettie nodded. 'Good.' She handed Mia the present.

'Oh, Hettie, you shouldn't have. And you Fred. Thank you,' Mia said.

'You don't know what it is yet, deary,' Hettie winked.

'Whatever it is, I'm sure I'll love it. We'll love it.' She smiled at Garrick and gently unwrapped the gift. 'Oh Hettie! It's wonderful. Look Garrick.'

It was a photograph of Sunbeam Cottage, clearly taken recently. Mia was standing in the doorway with a young Mattie by her side.

'Fred's been playing with his Photoshop, deary. Lori let me make a copy of one of the photos of Matilda and a photo of you, my dear, and Fred did whatever he does to make it look as if you're standing side by side. I hope you don't think it's a bit creepy, dear. I wasn't sure if you'd like it or not, to be honest, but Hector said you would and so did Prince Gustav and Fred did too,

87

so you can blame us all if you don't. Now I know you're not in it, Garrick dear, but somehow it didn't feel right.'

Garrick looked a tad surprised but he smiled and shook his head. 'I don't mind at all. And you're right. It's better with just Mia and Mattie.'

'I love it!' Mia said, a little tearfully. 'I really do. Thank you both so much. I'll treasure this forever.' She hugged them both and Franklin poured them a glass of champagne.

'Here's to y'all,' he toasted, meaning Mia and Garrick.

And everyone made a similar toast before Garrick looked into Mia's eyes and held his glass in the air.

'Here's to you, for saying yes, and for making me the happiest man in the world. And here's to us and a long and happy future together.'

Mia blew him a kiss and held her glass high. 'Here's to you for asking, and to us always being friends as well as lovers. And now, I think we have a party to get to.'

Chapter Nine

To Mia's surprise, Alexia was the first to congratulate them when she and Garrick walked hand in hand into The Frog and Lily. Not that she could hear much of what Alexia said above the cacophony of congratulatory voices.

'I hope you'll be very happy.' Alexia smiled, and it looked genuine.

'Thanks, Alexia. I hear you're dating someone. I feel as if I haven't really seen much of anyone lately.'

Alexia nodded. 'Yep. We should all get together and have a drink or a meal sometime. I'm working tonight so I'll catch you later.'

Freda flung her arms around Mia and said she couldn't be happier for her. Alec wished them well, in his usual gruff but friendly manner, and Toby said that he hoped this meant Garrick would be joining the rugby team on a permanent basis.

It took at least an hour for all the people in the pub to wish Mia and Garrick every happiness and it was clear that everyone in the village had turned up to the party. Even Tom made a point of saying how happy he was for Mia. And how truly beautiful she looked. But he added: 'If you change your mind, I'll be here, Mia. Or if you simply want a friendly ear, feel free to call on me, anytime, night or day.'

'Thanks, Tom. I appreciate that. How are you? I haven't seen you for a while?'

He shrugged. 'Good days and bad. Good days and bad. I hear Lori is leaving tomorrow. You'll miss her, obviously.'

He clearly didn't want to talk about himself.

'Yes. I'll miss her dreadfully. But it's wonderful to see her so happy. And she'll be back before we know it.'

'Back in plenty of time for the wedding, I hope. You must be excited. I'll admit, it was a bit of a shock when Garrick asked me, and said he wanted the very first date I had.'

Mia laughed. 'It was a bit of a shock for me too. Not that he asked you, but the date. I hadn't expected it to be so soon.'

'Nor had I. I mean. It surprised me when he said that date was perfect. He overheard me telling Phillip, the organist, to take it out of his diary as I'd just got the email cancelling it, and Garrick immediately jumped on it and asked if the two of you could take it instead.'

'Well, I nearly killed him, I can tell you, but as he says, what's the point in waiting?'

'I think there's every point. Oh. I mean in many cases. Not in yours, of course. You and Garrick have known one another for most of your lives, but some people rush into relationships without thinking them through and change their entire future, only to find out it doesn't always last. Oh heavens! I didn't mean Lori and Franklin, either. I'm so sorry, Mia. I'm making a bit of a mess of this, aren't I? I think I'll go and get myself a drink and have another word with Jet.'

'Jet? Jet's here? You've spoken to him?' Her eyes scanned the room but she couldn't see him anywhere.

Tom glanced around too. 'He was. I was speaking to him only a few moments ago. I was saying how lovely you looked and he said that you always looked lovely. That you were a beautiful woman and he hoped Garrick knew how lucky he was.'

'Yeah right.'

'I beg your pardon.'

Mia laughed. 'Oh come on, Tom. There's no way Jet said that about me.'

Tom raised his eyebrows. 'I can assure you he did. And that wasn't all he said.'

'Oh? What else did he say?'

'He said that he wished he wasn't such a fool.' Tom gave her a curious look. 'Forgive me for asking this, but why are you so interested in what Jet said?' He stiffened. 'I do hope Jet hasn't been up to his tricks with you, Mia. He's a good friend to me and I trust him with my life, but I wouldn't trust him with my girlfriend, fiancée or even my wife. Don't fall into the trap of listening to his flirtatious talk, and don't fall into his bed. It may look like a bed of roses, but many women can attest that by the second night, it's a bed of thorns.'

'I have no intention of falling into his bed, Tom! But don't you think that's a bit overly dramatic? If it's true that he tells women what to expect, surely they have a choice?'

Tom shook his head. 'Do they? One look from Jet and it seems they often don't. I have no idea what it is but some women seem to think they can change him, and they can't, Mia. Jet's like his dad. Where women are concerned, he really has no heart.'

'There you are!' Garrick beamed at Mia. He was obviously a little the worse for alcohol. 'I've been looking for you everywhere. I hope you're not trying to talk her out of marrying me, Tom.'

'Not me,' Tom said, with a strange sigh. 'I'm not your problem, Garrick.' He gave Mia a sad sort of smile and walked into the throng of revellers.

'Do I have a problem?' Garrick asked, swaying to the left.

Mia reached out for him. 'Only in standing up. I think we should find a chair for you before you fall.'

'Too late! I've fallen for you. And we're engaged and we'll very soon be married.' He swayed some more and Mia tried to steady him.

'So there. And there's nothing anyone can do about it. Not anyone. Not even a … fortune-teller. Not even … *Her!* Okay? Not even *Her!*'

'Why would the fortune-teller want to do anything about us getting married?'

His brows furrowed and he waved a hand in the air. 'Not the fortune-teller. *Her!*'

'Okay. I think we need to find you somewhere to lie down.' She looked around, caught Franklin's eye and beckoned him to help her.

'What's the problem, Mia?' He grinned at her, then at Garrick. 'Leave him to me. C'mon.' He took Garrick's weight and walked off with him as if he were carrying his hat beneath his arm.

'Having fun?'

Mia recognised Jet's voice immediately and turned to face him, taking a deep breath as she did so.

'Yes thanks. You?'

He slowly looked her up and down and she made fists with her hands to try to stop the strange sensation running through her.

'Not so much.'

'Don't you like parties?'

'Not this one.' He took a swig of his beer.

'Why? What's wrong with this one?'

He met her look. 'You're getting engaged to the wrong man.'

Her mouth fell open but she snapped it shut. 'Really? And who, pray tell, should I be getting engaged to?'

He shook his head and shrugged. 'Not Garrick. Especially now you know you're not pregnant.'

'My getting engaged had nothing to do with whether or not I was pregnant. I told you that before.'

'Then what does it have to do with?'

'Being in love.'

'With Garrick?'

'Yes of course with Garrick,' she snapped.

He held her gaze for a brief moment, took another swig of beer, and then that twitch she longed to see appeared at the corner of his mouth.

'Are you going somewhere after this?'

'N-no. Are you asking me to go somewhere?'

He raised his brows. 'Why would I ask you to go somewhere?'

'You tell me.'

'Would you go if I did?'

She placed her glass on the table beside her. 'It depends where you want to take me.'

He laughed. 'Is this where you want me to say, I want to take you to the moon? Because if it is, forget it. I'm no astronaut.'

'So where would you take me? Let me guess. To heaven.'

He laughed again. 'Nope. Not a god, either. Although I think one or two women have said they think I am.'

'I bet.' She rolled her eyes and smirked. 'Hades was a god, you know.'

He gave a burst of laughter. 'The God of the Underworld.' He leant closer and she was sure she quivered, but she hoped he hadn't noticed. 'Now does that mean that you think I'm a devil, or does that mean that you think I'm hot as hell? I'm going with the second choice, obviously.'

'Obviously. I'm leaning towards the first.'

'Lean towards me and we can put our heads together.'

She tutted. 'In your dreams.'

'You know about my dreams? Wow! But I suppose you would. You feature in most of them.'

'And you in mine. But mine are called nightmares.'

He looked her up and down again and this time he let out a long, low whistle.

'To answer your question. No. I wasn't asking you to go somewhere with me. And if you really loved Garrick, you wouldn't want to anyway. I was asking if you were going somewhere because you look ... a bit too dressed up for The Frog and Lily.'

She tilted her chin up and met his eyes. 'Is that your way of telling me I look nice?'

'No. That's my way of telling you, you might get mugged on the way home. Those jewels must be worth a fortune.'

'You told Tom you thought I looked beautiful.'

His eyes narrowed slightly for a fraction of a second. 'I think I was referring to the jewels.'

She shook her head. 'I think you're lying. And that's a pity because you told me you always tell women the truth.'

Again, his eyes narrowed momentarily. 'I do always tell women the truth. When I want to go to bed with them.'

She gasped. 'Don't you want to go to bed with me?'

'Is that a trick question?' He raised his brows and grinned.

'No. Do you want to go to bed with me?'

'Now is that an offer?'

'No! Why can't you just answer?'

He took a deep breath and let out a heavy sigh, placing his empty glass next to hers on the table. 'Because I'm not sure either of us would like my answer. Congratulations, again.' Suddenly serious, he turned to walk away.

'We've set a date you know.'

He glanced over his shoulder. 'A date for what?'

'The wedding. Haven't you heard?'

He glared at her and turned to face her. 'No. That I hadn't heard.'

That surprised her almost as much as the expression on his face. He looked angry and hurt at the same time.

'Hettie knows, so I assumed everyone else would. And I'm surprised Tom didn't mention it just now.'

'So am I.' He glanced towards the crowd of people. 'When is it?'

'Do you want an invitation?'

'Now who's avoiding the question?'

She smiled triumphantly, although she wasn't sure why. 'It's next month. The 27th of October.'

'Next month! Jesus, Mia. What's the rush?'

'He loves me. You'll find this hard to understand because you've made it clear that you'll never marry anyone, but when two people love each other they want to spend their lives together. To share their joys and sorrows. To build a future and have a family. To love one another and make love to each other. For as long as they both shall live. Or words to that effect.'

'It sounds delightful. But what happens when one of them sees someone else they fancy? When one of them has sex with someone else. When one of them fools around with every woman under the sun. What happens when he runs off with another woman and leaves his wife and child to fend for themselves. Then leaves the other woman too and moves on to the next one. What happens then, Mia?'

He was scowling by the time he'd finished and his eyes almost matched the colour of his hair.

'I think you're talking about your dad, Jet,' she said, in a soothing tone. 'I think you're consumed with hatred for him. I think—'

'You think too much.' He glared at her. 'And I think it doesn't concern you.'

He turned and marched away and even when she called his name, he didn't look back.

'Mia?' Lori appeared beside her. 'Franklin's taking Garrick home and I'm going too. I need to finish packing, if that's okay with you? But there's no need for you to come. We'll take care of Garrick if you want to stay and have fun. Justin's arrived, so Ella's happy. Darling? Is everything all right?'

Mia shook her head. 'I'm not sure, Mum. I'm not really sure about anything.'

Chapter Ten

Yet again, Mia had to spend some considerable time persuading Lori to get on the plane to Texas – only this time, she didn't have the safety net of a few days; she only had a few hours.

She had changed into her nightdress the minute she got home, and put the jewels away. Franklin had put Garrick to bed, in the blue room, so that he wouldn't disturb Mia, tossing and turning in the night. Then Franklin said a prolonged good night to Lori on the doorstep while Mia went into the kitchen and put the kettle on.

Lori was looking anxious when she finally joined Mia.

'I can still cancel, darling,' she said. 'If you need to talk things through, I can stay. I'm worried about what you said in the pub.'

Mia shook her head. 'Forget what I said in the pub. I am sure of everything. Well, of most things. I'm sure I'm happy. I'm sure I want to be engaged, even though my fiancé appears to be snoring his head off and as drunk as a skunk. Do skunks get drunk? Anyway. I'll be fine and I really want you to go. Franklin will be back here to pick you up in just a few short hours. Do we really have to spend this time, arguing?'

Lori frowned. 'We're not arguing, darling. I'm simply concerned about you.'

'And I've told you repeatedly, there's nothing to be concerned about.' Mia sighed. 'I'm sorry. I didn't mean to snap. I think I'm just tired.'

Lori smiled. 'I understand, darling. You've had a lot on your plate over the last few months. You sit down. I'll make the tea.'

Mia gave Lori a hug before slumping onto a chair, and when the kettle boiled a second or two later, Lori made some tea.

'What were you talking with Jet about?' She placed the teapot on a trivet on the table and grabbed two cups. 'He looked rather angry when he walked away and, I have to say this, Mia, you seemed very upset.' She looked Mia in the eye. 'Is there something you're not telling me as far as Jet's concerned? He seems a perfectly pleasant man, and he's definitely been good to Franklin, and of course, to me by saying we can stay in the cottage on his farm, but I've heard a few rumours about him. He hasn't tried anything on with you, has he?'

'If only.' Mia stared at the teapot.

'What did you say?'

Mia shot a look at Lori. 'Er. If only people would stop thinking the worst of Jet, perhaps he would stop behaving as they expect him to.'

Lori frowned. 'I'm not sure I follow that, darling.'

'What did Dad used to say? Tell a dog enough times that it's a bad dog, and it'll be a bad dog. Tell it that it's a good dog, stroke it, give it love and food and treats and it'll love you, watch over you and stay by your side for the rest of its life.'

Lori poured the tea. 'I'm not sure Jet would like being called a dog. But maybe he would. I'm still unclear of the point you're making and frankly, I've had a few too many glasses of champagne this evening myself to work it out. But I assume it's got something to do with you thinking that Jet's not as bad as people say he is. Which is lovely, darling, but it doesn't answer my question.'

Mia sighed. 'We were talking about weddings. And then we got onto the subject of his dad and it's not a happy topic as far as Jet's concerned. That's all. I said something I think may have upset him. But enough about Jet. You're going to Texas in a few hours and you need to get some sleep. So let's make the most of the time we have together. We'll drink our tea and have a girly chat. Just the two of us. I'm pretty sure Ella won't be back tonight.'

'Let me just say one more thing, darling.' Lori took Mia's hand in hers and looked her in the eye.

'I told you I knew the moment I saw your father, that I was going to marry him. I told you I knew when I saw Franklin, that he was going to be important in my life. You've known Garrick almost forever, and I know you had a crush on him when you were a little girl, which I don't think you ever really got over. But a crush is a very different animal from Love, Mia. Garrick's a wonderful man. He's kind and loving, thoughtful and hard-working. He loves you, that's obvious to anyone. And I'm certain you love him. The thing you need to ask yourself, perhaps you both need to ask yourselves – and preferably, before the wedding, is do you love each other enough? Marriage is hard sometimes. If either of you has any doubt at all, then you shouldn't be doing this.'

'Everyone has doubts before their wedding, Mum. Don't they?'

'No, darling, they don't. Not if they truly love each other. The only ones who have doubts, as far as I'm concerned, are the ones who weren't completely sure in the first place. Sometimes people marry for the wrong reasons. Because they think they should. Because their friends are all getting married. Because they've reached a certain age. Because they don't want to be alone. Because they've been friends with someone all their lives and they mistake their feelings for Love. There are a million reasons people get married. But there should ever only be one. Because you love the other person so much that, even though you could live without them, you don't want to. That's it. You should only marry someone if you're absolutely sure there isn't someone else you'd rather be with.'

'I'll bear that in mind.'

'What does that mean?'

'It's means that I love Garrick and I want to be with him. Now please can we change the subject?'

'Yes, darling. But don't forget, just because the date is set, the dress is bought and the invitations are being printed, until you say yes and sign that register, you can walk away at any time. You can walk away afterwards, but it's better to do so before. Less complicated and certainly less expensive. Now, I know we'll be catching up every day, but what are you going to do while I'm away?'

Mia smiled and hugged and kissed her mum. 'I'm going to see if I can find those damn diaries. I know we've searched everywhere but I may have to start taking floorboards up because they must be somewhere. I'm also going to see if I can find out anything else about the SOE, online, and see if there's somewhere or someone I can write to. I know it said it was disbanded after the war and the records were dissolved but someone must know something, otherwise how could there be all the stories and accounts we've read? I know that MI6 was once called SIS or the Secret Intelligence Service, so maybe I can find more information about that. But the most important thing I'm going to do, is get myself into that sea. I may not be swimming again by the time you get back, but I'll definitely have paddled. And I'll do that sooner rather than later because now that it's September, the weather may start to turn.'

'Oh darling. I'm so proud of you. But make sure someone's with you, won't you? Panic can take over at any time until you gain your confidence, and it's the panic that does the harm.'

'That's exactly what Jet said. But we're not going to start talking about Jet again.'

Why couldn't she get that damn man out of her head?

Lori gave Mia an odd look. 'No darling. Although I have a feeling we will be, long before I get back.'

Chapter Eleven

Franklin came for Lori at eight on Sunday morning to catch the eleven-twenty-five, British Airways flight from Heathrow to Dallas and in spite of having the hangover from hell, Garrick tramped down the stairs in time to say goodbye.

'You look awful, Garrick,' Mia said, trying not to laugh. It was self-inflicted, after all.

His hair was sticking out all over the place, his eyes were red dots beneath half-closed lids; he was gripping the banister so tight that his knuckles were turning white, which was the complete opposite of his face. That had a distinctly green tinge to it.

'That's better than I feel,' he mumbled.

'Go back to bed,' Lori said. She did laugh.

'I wanted to say goodbye.' He swayed at the foot of the stairs and looked as though he might fall over. 'And now I have, I'm going to crash out on the sofa. I don't think I can make it back upstairs.' He shuffled into the living room, giving Lori a quick kiss on the cheek on the way.

'Don't I get one?' Mia frowned at him. 'We've only been officially engaged for a few hours and he's ignoring me already,' she joked.

'Sorry.' He turned and came towards her but she backed away.

'I was joking, Garrick. You look as if you're about to throw up. Please go and lie down. I'll bring you an aspirin and some water in a minute.'

He made a grunting noise and gave a tiny smile before turning and padding into the living room where he collapsed on the sofa.

'Looks like you're in for a real fun day,' Franklin said. 'Want me to carry him upstairs? The guy's asleep already.'

Mia looked at Garrick and nodded. He was snoring and his arm had flopped off the edge. His body threatened to follow the same course.

She laughed. 'If you don't mind. He's going to be on the floor any minute and I can't get him up from there.'

Franklin handed his hat to Lori and within seconds had picked Garrick up and carried him back upstairs.

'I'll miss you, Mum,' Mia said, hugging Lori while they waited for Franklin to return. 'Have the time of your life and don't worry about me even for one minute. Okay?'

Lori gave her a tearful smile. 'Okay, darling. You have fun while I'm gone. And think about what we discussed last night. Life's too short for regrets.'

'I will,' she promised. 'Hey! Isn't that Ella?'

'Lori!' Ella yelled, waving her high-heeled sandals in the air and running barefoot across the grass surrounding the duck pond. 'I want to say goodbye.' She picked up speed and arrived at the door, panting and breathless. 'Bloody Nora, I'm unfit.' She hugged Lori, and as Franklin had returned, she hugged him too. 'You take care of Lori,' she told him.

'Count on it,' he said, hugging Mia.

By the time Lori and Franklin got in Franklin's car, all four of them had tears in their eyes.

'Where's Garrick?' Ella asked as she and Mia waved Lori and Franklin off.

'In bed. He came down to say goodbye, looked like death and collapsed on the sofa. Franklin took him back upstairs where he'll no doubt spend the day, snoring.'

'Bad as that?'

'Worse.'

Ella laughed. 'And he has the nerve to lecture us on drinking too much.'

'I think this is the first time I've seen him this drunk in all the years we've known each other.' Mia watched Franklin's car turn onto Seaside Road, and when it had gone, she closed the door. 'I need coffee. Want one?'

'Several.' Ella followed her to the kitchen.

'Everything's okay with you and Justin, I assume?'

Ella shrugged. 'I'm not sure. Last night was great but there was something about him. I don't know what, so don't ask me but it felt different somehow.'

'The sex was different, or he was different?' Mia filled the kettle and cleared away the coffee cups from earlier.

'Both. Usually we fool around and laugh and joke. Last night it seemed as if the fun had gone out of our relationship. He was very attentive and pretty passionate but afterwards, he turned over and went to sleep. Anyone would think we're married. And when I said that to him this morning, he looked at me as if I'd told him I had a sexually transmitted disease, so no morning romp for me! I would've stayed and had it out with him. No pun intended.' She grinned. 'But I wanted to see Lori before she left so I told him we need to talk later and came running over here.'

'Perhaps he's tired because he's been so busy lately.'

'Or perhaps he's been so busy lately because he's trying to avoid me.'

'Is that what you think?'

Ella shrugged again. 'I honestly don't know. He's just being weird, that's all. And I want to know why.'

Mia made coffee and handed a mug to Ella before sitting on the chair she'd vacated to see her mum off. 'Garrick's been acting weird, too.' She grinned. 'Perhaps it's the time of the month.'

Ella grinned back. 'Garrick's been acting weird ever since he came back from Scotland. Oh bugger! I didn't mean it like that. What I meant was that he hasn't been his old self. Since he's been seeing you he's been better, but there's still something off about him. Like he's holding something back. Sorry. I shouldn't have said anything. It's probably me who's being weird, not him.'

'No. I'm glad you did. If something's wrong, I'd rather know about it.'

'I'm not saying anything's wrong, exactly. It's just that it feels as if he's been waiting for something to happen. Perhaps falling so deeply in love with you took him by surprise and he's been worried about your relationship going the same way as his last one or something. Perhaps that's why he got so drunk last night. Now that the engagement is official, he felt he could finally relax. I know he's been worried about you and Jet.' Mia choked on her coffee and Ella gave her an odd look. 'You do that every time I mention that man's name.'

'I don't! What do you mean he's been worried about me and Jet? There is no me and Jet. We're simply friends. Although I'm not even sure we're that.'

'Oh come on! This is me you're talking to. I've been your best friend since we were running around the garden in just our knickers. Oh wait. We still do that.' She laughed. 'But seriously, Mia. It's pretty obvious you like Jet. And I think if Garrick hadn't come here with us, you and Jet might be having an engagement party, not you and Garrick.'

'Now that is ridiculous, I can assure you. For one thing, other than some silly flirting on his part, he hasn't so much as hinted that he'd like to date me. For another, I've never in my entire life, met a man who is so anti-marriage, anti-relationships, anti-almost everything involving any hint of couple-dome, it's almost unbelievable. That man would rather have a serious bout of the plague than a serious girlfriend. Talk about baggage. He's got more than the whole of Heathrow airport. Believe me, Garrick has nothing to worry about as far as Jet's concerned.'

'Okay then. I'm glad I mentioned it.' Ella threw Mia a sarcastic look and nudged her arm.

Mia grinned and drank her coffee. 'Actually. He did say something weird last night.'

'Jet?'

'No. Garrick.' She put her mug on the table and leant forward. 'I can't remember what we were talking about, and he was very drunk at the time, but he said something like, "We're engaged now and going to be married very soon. And there's nothing anyone can do about it. Not anyone. Not even a fortune-teller. Not even *Her!*" And he really emphasised the 'Her' bit. In fact, he said it twice. I thought he meant the fortune-teller, but I wasn't sure. It was as if he was talking about someone else. For a moment, I thought it might be Alexia and then I realised how foolish that was. Garrick ended their relationship. Then suddenly, Fiona popped into my head. Don't ask me why, but I think he meant Fiona.'

'Fiona!' Ella was clearly surprised. 'Why would he be talking about her? Don't forget, he ended their relationship too.' She frowned and took a large gulp of coffee.

Mia nodded. 'I know he did. But only because she doesn't want children. Not because he stopped loving her.'

'What?' Now it was Ella who choked on her drink. 'Did Garrick tell you that?' she finally managed.

'Yes. And he made it clear that if I didn't want children, our relationship would have to end too. Your brother really wants kids. Far more than you do.'

Ella sighed. 'I know he does. I told you. He's weird. But he really said that? About dumping Fiona because she doesn't want kids? There was no other reason?'

'Yes, he said it, and no. No other reason that he told me. But he did say that he was still in love with Fiona when he came here and that the reason he dated Alexia was because she looks so much like Fiona and he thought a fling with Alexia might get Fiona out of his system. But then he fell in love with me. Which he obviously wasn't expecting to happen.'

'Bloody Nora. So, excuse me for asking this, but how does he feel about Fiona now?'

'Er. I don't know. I haven't asked. He may still love her, I suppose, but hopefully, he loves me more.'

'I should bloody well hope so too. And of course he does. He asked you to marry him, didn't he?'

Mia took a deep breath. 'Yes. But he proposed to Fiona first.'

'He did what?' Ella's face was the colour of fire and it looked as if a volcano was about to erupt inside her.

'That's when she told him she didn't want kids. Apparently, they hadn't discussed it before because he'd simply assumed she would. You know. Like most people assume that just because you're a woman you'll obviously want kids. Not every woman does, but people think women who don't are odd somehow. He assumed she would, so he didn't ask. But when he proposed she must've told him. He didn't tell me exactly what she said and I didn't ask. But that was it as far as he was concerned. No kids. No marriage. That's why he left and came back down south.'

'Bloody Nora doesn't quite cover this, does it? I love my brother dearly, but what an absolute dickhead! I'm surprised she didn't smash something over his head. You can't stop loving someone just because they don't want the same things as you do.'

'No. But you can decide you don't want to spend your life with them if they don't want what you want. Especially if what you want is so important to you. Take Justin, for example. You love him and we both know you've already decided you'd like to be Mrs Swann-Lake.' Mia grinned. 'But what if he said he didn't like your friends and you'd have to give them up to be with him. Would you do it?'

'Of course I wouldn't. But if he loved me, he wouldn't tell me to do that.'

'He might, if he really, really hated your friends and couldn't bear being near them. Okay, that's probably not a good example, but what I'm saying is that you can love someone but know that you simply can't be with them because ultimately, it would make you both unhappy.'

'Then all I can say to that is that you don't love that person enough. Because if you did, you would want to make it work. To reach some sort of compromise that makes you both happy and lets you both have what you want.'

'I agree. But you can't do that with children, can you? And if you put another's person happiness before your own, you may end up being unhappy and bitter and resenting them. I'm not sure Love can overcome that. What we need to do is find someone we're on equal terms with, and that when it comes to the really, really important things, we want what they want, or as near as damn it. Does that make sense?'

'I think so. But I'm not entirely sure. It's far too early in the morning to try to be philosophical.'

'I'm being practical.'

'It's too early for that, too.' Ella got up and refilled the kettle. 'So, I'm assuming that you and Garrick are on equal terms. That you both want the same things in life. And that you love each other enough to make this work.'

'I think so.'

'You think so? Bloody Nora, Mia. I love you both, so I mean this sincerely. If you've got any doubts. Any doubts at all, especially bearing in mind what you've just been saying, you'd better say something pretty soon. I'll still love you, I promise. But the wedding is only weeks away and it may be amusing in books and films, but being stood up at the altar isn't fun for anyone. And I don't want my brother to have to go through that.'

'I wouldn't do that to Garrick! You know me better than that.'

Ella shrugged. 'I thought I knew my brother, but this morning's conversation has been a bit of a revelation. Sometimes it seems we don't know people as well as we think we do.'

'And sometimes, we don't know ourselves as well as we think we do, either.'

Once again, she was thinking of Jet bloody Cross. Not the man she was going to marry.

Chapter Twelve

Mia was determined that from now on, she would think about no one but Garrick Swann. He spent most of Sunday recovering from his hangover but by lunchtime, when she took him a cup of tea and the dry toast he had requested, they chatted about the future for a short time.

'Where are we going to live?' she asked, sitting on the edge of the bed. 'Once we're married. I've got to stay here until the year is up, so I assume we'll live here until then. But after that? Before I came here, I thought that if I could see the year out, I'd sell up afterwards and move back to London. But now that Mum's moving down here, that sort of changes things.'

He smiled wanly, still clearly not feeling great. 'We'll definitely live here until you inherit it free and clear. After that, I don't mind where we live. To be honest though, as much as I like this cottage and the village, it would be nice to live somewhere with more than one pub and with possibly a few shops, and restaurants. Perhaps a theatre or two and a cinema.'

'Really? You were the one who said you'd be happy living in a place like this and that it would be me who would miss the bright lights and shops. Has living here changed your mind?'

'It's a wonderful place to spend a few months or so, but to live here forever, seeing the same people, day in, day out?' He shrugged. 'Well, I think that may get old after a while, don't you? We wouldn't have to move far. Just far enough away so that we didn't keep bumping into the same people every time we went for a walk, or something.'

Mia frowned. 'Does this have anything to do with Jet Cross by any chance? Ella told me she thought you were worried that there might be something between him and me. There isn't, Garrick. Not like that, anyway. I love you. I'm marrying you.'

He sighed deeply. 'I did have worries. Until you said yes. But I would still prefer you not to be in the man's pocket.'

'I'm not in his pocket.'

'Okay. Perhaps that was the wrong word. I would prefer to know that every time you went on the beach, you wouldn't be bumping into him.'

'Don't you trust me?'

'Yes. Jet, I'm not so sure about.'

'You were the one who said that I shouldn't believe everything I hear. That he was a great guy and had worked really hard to get where he is. That he didn't have time to mess around with all the women he's accused of messing around with, or words to that effect. Are you saying you've now changed your mind about him, as well as the village?'

'I'm saying that I've seen the way he looks at you sometimes. And I'm not sure I like it.'

Mia jumped up and glared at him. 'Not sure you like it? Frankly, I think you're imagining it, but even if he does look at me in a certain way, surely that doesn't matter? What matters is how I look at him.'

He coughed lightly and straightened the duvet cover. 'Yes. And I'm not sure I like that either, sometimes. In fact, I've been meaning to have a word with you about it.'

Mia blinked several times. 'Have a word with me about it? Are you serious? You're clearly still hungover and not thinking straight. Go back to sleep. We'll continue this discussion later. But not about Jet bloody Cross. Merely about where we're going to live.'

'Mia!'

She hurried out of the room and slammed the door behind her, running down the stairs as fast as she could and heading towards the decking.

That was a good start, wasn't it? They'd only been officially engaged for a day and already they were arguing about another man.

'What's up?' Ella asked as Mia dashed through the kitchen.

'Nothing. I just need some fresh air. I'll see you later.'

She ran the length of the garden and sprinted over the dunes, only stopping when she reached the flat expanse of sand. The tide was out and the sun was still high; there was hardly any breeze and what there was, was warm: like standing in front of an oven with the door open. Along the shore, a group of children played gleefully, jumping in and out of the gentle waves, their short legs not long enough to clear them. The school summer holidays would be over this week and they were no doubt making the most of their last few days of complete freedom. Oh, to be that carefree again.

What did she have to do to convince not only Garrick but also Ella that she had no interest in Jet Cross as far as romance was concerned?

More importantly, what did she have to do to convince herself?

'Arghhhhh!' She screamed at the top of her lungs.

One or two of the children stopped jumping and looked towards a group of adults, further up the beach.

'Sorry,' Mia shouted, giving a friendly wave and hoping they were visitors, not locals. She didn't want everyone in The Frog and Lily to hear that the day after her party she was standing on the shore, alone, screaming her head off. She'd seen a couple of kids who lived in the village, although she hadn't said more than a word or two to their parents, but she didn't recognise these children or the adults on the beach. But not everyone spent their time in the pub, or went to choir practice and even last night, there were people at the party she hadn't actually 'met'. She should make more of an effort to get out and about and meet them. Soon, the children were screaming too, the only difference being that their screams were of delight.

The water looked so inviting. If only she had someone with her, now would be the time to finally face this fear. To put her toes in the warm water and instead of feeling terror, experience the delight the children were. She walked towards them, and as she did so, she felt the smile form on her lips. The children were so small and yet not one of them was frightened. Even when a slightly larger than expected wave caught one of the little girls off guard and made her stumble, she didn't cry or stand paralysed with fear. And then another knocked her over and she disappeared beneath the water. Instinctively, Mia raced to her aide and was about to scoop the child up, but she reappeared and shrieked with laughter. One of the adults appeared a second later.

'Be careful Lulu,' the woman said, smiling at the delighted little girl and shaking her head. She turned to Mia. 'Thanks for coming to her rescue, but she's always doing that. I swear someone took my baby in the hospital and exchanged her for a mermaid.' She laughed. 'I hope they weren't expensive.' She nodded her head towards Mia's feet and Mia almost screamed herself.

But not with delight. She was ankle deep in water and she hadn't even realised she'd gone in.

'Are you okay?' the woman asked. 'You've gone really pale. Is it your shoes? They were expensive, weren't they? I'm sorry. Lulu, apologise to the lady. You've made her ruin her lovely shoes.'

'Sorry lady,' the little girl said.

And Mia burst out laughing.

'Oh God! I'm so sorry.' She gave the woman a pleading look. 'It's not my shoes. I'm terrified of water. Or at least, I was. Let's see if I can move?'

She wobbled slightly and the woman stretched out her hand but couldn't reach her.

'Blimey!' the woman said. 'Do you need my help?' She bent to take off her shoes. 'Lulu. Take the lady's hand. Now, Lulu. The lady's scared.' Her voice was loving but firm and Lulu looked surprised but she did as she was told.

'You're safe. Lulu's here,' Lulu said, sounding like a grown up and her mother smiled.

'That's what I say to her,' the mother said.

'Want to get out?' Lulu asked.

Mia moved one foot and then the other. 'I'm not sure. Would you hold my hand for a little while longer? I'd like to see if I can stay here.' She glanced at Lulu's mum. 'Is that okay? I promise

I'll let go if I feel panicky or anything. Or if Lulu does.'

The mum laughed. 'A ten-foot wave wouldn't panic Lulu. But hold on. Girls!' she shouted to her friends on the beach. This lovely girl needs our help. Come on.' She kicked off her shoes now they were unbuckled and walked towards Mia, making sure not to splash, Mia couldn't help but notice. She took Mia's other hand in hers and smiled at her.

'Nothing to it,' she said.

Mia smiled back. 'Easy for you to say, but yes, you and Lulu are making me realise that.'

The three other girls were about to rush into the sea but Lulu's mum stopped them.

'Slowly, girls. Fear of water.' She nodded her head to Mia. 'What's your name?'

'Mia. And yours?'

'Susie. You can let go now Lulu and go and play with the others.'

'Thank you, Lulu,' Mia said.

'You're welcome.' Lulu let go and ran back to her friends a few feet away.

Mia grinned. 'She's adorable.'

'She's a little minx. But yes, she is rather wonderful. Okay, this is Dee, Anna and Barb. Girls, meet Mia.'

'Hi Mia,' they said, as Anna took the hand Lulu had released and the other two stood close by.

'Why the fear of water?' Susie asked.

'I almost drowned when I was six.'

121

'How?' Anna queried.

Mia took a deep breath and tried to forget she was standing ankle-deep in water.

'We were on holiday and I was on the beach with my mum, at Camber Sands, which I think is only about thirty miles or so from here. She'd left me playing on the sand. I was a good swimmer, so she wasn't worried about me going into the water. I don't know if you've been to Camber, but the tide goes out a long way. Anyway, it's got pockets of that awful sinking sand. You know? That quicksand stuff. Most of the areas are signposted but I got caught in one that wasn't. I struggled, which you shouldn't do. It actually doesn't suck you down, but struggling can make you sink deeper, which is what happened to me. On top of that, there was a rip tide. I would've drowned if it hadn't been for my dad, who had, thankfully, decided not to play golf after all that afternoon, and to come and join us instead. He heard me scream and saw that I was in trouble and he, together with a doctor who was there with his family that day, managed to rescue me, but not before I'd gone under the water. I had to be resuscitated and I was taken to hospital. I don't remember much about that but I was terrified of water after that day. I wouldn't even go in a bath for years. Only the shower and even that I hated. Mum had to hold my hand until I was about eight, I think.' She gave a snort of laughter. 'God. I'm such a wimp. We lived in London so I've rarely

122

been to the beach since then, or a swimming pool either.'

'What about holidays?' Barb queried. 'Where d'you go on holiday?'

'Usually a city or somewhere inland. Basically, as far away from water as I can get.'

'So what are you doing here then?' Dee said. 'This is a beach, or hadn't you noticed?' Her laugh was warm and friendly.

'I'm living in my great-aunt's cottage.' Mia pointed towards Sunbeam Cottage. 'It backs onto this beach.'

'Bummer,' Anna said. 'I could think of worse places to live though.'

'So can I,' Mia said. 'I'm determined to beat my fear and I've been coming to the beach almost every day. This is only the second time I've had my feet in the sea since I arrived in May. The first was by accident and this time was because I didn't think about it.'

'Why don't you take your shoes off?' Barb suggested. 'We'll hold you steady.'

All four of them held Mia as she removed her shoes and she tossed them to the shore. It was a little scary to feel the sand against her bare feet but it definitely wasn't sinking sand, and within seconds she was wiggling her toes in the soft grains.

'Want to go a little deeper?' Anna asked. 'We'll make sure you're safe. Barb spent a year in Australia working as a life guard. And there're sharks in the water there so there's good reason to be terrified.'

'Not helping,' Susie trilled. 'No sharks here, Mia. Nothing at all to be afraid of, in fact. And there's no sinking sand around this part of the coast. But it's up to you.'

'I don't want to spoil your day. I'll get out now and leave you to enjoy yourselves.'

'Don't be a silly sod,' Anna said. 'You're not spoiling anything. Do you have a swimsuit beneath that dress?'

'No.'

'Okay. No point in you going home to get one, you can borrow one of mine. I always bring about four with me. And before you ask, one is for swimming, one is for sunbathing and the other two are for flirting in front of any gorgeous men who might be around. If you're living here, you'll already have met some, I expect. This village is bursting at the seams with single guys.'

'I noticed,' Mia said. 'We couldn't believe it when we arrived.'

Anna grinned. 'So are Little Whitingdale, Little Stelling and Stellingfold Heights. My gran, who lives in Little Whitingdale, says it's because a white witch cast a spell that four out of every five babies born during the months of November, December and January each year would be male. It was after the First World War apparently because so many guys died from all the villages that there was only about one man to every ten women.'

'Is that why? Bloody Nora, as my best friend would say.' Mia laughed. 'I've been to Little Whitingdale.' She remembered that was where she went with Ella to see Justin's show and to meet Bear on that blind date. 'I haven't been to the other villages you mentioned.'

'Well, if you're single, go. Oh. You're not. I've just seen the ring.'

'I got engaged last week, but we only made it official yesterday. We had a party in the pub.'

'To someone local?' Susie asked.

'No. To someone I've had a crush on for years but we only recently got together. His name's Garrick and he and his twin sister, Ella who's my best friend, came down here to stay with me for a while.'

'And Love developed from there,' Barb said, sighing for dramatic effect.

'Yes.'

'Have you met Jet Cross?' Anna asked.

'You know Jet?' Mia was astonished.

Anna grinned and sighed. 'Not as well as I'd like to, but yes. I've met him a few times. Little Pond Farm cheese is the best cheese in the world. Have you tried it?'

'Yes. It's delicious.'

Anna fluttered her eyelashes and pretended to swoon. 'And to think the man makes it with his bare hands. It's enough to make the stuff an aphrodisiac. And this, coming from someone who's allergic to dairy!' She laughed.

'Have you ever, I mean, has he ever asked you out or anything?'

'No. Sadly not. He did date a friend of mine once though. By date, I mean they slept together a few times. She was heartbroken when it stopped. But he'd told her he didn't want a relationship so she wasn't surprised. It's just that, to use her words, "once you've spent a night with Jet Cross, you want to spend every night with him". I'd be happy for one night. But enough about men. Look where you are.'

Mia glanced down. The water was almost touching the hem of her dress, and that was above her knees.

'You okay?' Susie's voice was reassuring.

Mia nodded. 'I think so.'

'Great,' Anna said. 'Let's get you out and into a bikini and then we can see if you can put this fear behind you, once and for all, by swimming. I've got an idea.'

Mia shook her head. 'No. I can't do that. I can't go deeper.' Panic was creeping into her voice.

'You've got this far without a problem,' Dee said. 'Give it a try. If you can't do it, you can't. But if you can, we're here and we'll take care of you.'

'Come on, Mia. Take a chance,' Anna coaxed. 'When we women put our minds to it, we can do anything.'

An image of Mattie popped into Mia's head. She still wasn't certain about Mattie's past but she was convinced that Mattie was one hell of a woman. Mia was her great-niece. She must have a bit of Mattie's determination and possibly courage somewhere in her blood, mustn't she?

'Okay. Let's try it. But are you sure you don't mind me borrowing a bikini?'

'Nah. And if you get in up to your waist, I'll let you keep it as a reward. It's a really lovely one. But I've got loads more at home. Some girls buy shoes. I buy bikinis.'

'I'll pay you back.'

'No, you bloody won't! It's a gift – but only if you get to your waist.'

They all helped Mia out and held towels around her while she changed. Not that there was anyone about, but you can never tell who might be watching when you least expect it. Like Jet had been that night she had danced beneath the moonlight.

'Okay,' Anna said. 'This is the idea I mentioned.' She promptly handed her friends some water wings, a crocodile and a dolphin to inflate. 'We'll hang on to you and you can hang on to these. Just until you feel confident.'

'Thank you, Anna. Thank you all. This is a dream come true.'

'That's what I'll be saying if I ever get my hands on Jet Cross,' Anna replied.

'Happy to help,' the others said.

And a few minutes later, Mia was wading slowly into the sea with a large, smiling, plastic dolphin and a similar-looking crocodile under each arm and water wings on her wrists. They were made for children so wouldn't go any higher but just wearing them made her so confident that the girls didn't even have to hold her hands. The children looked askance when they saw her with their toys, but they were soon cheering her on. And when a kid of five and some even younger shows you that swimming is simple but doesn't have to look graceful, you'd be hard-pushed not to try it.

'I'm scared, I'll admit but I'm going to do this.'

Mia stood up to her waist in water and slowly eased herself lower, whilst her new friends clapped and cheered. Her heart pounded against her chest, her tummy did belly-flops and she was sure she'd scream and run at any minute. But she didn't. And when she got her shoulders beneath the sparkling, azure water, she held tight to the dolphin and the crocodile and lifted her legs off the sand.

It might have only been for a second or two but she had finally done it. And Anna had taken a photo of Mia on her phone.

'I'll send it to you if you give me your email address. Then you'll have proof that you've done it. No point in trying to send a text message because it won't get through. Now let's see if you can do it with only the water wings.'

To Mia's amazement, she did. She also took a few tentative strokes of breaststroke.

'You're swimming, Mia!' Susie cheered, as Lulu splashed about in a type of crawl, beside her. 'You've done it!'

'I have, haven't I? Oh my God! I can't believe I'm finally back in the sea. After all these years. And it's all because of Lulu.'

'No,' Susie said. 'It's because of you. Lulu just gave you a reason to not think about your fear for a moment. You're the one who's faced it and conquered it.'

'But I couldn't have done it without all of you. I know the kids will want to get home this evening but if I arrange a barbecue or something next weekend or whenever you're free, will you come? I'd like to say a proper thank you. And I'd like you to meet Garrick and Ella.'

'There's no need,' Susie said. 'But yeah. That would be great. And next weekend is perfect.'

'And obviously that includes your husbands, partners, or whatever. And the kids, of course.'

'I don't suppose you could invite Jet, could you?' Anna asked. 'Or one of the other local single guys you know. I know that's a bit cheeky of me but I don't have a significant other.'

Why did the thought of inviting Jet for Anna make Mia shiver? Or perhaps the water temperature was dropping.

'I'll ask,' Mia said. 'I'm sure one, or maybe all of them will come. Tom, the vicar's lovely and he's single. Jet, of course. But I think Toby and Bear are dating people now. I'll sort something though. It's the least I can do after all you've done for me today. I'm enjoying this so much, I really don't want to get out. And I never thought I'd be saying that about the sea.'

Chapter Thirteen

It was typical of the man. Jet Cross was always popping up unexpectedly but the minute Mia wanted to talk to him, he was not around. Perhaps he was busier than usual now that Franklin wasn't at the farm, although he must have made alternative plans because he had always expected Franklin to be leaving at the end of August. She was tempted to simply not bother inviting him to the barbecue, but Anna had been so kind and generous and Mia didn't want to let her new friend down. Would Jet even accept the invitation, if she did get to ask him? And if he did, would he show any particular interest in Anna? He'd met her before, according to Anna, and he hadn't asked her out, but with her long, sleek jet-black hair, wide deep blue eyes and fabulous figure, surely she was any man's idea of the perfect woman? If Jet thought any woman was perfect, that is.

At least things were getting back to normal with Garrick and Mia was thankful for that. After their row on Sunday, neither of them mentioned the subject again. There was no rush to decide on their permanent residence because Mia had to remain at Sunbeam Cottage until at least the middle of next May to adhere to the terms of Mattie's will.

Neither did Garrick mention his concerns regarding Mia and Jet. When Mia told him and Ella on Sunday evening about her afternoon, the friends she had met, the fact that she had finally been swimming again after so many years, and that she was having a barbecue the following weekend to thank them and would be inviting some of the locals, he didn't ask if Jet would be invited. Even when she told him that Anna fancied Jet and had specifically requested that he be there, Garrick didn't comment.

And, having had her contraceptive injection whilst in town the day she had bought her wedding dress, even their sex life would be good again before too long. They had to wait a few more days to be sure it had taken hold but the mere fact she would not have that added worry of extra precautions for much longer was a weight off her shoulders.

The thing she found the most surprising was that when she woke up on Monday morning, with the warm breeze dancing with the curtains at her bedroom window, all she wanted to do was go for a swim in the sea. The fact that Garrick was happy to go with her, reminded her why she loved him.

Not that she should need reminding but it didn't hurt, she supposed. Anna had told her to keep the water wings as well as the bikini, so with Garrick by her side her confidence remained high. And when he suggested they make love in the water, and she said no, it wasn't due to nerves – it was the fear of being seen. Knowing the workings of the Universe, it would no doubt have been by Jet.

On Tuesday, Ella went with her and was astonished by her progress.

'After almost thirty years, you finally get back in the water, and now we can't get you out,' she said. But she was clearly happy for Mia.

'How are things with Justin? Getting back to normal?' Mia asked, as they dried themselves.

Ella shrugged. 'Since Saturday night, it's been okay, but it's not the way it was. At least he's no longer making excuses not to see me but things have definitely cooled.'

'Well it is Autumn,' Mia joked.

'Then I'm not looking forward to Winter. Seriously, I'm not sure what to do. If he's going off me I'd rather he said so, but when I ask if something's changed he merely tells me it's all fine.'

'I don't know what to suggest. Either wait and see or end it yourself. There's no point in being unhappy.'

'I'm not unhappy exactly, simply not as happy as I was. I'll give it another week and see.

But he still won't tell me what the fortune-teller said.'

'God, Ella. You're not still thinking about that fortune-teller, are you?'

'Yes,' she said. 'Aren't you?'

Which naturally, made Mia think about the woman. Only the predictions for Lori and Franklin had come true so far. Oh, and Tiffany, Jet's stepsister. Although the woman had been right about Mia overcoming her fear. But the person she can't trust? Was that connected to those unwanted gifts and the card? And Love not being where she was looking for it – had that been about her infatuation with Jet? Had she been looking for something from him that he would never give? None of it made sense.

On Tuesday night, she hoped to see Jet at choir practice but he didn't turn up.

'Have you seen Jet since Saturday, Tom?' she asked, during the break.

'No. But he's got a new man helping out at the farm so perhaps he's busy training him. Why?' Tom handed her a glass of orange juice.

'Thanks. I'm having a barbecue on Sunday afternoon and a new friend wants Jet to come. She's got a bit of a crush on him.'

'I'm sure she's not the only one.' He grinned, but Mia didn't think he meant that as a friendly jibe.

'You're invited, obviously, and I really hope you'll come. If you want to bring someone, feel free.'

'The only person I want is already taken. But thank you. I'll look forward to it.'

There was nothing she could say to that, so she drank her juice until Tom walked away to hand out refreshments to the others.

She invited Toby, Alexia and Bear and also their new loves, and Hettie and Fred, of course. Before she knew it, she had invited almost everyone in the village. The one person she hadn't yet invited, was Jet. And he was the one person Anna had specifically asked for. She had to bite the bullet.

On Wednesday, after an early morning swim with Garrick, she walked to Little Pond Farm, merely telling Garrick she had more people to invite, but she didn't tell him who, or where she was going. At least it wasn't raining this time. Certain that Jet would be in one of the barns, she bypassed the house and went directly to the chicken barn.

'Hello!' She knocked on the door as she had the last time and knocked again when no one came. After the third time, she wandered down the path. No mud, just dry earth today and slivers of what was possibly hay, or straw, or something farm-like. As she walked, a children's song about a farm popped into her head but she couldn't recall the words so she made up some of her own.

Something rumbled and roared close by and she headed in that direction, singing to herself and playing hop-scotch between the light brown strips of whatever it was. She leapt over the white chain across the path and then the red chain. The noise grew louder as she rounded the end of the barn and she saw something flash in the sunlight.

'Mia!' She heard Jet's terrified shout and a second later a screeching, crunching sound and a second after that, there was a thump in her side and strong arms throwing her to the ground. 'My God, woman. You could've been killed! Didn't you see the chains? Didn't you read the signs? What the hell are you doing?' He was lying half on top of her and glaring into her eyes.

'I was looking for you. Don't yell at me. I can't breathe. Can you please get off me?'

He got to his feet, grabbed her unceremoniously by the arm and yanked her up. Only then did she fully comprehend the danger she had been in. Rows of whirling metal blades slowed to a stop and glinted in the sunlight, exactly where she had been standing. If not for the fast reaction of the driver of the vehicle the blades were attached to, and Jet putting himself at risk by getting between the blades and her, she might be in pieces right now. Literally. Her knees buckled beneath her as that sunk in but once again, Jet caught her in his arms.

'I'll get her to the house. Thank God for your quick action, Pete. You saved her life and mine.'

'Saw her in the nick of time,' Pete said. 'You okay, love?'

Mia nodded slowly, still in shock. 'Thank you. Sorry. My fault.'

'Yes,' Jet barked. 'Entirely yours. Come on.' He wrapped one arm around her and half marched, half carried her to the house. Only when they were inside, via the kitchen, and he sat her down on a chair, did he speak to her again. 'What in God's name were you thinking? You don't simply walk around a working farm as if you're out for a stroll. There's machinery here. Dangerous machinery. That harvester nearly sliced you into pieces. And me too. Jesus, Mia. Don't ever, ever do that again.'

'I'm sorry. I didn't know. I thought you just kept cows and chickens and that you made cheese and butter and sold milk and eggs. How was I supposed to know that you had a death machine on wheels?'

'The fields of hay might've been a clue, to most people.'

'Most people? Only if they know about bloody farming, which I don't. I don't suppose you know anything about accounting, but I do. And I wouldn't shout at you for coming to see me in my office. Not that I work there now so you couldn't.'

The tiniest of twitches tugged at his mouth but he glowered at her. 'Calculators can't kill you. Farm machinery can.'

'I don't know. I almost died of boredom working there. But there's no need to keep

shouting. I'm not deaf. I am still in shock though.'
She put one hand on her chest. 'I may die of a
heart attack and then you'll be sorry.'

He grinned. 'At least you still have your sense
of humour.' Serious again, he turned away. 'But
that's about the only sense you do have. I don't
know what you could've been thinking wandering
around like that.' He went to a cupboard and
poured her what she could see was a small glass of
brandy. 'Drink this.'

'I don't like brandy.'

'I don't care. Drink it.'

'No! First you try to chop me to bits, now
you're trying to poison me. I'm going home.' She
stood up but he shoved her back down, albeit fairly
gently.

'Brandy isn't poison and you're not going
anywhere until you've drunk this. It's supposed to
be good for shocks. Then I'm driving you home.'

'I can walk.'

'Not on my farm, you can't. Stop arguing.
Drink it. I'm serious, Mia. Don't think I won't
pour it down your throat if I have to, because I
will.'

'Fine.' She took it and drank it. 'Ooh! That's
rather nice.'

His brows shot up and his mouth fell open.
'So much for not liking it.'

'I've never had it before. It's just the smell I
don't like.'

He sighed and shook his head.

Mia handed him the empty glass. 'Thank you for saving my life, by the way.'

'I hope I never have to do it again. I don't know about you having a heart attack but I died a thousand deaths when I saw you in the path of that thing. Jesus, Mia. For a split second I didn't think I'd get to you in time. I wouldn't have, if Pete hadn't had his wits about him. He was just testing the blades, so thankfully, he wasn't moving forward at full speed, but even so. You really don't know how lucky you are.'

'I'm sorry. And I'm sorry I worried you.'

'Worried me? I've never been so terrified in my life. The thought of anything happening to you is more than I can bear.'

It was hardly the time or the place but she couldn't help herself.

'So you do like me then?'

'Like you? I …' He stopped and sucked in a breath. 'I was thinking about the insurance claim. Killing someone on my farm would send my premiums sky-high. Not to mention I could very well be charged with manslaughter. Even though the signs clearly state: 'Do not pass. Dangerous machinery ahead.''

She grinned at him. He wasn't thinking about insurance and they both knew it.

'Did they? I honestly didn't see the signs. I did see the chains.'

'And you didn't think they might be there for a reason? Other than for you to simply jump over.'

She shook her head. 'This is the first farm I've ever been to and last time I only saw the cow shed and the chicken barn.'

'It was almost the last. Why did you say you were here, anyway?'

'Oh. To invite you to a barbecue.'

He suddenly burst out laughing. 'A barbecue? You were almost barbecue-sized portions yourself. A barbecue.' He shook his head and grinned. 'Couldn't you use the phone, or send an email?'

'I don't have your number or your email address.'

'I'll give them to you. Next time you want to come here, make an appointment. I'll make sure all the machinery is turned off and the chains are too high for you to get over. And I'll meet you at the gate. Why are you having a barbecue? Another celebration?'

'No. Well yes, actually. I can swim! I mean, I've been swimming. Last Sunday, in the sea. And every day since then.'

He blinked several times. 'In the sea? Swimming? You've overcome your fear?'

She nodded. 'Yep. Isn't it great?'

'It's wonderful. So you took the plunge? You said you would that night I saw you dancing in the moonlight, but I didn't think you'd be swimming already. That's really great. Congratulations.'

'I was a good swimmer, especially for a kid. I just haven't swum for years. I'd forgotten how much I enjoyed it. Actually, it was by mistake. I saw a little girl get knocked under the water by a wave. A little wave but I panicked and ran to save her. I was in up to my ankles and I didn't even know it.'

'Wow. Is the girl okay?'

Mia laughed. 'She's absolutely fine. She came up screaming with delight. It was me who was screaming in terror. She had to hold my hand. But when a five-year-old tells you you're safe with them, it makes you realise what a twit you are and that it's time you did something about it. Her mum Susie and Susie's friends came and held me and walked me in and then gave me a bikini and some water wings. Yes, kiddies' water wings and an inflatable dolphin and crocodile and voila! I swam.'

His eyes gleamed as he looked at her and the smile on his face was warm and genuine.

'I'd like to have seen that.'

'I looked a real sight, I bet. A grown woman with two inflatable toys and water wings holding her up. What a picture.'

'No, I meant I'd like to have seen you in a bikini.'

She tutted then smiled. 'You can. Anna, one of the women, took a photo. She's emailed it to me, I can send you a copy if you like.'

He grinned and put the empty glass in the dishwasher. 'I'd like that. I can print it out and stick it on the wall beside my bed.'

'Very funny.'

'Who's joking?'

She stared at him for a moment and he held her gaze.

'Anna, the woman I mentioned, has a thing about you. She'll be at the barbecue on Sunday.'

He stiffened. 'Trying to set me up?'

'No. Just telling you that a beautiful, single woman who can't wait to jump into bed with you will be at my cottage on Sunday.'

'There's only one beautiful woman in your cottage that interests me, but she's not single, sadly. I'd better get you home and then see if there's any damage to the harvester. They're not made to stop that fast.' He turned away.

'Jet?'

'Yes.'

'Did you mean me? Or were you messing about again?'

He looked at her and shook his head. 'I meant you. You know I did. But there's no point in dwelling on it, is there? And I still wouldn't change my ways, so don't think I would.'

'So you want me, but only for fun and then it'd be over?'

'Yes. And we both know you're not the type of girl who could handle that. You want Love. You want romance. You want the whole Prince Charming and the castle. You've got that with Garrick. I can't offer you what he can.'

'No. You think you can't offer me what he can. But perhaps you're simply not ready to. Perhaps you're merely scared.'

'Oh dear God. I knew it was a mistake to tell you. I'll never be ready to settle down. I thought I'd made that clear.' He shook his head. 'Come on. Let's get you home. I've got work to do.'

Mia watched him walk towards the door. Could she pretend she didn't feel well enough to go just yet? No. That wasn't fair to anyone.

He held the door open for her. 'So who's this Anna woman and what's she like?'

Mia looked at him and smiled. 'She's stunningly beautiful, long legs, great body, long sleek black hair. As you're not interested in her mind, her conversation or her other skills, I suppose that's all you need to know.'

'Sounds perfect.' He closed the door behind them. 'I'm looking forward to Sunday already.'

'So am I,' she lied.

They walked around the side of the house, to his car and when they got in, he took a business card and a pen from the glove compartment. He scribbled on the back and handed her the card. 'Mobile, email, home phone. Call me on the landline if you want to come again. And don't forget to email the photo. I really do want to see it.' He started the car and headed down the drive.

'Talking of photos, I've just remembered. So much has happened since then and I know it's weird but I completely forgot. The solicitor came

143

to see me last Monday, not this one just gone, the one before. It was a bit of a surprise, especially as it was Bank Holiday, and he hadn't called beforehand. Anyway, he gave me Mattie's laptop back. And you'll never guess what. She had photos of everyone in the village, including you and even some of you and your mum. Some of which, I don't think you knew were being taken.'

He braked hard and Mia fell forwards, but his arm shot in front of her and held her back.

'Put on your seatbelt. You've nearly died once today. That's quite enough. What do you mean by that?'

'Precisely what I said.' She clicked the seatbelt into place and looked at him. 'She'd taken pictures of everyone in the village throughout her years of living here, it seems. There're a lot and I haven't been through all of them but I did see photos of you with your mum. And from the way the photo's been taken, it looks as if you weren't aware. Not just you, of course. Lots of others too.'

He furrowed his brows. 'That's odd. But I would really like to see those, if I may.' He let off the brake and drove forward.

'Of course. I'll load them onto a USB and give it to you on Sunday. Oh.' She shifted in her seat and grabbed his arm. 'But that's not all.'

'Mia! Are you determined to kill yourself today?' He yanked on the handbrake and turned to face her. 'Okay. Now tell me.'

'Mattie had some super-duper Spyware on there. One that she or someone else had installed to watch me, get access to my emails, and all my social media accounts. In fact, everything I did online. That's creepy, isn't it?'

'Mattie watched you?' He was clearly astonished. 'And monitored what you did? Yeah. That's creepy. Just you?'

Mia nodded. 'I suppose she really wanted to find out all about me before she left me her cottage.'

He frowned and shook his head. 'But spying on you is a bit over the top. Surely there were other ways she could find out about you? Like write you a letter. Or pick up the phone and ask. And where did she get the stuff to spy on you?'

Mia smiled. 'That's exactly what I said. About the letter bit I mean. But wait until you hear this. The reason she used the Spyware stuff is because … Mattie was a spy in World War Two! At least we think she was. We think she may have been recruited by the SOE. Or may have worked for SIS which then became MI6.'

He stared at her but didn't say a word.

'You don't believe me, do you? Why does everyone find that so far-fetched? Lots of ordinary people did extraordinary things in those days. And we think she may have worked for MI6 after the war, too. I suppose you think I'm crazy.'

'Actually, I don't.' He met her eyes and smiled. 'Think you're crazy, that is. And I do believe you. That would explain a lot. She certainly liked secrecy. Although I can't imagine Mattie as a spy. Perhaps there's some other explanation.'

'Well, in one of the photos, we found a picture of a pile of diaries. Mattie's diaries. But we've searched everywhere and can't find them. I'm making it my mission to do so.'

'Mission?' He shook his head and let off the brake, pulling out onto Seaside Road. 'So you're really getting on board with the whole spy thing then?'

'Yep. And you'll laugh the other side of your face when I find them and prove I'm right. Will you let me out a few cottages down, please? I don't want Garrick to see me with you.'

'Why not?' He turned into Lily Pond Lane and stopped the car before he got to Hettie's.

'Thanks,' Mia said, and got out.

'Why not, Mia?' he asked again.

'Because he thinks we've got feelings for one another. And so does Ella.' She shut the door and ran towards Sunbeam Cottage and she didn't hear Jet drive off until she had reached the front door.

Chapter Fourteen

Mia didn't see Jet again until the barbecue on Sunday and as Garrick seemed to be watching her every move, she didn't get much chance to talk to him. Not only that, Garrick introduced Anna to him the moment he arrived, and Anna seemed determined not to leave Jet's side. It annoyed Mia more than she expected, but Jet seemed rather pleased. The minute Anna disappeared to the loo, Mia handed Jet the USB stick.

'Here are those photos I promised you. You seem to have taken a liking to Anna.'

'Thanks for these.' He slipped the stick into the pocket of his jeans. 'What's not to like? You're right. She is gorgeous. Did you tell Garrick you nearly died on my farm?'

'No. And don't you, either.'

'You haven't sent me the photo of you in the bikini. Send that, I'll keep quiet. If I don't have it by five this evening, I'll tell Garrick everything. That's how spies talk, isn't it?' He grinned.

'Pillock. I'll send it. The reason I haven't is because I didn't want Anna to see my photo plastered by your bed when you take her there tonight. Which I assume you will be.'

'How considerate.' He laughed. 'You think I'm joking, don't you?'

'About taking Anna to bed? No.'

'About the photo. I'm deadly serious.'

She looked into his eyes. 'No, you're not. Only a twelve-year-old would plaster a photo on a wall. I know it's all a joke.'

'A twelve-year-old, or a man deeply in love,' he whispered.

'Okay. Very funny. We both know that's not true. I thought you said you never lie.'

'I don't. Ah, here comes Garrick.'

'And here comes Anna. Have fun.'

'I intend to.'

'So do I, Jet. So do I.'

But by the time the sun dipped into the sea and the first mists of Autumn rolled in across the dunes, Mia wasn't having any fun at all.

Jet, on the other hand, seemed to be having plenty. And he hadn't looked in Mia's direction for at least the last three hours.

Not that she kept looking at him and checking, of course.

Which was even more annoying, because she didn't see him leave. But when she looked around for Anna, she also seemed to have left. And it didn't take a genius to work out in which direction she had gone, or who she'd gone with.

Bloody Jet Cross. He was starting to get on Mia's nerves.

•

Chapter Fifteen

The weather was definitely turning cooler; as well as evening mists becoming more frequent, on a couple of mornings the garden had sparkled with dew. Mia wouldn't be able to swim for very much longer so she was determined to make the most of every time she could. By the end of the following week, she was even able to venture in alone. Lori was so proud of her and Mia had spoken to her every day since she'd called to tell her on that first Sunday.

'Everything else okay?' Lori asked on the Saturday morning, a week after the barbecue.

'Yep. Everything's fine. Better than fine. Things have improved with Ella and Justin and they seem to be back to where they were before the Village Fête and that damn fortune-teller. Garrick's working hard and I'm still doing research about the Second World War. It's really interesting to read about all these incredible women. I still haven't found the diaries though.

Everything okay with you? Why are you up? It must be about four in the morning in Dallas.'

'It is, darling. Everything's perfect. Absolutely perfect. But I had a strange dream and I'm missing you, so I thought I'd give you a call. I'm even missing Hettie. Give her and Fred my love, won't you? And Ella and Garrick, too. Have you seen much of Jet?'

'Not since the barbecue last Sunday. He's seeing one of the girls I told you about. Anna. She's gorgeous, so who can blame him, but she's also crazy about him so I hope she doesn't get hurt.'

'Perhaps Anna will be the one to change him?'

'He won't change. He's too determined not to.'

'I don't believe that, darling. He simply hasn't met The One.'

'He definitely doesn't believe in The One. He thinks I'm mad because I do.'

'And is Garrick still The One for you?'

'Yes. Of course he is. Oh. There's someone at the door. I've got to go, Mum. I'll call you tomorrow. Love you. Give my love to Franklin.'

'Love you too.'

Mia hung up the landline phone and went to the door. She wasn't expecting anyone this morning and as Garrick had gone to the wood merchant and Ella was helping Justin in the bakery, neither were they. It was chilly in the hall but when she opened the door, the temperature dropped off the scale.

'Hullo, Mia. It's been a long time since I've seen you. I hope you're not put out with me turning up unannounced but I heard Garrick and Ella are staying with you.'

And suddenly the fortune-teller's words rang out in Mia's head. A cold wind from the North, she'd said. But Mia hadn't understood what she meant until this very minute.

'Hello, Fiona. You look exhausted,' Mia said, her gaze travelling down to the light raincoat stretched tight across Fiona's tummy. 'You'd better come in and sit down.'

Fiona stepped into the hall and smiled. She had a suitcase with her. 'Thank you, Mia. It's been a long journey. I caught the overnight from Aberdeen. I've been travelling since eight last night.'

'Let me take your coat.'

Mia was struggling for words. Why on earth was Fiona here?

Fiona pulled off her coat and handed it to Mia. 'I was going to send Garrick a text because I couldn't get him on the mobile, but I thought it'd be better in person.' She gave Mia a nervous smile.

'Go through into the living room and sit down.' Mia pointed to the open door. 'I'll go and make some coffee.'

'Tea, if you don't mind.' Fiona stopped just inside the living room doorway. 'How is he, Mia?'

Mia turned and took a step towards her. 'Garrick? Oh. He's fine.'

Fiona walked to the sofa. 'I'm not quite sure how to break this news.' She perched on the edge, looking rather uncomfortable.

Against her better judgment, Mia followed her in. 'Oh?'

'I know it'll be a shock.' Fiona fiddled with the hem of her dress. 'It's been a shock to me too. But I've put it off for too long already. And it's only fair he knows.'

Mia couldn't take this. 'I'm sorry, Fiona, but why does Garrick need to know you're pregnant? I assume you are pregnant, from the way you were standing. But you've both moved on since you split up, so there's no need to break this news to him. He'll be happy for you and wish you well, I'm sure.'

Fiona frowned. 'I don't think you understand, Mia. I'm not here to tell Garrick I've moved on. I'm here to tell him I'm having a baby. His baby.'

Mia couldn't have heard her correctly. 'Sorry. Whose baby?'

Fiona looked surprised by the question. 'Garrick's, of course. Garrick's and mine.'

'What? No. It can't be.' The room must be spinning. Mia stumbled to a chair opposite the sofa. 'It's not possible.' She dropped onto the seat and stared at Fiona.

Fiona shook her head and her long red curls cascaded over her face. Even tired, she was stunning. And she did look so much like Alexia. Or Alexia looked like her. But why was Mia thinking about that? Fiona couldn't be expecting Garrick's baby. She simply couldn't be. They'd been apart for far too long.

'I know I don't look it and that's been half the problem. I had no idea myself until a couple of weeks ago. I'd been putting on weight but I thought that was due to overeating and lack of exercise. Our break up was hard on both of us and I simply threw myself into work. I've been stuffing my face with pizza and ice cream and eating all sorts of unhealthy junk. It sounds ridiculous, I'm sure, but it didn't even register with me that I hadn't had a period for months. I stopped taking the pill shortly after Garrick left so I thought my hormones had just gone haywire.' She gave a little laugh. 'Little did I know! I put it down to stress. I wasn't having morning sickness. And I didn't know any other signs. I was on the pill when we were together so pregnancy never entered my head. It was only when a close friend of mine mentioned that she thought I might be that I went and had a test.'

'A test? They're not always accurate, are they?' Mia was grasping at straws. This couldn't be true. It simply couldn't be.

'Virtually one hundred per cent. But I had another, with the doctor, just in case and that confirmed it. I'm five months pregnant, almost to the day.'

'Five months? But … but Garrick told me you hadn't had sex for months!'

She frowned again. 'Did he? I don't know why he said that. Although it had been about five weeks or so. He's obviously told you all about it. I know that's what he's like. After he proposed we thought we could go on. Work something out about the kid issue, but we couldn't. And during that time, I know I let my routine slip and probably forgot to take my pill. The night he left to move back home … Well you know how it is. We spent our final night together and that's when this little darling happened.' She rubbed her tummy and smiled lovingly at her bump.

'But you don't want kids. That's why you split up.'

'Aye. That's right. I didn't want kids. Or didn't think I did. I was one hundred and ten per cent certain of that. But the strangest thing is, when I got the result, somehow, deep inside, I realised I had known. And not for one minute did I think I didn't want this child. Not for one second, even. But as I said, it was too late to do anything when I found out in any case. I still love Garrick, and I'm hoping he still loves me. I'm here to ask if we can pick up where we broke off. You've known him all his life, Mia. I know he'll be shocked, but I think he'll be pleased. Don't you?'

Mia slowly and unsteadily got to her feet but how she walked she had no idea. Her knees were buckling beneath her and her feet were lumps of lead. 'I've no idea what he'll feel, Fiona. I'll go and make some tea. Stay there and rest.'

How was she being so cool? So polite? This woman had turned up on her doorstep. *Her doorstep.* And had ripped her future to shreds.

What on earth could she do? She couldn't get hold of Garrick. There was no phone signal. But neither could she sit in the living room playing host to Fiona without telling her the situation. Fiona had been honest and completely open with her. Far too open for Mia's liking, especially as they weren't exactly friends. They'd only met a few times over the years. But how could she say that Garrick was now engaged and in just over one month, he would be marrying her.

Or would he? Now she must be having a heart attack. She couldn't breathe, her palms and forehead were sweaty and her heart was pounding in her chest. No. It was simply a panic attack. Which was a pity given the circumstances. A heart attack might solve all their problems.

But she mustn't think like this. The problem was, she couldn't think at all. There was only one thing she could do. She would have to go and get Ella.

Chapter Sixteen

Ella was even more shocked than Mia, if that were possible. Although she did say, 'Bloody Nora! How the hell could that fortune-teller have possibly known that. She'd said I'll soon be an aunt and she was right. You know what this means, don't you?'

'It means I'm heartbroken and all you can think about is how this will affect you. What about me, Ella? What about Garrick? What about our wedding?'

'You're right. I'm sorry.' Ella linked her arm through Mia's. 'Did you tell Fiona you were coming to get me?'

Mia shook her head. 'I didn't tell her anything. I just ran out. She thinks I'm making tea. But I couldn't go back in there again and look at her, especially as she's carrying Garrick's child. God, Ella. How can this be happening?'

'I've no idea. But we'll have to face it and deal with whatever happens. The important thing is to get hold of Garrick. Do you know where he is?'

'Yes.'

'Then why don't you go and find him and break the news to him. I'll come back with you now and sit and keep Fiona company.'

'Okay,' Mia said. But as they walked out of Justin's bakery, after Ella told him there was an emergency she had to deal with, and crossed the green, heading towards Sunbeam Cottage, they saw Garrick's van in the drive.

'Oh my God,' Mia said. 'He's home.'

'Bloody Nora.' Ella looked at Mia. 'What do we do now?'

'I don't know. Do you think we should leave them alone for a few minutes? I don't really want to but I can't face walking in there and seeing the look in his eyes. I can't believe this, Ella. I really can't believe it. I want to sit right here and cry.'

Ella squeezed her hand and tightened their linked arms. 'No you don't. You're Mia Ward, and you can handle anything. You've faced your fear of water. You can deal with this. Whatever happens. It's Garrick I'm worried about.'

'I'm not sure I can. And I'm worried about him too. This will devastate him, Ella.'

'I know. Come on. You have a right to be there. You have a right to know what Garrick plans to do.'

'I think we both know what he'll do. If this is his kid, and I can't see Fiona lying about it, he'll go back to Fiona. I know he loves me, but I know he still loves her. And now, he'll love her again. I'm sure of it.'

'Let's wait and see. It's not over till the fat lady sings. Sorry. Not a good thing to say given the situation.'

Chapter Seventeen

'Why didn't you tell me?' Fiona glared at Mia when she walked back into the living room. 'Garrick's gone upstairs to see if you're there. Why didn't you say you'd got engaged?'

'Mia!' Garrick hurtled down the stairs and rushed to Mia's side. 'I had no idea. Believe me.' He looked as distraught as she felt.

'I know you didn't. Fiona's explained everything. In great detail, I might add.'

'Whereas you explained nothing. You should've told me, Mia instead of letting me go on about how Garrick and I would get back together. Obviously now we won't. I wish you'd said. I would've left before he saw me.'

'Obviously what? What do you mean, you won't get back together? We're only engaged. We're not married and we're definitely not having a child.'

'Only engaged?' Garrick screeched, grabbing her shoulder and turning her to face him. 'Only engaged? I love you Mia. I can't just walk away and leave you.'

'You mean … you'd choose me? What about the baby, Garrick?' She stared into his eyes and saw the turmoil he was feeling.

His hand slid from her shoulder and he shook his head in an obvious state of shock. 'It's my baby and I'll obviously want to be a part of the child's future. But … Fiona and I have split up.' He shot a glance at Fiona. 'We can't just pick things up again and pretend none of this has happened, because it has.'

Mia took a few steps towards the hall, then back again and paced back and forth for several seconds as everyone else fell silent, all clearly lost in their own thoughts.

'I think this has been a massive shock for all of us,' she finally said. 'And it hasn't really sunk in for me so I know it can't have for you, Garrick. I love you too, but I know you well enough to understand what this child means to you. I can't come between you and the family you want so much. Not unless you're absolutely sure that's what you want. With no regrets. And I don't think you can make that decision now. I don't think any of us can.'

'What are you saying?' Garrick walked towards her but Mia backed away.

'I can't believe I'm saying this, but I think Fiona should stay here and we should all spend the afternoon thinking about it and sleep on it tonight.

We can discuss it in the morning and see if any of us feels differently then.'

'I don't think I should stay here,' Fiona said, struggling to her feet. 'I'll go back to Aberdeen. You two can decide and let me know.'

'No,' Mia said. 'You're not going anywhere. You look exhausted and now you've had as big a shock as we have. You're staying here and that's that.'

'Mia,' Fiona said, smiling wanly. 'Can't you see how ludicrous a situation this is?'

'Of course I can. I'm not an idiot. But it's not just you two this child affects. It's also me. And I want the best for all of us. Including the baby. Now if you'll excuse me, I need to go and call my mum. Ella, will you take Fiona up to Mum's room and get her settled. And Garrick, take Fiona's case upstairs, and then I expect she'd like something to eat. Please don't argue with me. This is my cottage. My rules. I need to go.'

'Mia?'

'Not now, Garrick. Please, not now.'

She walked away and despite saying she was going to call Lori, she trudged into the garden, but Garrick followed her.

'I said not now, Garrick,' she pleaded, tears pricking her eyes.

'I know what you said but you're not being fair to me. This is just as much of a shock to me you know. I didn't want this. I didn't ask for this to happen. I love you, Mia. I meant it when I said that. I love you. Yes, a small part of me still loves Fiona, but not enough to leave you for her.'

'Not even for the baby?'

He hesitated. 'I … No. Not even for the baby.'

She shook her head. 'Don't lie to me or yourself, Garrick. It's not fair to either of us. You hesitated when you answered. You're already having doubts.'

'Jesus Christ, Mia! Give me a break. I feel as if a building has collapsed on top of me. I can't breathe and I'm struggling in the dark to find a way out. My chest is caving in under the pressure. That's what this feels like.'

'I understand that. But that's the point. You're torn. You don't know what to do or which way to turn. You can't just find out something like this and simply say, "Oh okay. Well, never mind, I'll marry Mia and go and see Fiona and my baby at the weekends." It doesn't work like that. Marriage is hard enough without that pressure. And even though I trust you, I know you still love her. Imagine how I'll feel every time you go to see the mother of your child and play happy families. Imagine me sitting here waiting for you and wondering if one day, you won't come back to me.'

He nodded. 'I understand that. I see your point. But I don't know what to do.'

'Nor do I, Garrick. Dear God. Why did you have to have sex with her when you broke up? You told me you hadn't had sex for months.'

He shrugged. 'We hadn't. For several weeks, at least. But you know how it is. We still loved one another. We weren't breaking up because we'd fallen out of love. We were breaking up because we wanted different things. The last time we saw each other to finally say goodbye, well. It just sort of happened. One thing led to another and we had goodbye sex.'

'Goodbye sex? Bloody hell. Why couldn't you just wave at one another? Or kiss each other goodbye? Or shake hands, or something? Why did you have to have sex with her to say goodbye? I don't have sex with people I say goodbye to. Ever.'

'Okay. But shouting at me isn't helping, is it?'

'No. Actually yes. It's making me feel better. Now please leave me alone to think. I need some time. We both need some time. Sorry. We all need some time.'

She ran down onto the beach, where the sand shimmered in the morning sunlight, and the gentle waves lapped the shore. She stared at the horizon, watched a gull soar overhead and then she crumpled in a heap and cried until she could cry no more.

Chapter Eighteen

Mia managed to avoid Garrick and Fiona for several hours, locking herself in the attic room after sneaking back into the cottage. Yes, it was wrong. Yes, it was selfish. But seeing Garrick so distraught, so torn, was not helping her to think things through. And seeing Fiona – and her baby bump – would only make the outcome seem more inevitable. Garrick had made it very clear how important having a family was to him and how much he wanted children. Would he really be able to walk away from the mother of his child? It seemed highly unlikely. And would Mia want him to? As both he and Fiona had said, they had not split up because they no longer loved one another; they'd split up because they wanted different things. Now they wanted the same thing, and in less than four months' time, they would have it. A bouncing baby boy or girl.

Okay, things had changed since they had split up. Mia loved Garrick and he loved her, obviously more than she had realised, if his first reaction was to say he wanted to stay with her. But she had to be honest with herself. Hadn't she been having doubts? Not long ago she had admitted to herself that her feelings for Jet Cross were not as platonic as she thought they were. No matter how hard she tried, she could not get Jet out of her head.

She had hoped it was all just silly banter. A bit of harmless flirting between them. But it was more than that on her part. And if what Jet had said to her the other day at Little Pond Farm was anything to go by, it was also more than that on his. What did that say about her relationship with Garrick?

If Jet wasn't so hung up on not getting involved romantically, would he have asked her out long before Garrick proposed? And if he had, would she have said yes? Or, if she was the sort of woman who was happy with simply having fun, no strings attached, would she and Jet have tumbled into bed the first time she had looked into his eyes just four months ago?

How could she honestly ask Garrick to give up the chance of being with his child in Scotland, to stay here with her, if she had doubts like this? How was that fair to any of them?

Fiona still loved Garrick. That was obvious even before she had actually said so. Fiona wasn't here because she couldn't face the thought of raising this child alone. She was not the type of woman to be fazed by lone-parenting. If she had to do this alone, she would, and she would make a bloody good job of it, Mia was certain of that. Fiona was here because she genuinely believed Garrick would be pleased to see her … and because she wanted to raise her child – their child – with the man she still loved.

'Mia?' A knock on the attic door was accompanied by Ella's voice. 'You can't hide up there all day and night you know. It's four-thirty and you haven't eaten since breakfast. And don't pretend you're not there because I know you are. The coast is clear. Garrick and Fiona have gone for a walk on the beach. Although I don't know if that's something you want to hear or not.'

It wasn't. But what did she expect? You can't leave your fiancé and his pregnant ex alone for hours on end and not expect them to talk.

'Fine. I'm coming down.'

Mia clumped down the stairs and unlocked the door, smiling gratefully when Ella handed her a large glass of wine.

'I assumed you'd be needing this.'

'You know me so well.' Mia gulped down the contents, hardly taking a breath.

'I should've brought the bottle.' Ella shook her head and linked her arm through Mia's, as they walked along the hall. 'They've only just left so they'll probably be a while. Come downstairs and talk to me. I promise you can run back and hide, if you really want to, the minute we see them return.'

'I want to phone Mum, anyway. If it's four-thirty here, it's ten-thirty in the morning in Dallas and I think I can talk now without bursting into tears. Have either of them said anything to you?' Mia unlinked their arms when they got to the stairs.

'Garrick's been going mad. He knew you were in the attic and I don't know how I stopped him from coming up and breaking down the door but I persuaded him you needed space. You all needed space. Fiona's been apologising one minute and cursing herself for coming here the next. Then cursing Garrick for not loving her as much as she thought he did, saying he wouldn't have rushed straight into a relationship with you if he'd really been in love.' Ella rolled her eyes. 'Neither of us has mentioned Alexia, obviously. Fiona would probably kill him. Not that anything really happened with her, but even so.' She tutted. 'It's all Uncle Bert's fault.'

'Uncle Bert?'

'Yeah. Mum and Dad are still away so when Fiona couldn't get hold of Garrick and decided she didn't want to send a text – not that he'd have got that either – she called the house and spoke to Uncle Bert. Like the numbskull my uncle is, he said Garrick and I were staying with you for the summer and gave her the address. It didn't occur to him to mention that turning up unannounced might not be a good idea. Or that Garrick had moved on and that he and you were engaged. Bloody Nora, wait until I get my hands on him.'

'It's not really his fault. The engagement was all a bit of a rush, wasn't it? Perhaps he didn't really take it in and with your Mum and Dad away, there was no one to remind him. But imagine if he had told her. She might have kept the child secret and raised it on her own, deciding if Garrick has moved on, he wouldn't want to know. But he has a right to know. Not that I think Fiona would've done that. Oh I don't know. It's all so confusing. So unbelievable. Such a bloody mess.'

'It could've been worse.' Ella grinned as they reached the hall and walked towards the kitchen.

'Oh really? How, exactly?'

'You could've been pregnant too. We all thought you were, remember? That would've really thrown the cat among the pigeons.'

Trust Ella to think of that.

She was right though. And as miserable as Mia was, she burst out laughing.

She had to be grateful for that, at least.

Chapter Nineteen

Mia had expected her mum to be as astonished by the news as she had been – which Lori was; but what Mia didn't expect was for her mum to say that it all might be for the best.

'For the best? How can it possibly be for the best, Mum?' Mia put the landline phone on handsfree and slumped on the sofa. 'I'm supposed to be getting married. The dress is bought. The church is booked. The invitations have all gone out.'

'I know, darling. But think how much worse it would've been if Fiona had turned up after the wedding. Or even during. At least you all have time to work things out. And, I know this is no consolation whatsoever, but the fortune-teller did predict this. And she's been right so far.'

'The fortune-teller? Why does everyone keep going on about that bloody fortune-teller? You're really bringing her up at a time like this!'

'Yes, darling, because I know you love Garrick and I know he's a wonderful man, but I honestly don't think he's the man for you.'

'What? Why didn't you say so before?'

'I did, darling. Not in so many words, I admit, but I tried to make you really consider your options. I simply wasn't convinced your heart was completely in it and I hoped that, with me not around, you'd think things through and come to that conclusion yourself. I love Garrick dearly, and I was dreading him getting his heart broken, but I don't think this has come as such a surprise to him as it has to you.'

Mia sat upright and stared at the phone. 'What does that mean? You think Garrick knew?'

'Not exactly. But I think the fortune-teller gave him a clear indication that something drastic was going to happen. He could hardly speak when he came out of that tent, remember? And when he did, he said something like, "The woman can't be right, can she?" And let's not forget, he was in a hurry to propose, but he was in an even bigger rush to set the wedding date. I know he'd bought the ring before and was planning to pop the question, but I'm convinced that whatever the fortune-teller told him, had something to do with his haste. The woman told Ella that she would soon be an aunt. Don't you think there's a very strong possibility the woman told Garrick he would soon be a father? Perhaps that was why he was so overjoyed when we thought you might be pregnant, and so

171

incredibly disappointed when you weren't. I assumed that his haste was because he was worried about Jet. What if he was worried about someone else entirely?'

'He wouldn't do that. He would've phoned and asked Fiona outright if he thought there was any chance of that. I'm sure he would.' She got up and grabbed the phone, heading towards the kitchen. This called for another glass of wine.

'There's only one way to find out, darling. Ask him. He loves you. We all know that. Perhaps he thought that if the two of you were married, nothing would tear you apart. I'm only guessing, of course. You'll have to ask him, to be sure. And whatever he says, think about what you really, truly want from your life. You're going to be a wealthy woman next year. You can do anything you want to, with anyone you want. I know you love Garrick but isn't it possible that you've let a long-held crush turn into something it was never supposed to be? That all the upheaval and excitement had you spinning and perhaps you landed in the arms of the wrong man? Only you can decide. I know you don't want to hurt him, but it'll hurt him more to lie. And it'll hurt you too in the long run. This is your life, Mia. You must live it as you want, regardless of how anyone else thinks you should. Promise me you'll do that, darling. I want you to be happy.'

'I will, Mum. I promise. And I can hear Garrick's voice so I'll talk to him right now and speak to you later. I love you, Mum.'

Mia hung up and waited for Garrick to come up the steps to the decking and into the kitchen. He was laughing and so was Fiona. Was that good, or was that bad?

'Mia!'

'Sorry, Garrick. I didn't mean to startle you. I was waiting for you and Fiona to get back. There's something I need to ask you.'

'Of course.' He swallowed hard and his Adam's Apple pumped up and down like a piston engine. 'Ask me anything. Fiona and I were just …' He coughed. 'It doesn't matter.'

Mia pulled out a chair and sat, and Garrick sat next to her, giving Fiona a sideways glance.

'D'you want me to go elsewhere?' Fiona asked, her face serious now.

'No. I think you should hear this too. And Ella. Where's Ella gone? Ella?' Mia glanced around and called out to her friend.

'I'm here.' Ella dashed along the hall into the kitchen and her eyes shot from Mia to Fiona to Garrick. 'I think we need wine. I'll get it.'

'Thanks. I was just about to do that,' Mia said.

Fiona sat at the farthest end of the table and no one said another word until Ella had placed the bottle and four glasses down.

'None for me.' Fiona raised her hand in a stop gesture.

'Bloody Nora. I forgot.' Ella frowned apologetically. 'I'll get you orange juice instead.'

'What did the fortune-teller tell you, Garrick?' Mia asked while Ella was finding the juice.

'Fortune-teller?' Fiona queried.

'Yes,' Mia said. 'There was a fortune-teller at the Summer Fête and she told us all some things we didn't want to hear. I want to know what she told Garrick.'

He swallowed again. 'I can't believe you're bringing this up now. Don't we have more important issues to deal with?'

'Yes. But I want to know. She told me that someone I loved would soon walk out of my life. That I couldn't hold them back. That some things are meant to be and some are not. I thought she was talking about someone else, but I'm now realising she meant you, Garrick. She told Ella she would soon be an aunt. What did she tell you? And please tell us the truth.'

He shook his head, sighed and ran a hand through his hair. He glanced at Fiona before meeting Mia's eyes. Taking a deep breath, he began. 'She said that I've met the woman of my dreams and that we'll have a lifetime of happiness together with a large family. But that she saw two women in my life. One past, one present. Present could be past and past could be present. That she heard a child's heartbeat. That I had to make a choice and it would be the hardest one in my life so far. She saw a wedding and the saying "marry in haste, repent at leisure" would not apply. If I married in haste, I would find true pleasure. True happiness. Providing I made the right choice. That's it. That's all she said. I can remember every last word.'

'And you thought that meant you should marry me in haste?' Mia's gaze locked with his.

Garrick nodded. 'Yes. And when I came home and Ella said you might be pregnant, it all made sense. But I also thought it meant Fiona would come back into my life and I was worried that what the woman was telling me was that I wasn't over Fiona.' He shot Fiona another glance. 'But if I married you quickly, I would be happy. We would be happy.'

'That doesn't make any sense, Garrick Swann!' Fiona snapped. 'No sense at all. And since when has an intelligent man like you listened to a fortune-teller's nonsense?'

Mia smiled lovingly at Garrick as Ella poured the wine. 'Actually, it sort of does. But I think you were trying to marry the wrong woman, Garrick. I think you're supposed to be marrying Fiona.'

'No!' Garrick jumped to his feet, knocking his glass over. 'No! I …' His voice trailed off and he closed his eyes tight for a moment.

'I think you know it's true, don't you, Garrick?'

'Garrick?' Fiona rose slowly to her feet. 'I have no idea what's going on here.'

'Bloody Nora,' Ella said, dropping onto a chair as the spilt wine formed a little pool in the centre of the table. 'I think what's going on is that Mia and Garrick are no longer engaged. Is that right?' She frowned at Mia.

Mia nodded. 'I think it is. Garrick and I love each other but we both know what the outcome of this will be and there's no point in dragging it out. Better to make a clean break now. It'll cause less pain in the long run.' She smiled wanly at Fiona and Garrick. 'What you two do from here is up to you, of course, but again, I think we all know what that'll be.'

'I love you, Mia.' Garrick turned to her and reached out his hand.

Instead of taking it, Mia slid the ring off her finger and placed it in his upturned palm.

'I know you do, Garrick. And I love you. But neither of us love each other enough. And deep down, we both know that you still love Fiona. If you stay here with me, you'll regret it. We all will. And none of us want that.'

He nodded slowly, sadly, as if his heart was breaking. 'I honestly do love you, Mia. But I also still love Fiona. Talking to her today has made me realise just how much.' He gave Fiona the briefest smile, but that smile held so much love, Mia could see that.

'You love me?' Fiona asked, looking bewildered. 'Enough to marry me? Is that what you're saying? But earlier you said you'd choose Mia over me. What's changed your mind?'

'Nothing's changed his mind, Fiona,' Mia said. 'He never got over you. He's loved you all along. But he loves me too. It was a shock, you coming here. None of us knew what to do, or say, or how we really felt. It took a few hours for reality to settle in. But now we do know. And this is right for all of us. Painful, but right. You can stay the night, as planned, but I hope you'll understand that I'm not ready to chat over dinner.' She looked at Garrick and smiled sadly. 'I'll always be your friend Garrick and I hope you'll always be mine. Make yourself at home, Fiona. I truly wish you every happiness. Now if you don't mind, I'm going to my room, with a bottle of wine, and I'm going to phone my mum again. I think I'll probably stay there for a couple of days at least.' She turned to walk away.

'Mia?' Garrick said. 'Are you okay? Is this really what you want?'

Mia turned back to face him, tears pricking at her eyes. 'Yes. But I don't think it matters what I want. Oh. Can somebody please tell Tom we need to cancel the wedding?'

Garrick nodded dolefully. 'I'll do that.'

'I'll do it,' Ella said, 'You should stay here and sort things out with Fiona.'

Chapter Twenty

'I really don't want to go,' Mia said, pulling back from Ella and shaking her head. 'I know it's been two weeks since Garrick left, but I still don't think I'm up to this.'

'You've got to face everyone sooner or later and it may as well be sooner. I can't keep people at bay forever. Hettie almost ripped my throat out when I told her you weren't seeing anyone. Okay, perhaps that's a slight exaggeration, but she hasn't been happy. Tom's called round at least eight times. Freda and Alexia, twice. Even Bear's been round more than once to see if you're okay. In fact, I think I've had to turn away everyone in the village, or tell them not to call round.'

'But not Jet.'

Ella sighed. 'No. Not Jet. But everyone else. And they all understood when I said you needed a little time. But you've had that now and nobody likes a misery, so it's time you showed your face. Besides, there'll be such a crowd on the beach that no one will even notice you. And they'll all be looking at the fireworks anyway. You can't spend the rest of your life hiding in that attic room.'

'I know. And I wasn't hiding. Nor was I being a misery. I was searching for Mattie's diaries and reading more about the SOE and all the incredible things women did during the war. It's fascinating.'

'Of course you were.' Ella gave Mia a disbelieving look. 'Lori gets back on Monday. Do you really want to tell her you missed the highlight of the year in Little Pondale? Tonight's a big deal for the village. Don't give me that pathetic look.' Ella sighed. 'Okay. What would Mattie do? Would she skulk indoors while the entire village celebrates its Millennium?'

'Okay, okay. I'll come. But if one person says they feel sorry for me, I'm going to punch them on the nose, come straight home and drink an entire bottle of wine.'

Ella shrugged. 'That sounds perfectly reasonable to me.' She linked her arm through Mia's and walked into the garden. 'This could be fun. Although how they know this place has been here since September 29th 1018, is beyond me.'

'It says so on the foundation stone in the church. I remember Hettie mentioning it once during a conversation she and Mum were having about the village and the curse of Frog's Hollow. Hettie said the village was here long before the church and that it dates back to the Dark Ages.' Mia giggled. 'She even said that Alfred the Great came here, but there is no way she could possibly know that.'

'Perhaps he signed the visitors' book at The Frog and Lily,' Ella joked. 'That place has definitely been here since the Dark Ages. At least the toilets smelt as if they had when Justin and I were in there at lunchtime. This Indian Summer they say we're getting couldn't have come at a worse time. They're digging up the lane to put in fibre optic cables, apparently. Can you believe that? Little Pondale is joining the twenty-first century. Anyway, the workmen hit a pipe outside the pub this morning and God, does the place pong.'

Mia glanced at her. 'You didn't mention that earlier.'

'Sorry. I forgot. I only found out when I almost fell down a hole the workmen had dug and hadn't got around to cordoning off. Then Alec confirmed it. But it went out of my head when Alexia reminded me about the fireworks tonight, and I was so intent on getting you to come, that I completely forgot about everything else.'

'Oh? Is there anything else you've forgotten to tell me? The way you said that made it sound as if there is.'

Ella shook her head. 'Nope. No other news.'

They continued walking over the dunes and onto the sand. The tide was out and the moon was on the wane. A gentle breeze played with Mia's hair and the gulls overhead soared silently for once. Twilight was giving way to night and myriad stars filled the sky. In the distance, Mia could see the villagers crowding around a bonfire even though it wasn't in the least bit cold. Part of the festivities, obviously. It was the perfect night for romance – if you had someone to be romantic with. And once again, Mia missed Garrick and the feel of his arms around her. The kiss of his lips. The touch of his hand. She took a deep breath and tried to think of something else.

Would Jet be here tonight?

'Oh wait,' Ella interrupted Mia's thoughts. 'You did see the message I took when you were in the shower this morning, didn't you? Only you haven't mentioned that, and as you were just talking about Mattie, you probably would've, if you'd seen it. I scribbled it on the notepad by the phone in the living room. I was late to meet Justin, so I couldn't stop.'

'No.' Mia stopped in her tracks. 'What message? Someone called concerning Mattie and you forgot to tell me? Ella! You know how important this is to me. How could you forget? Who was it and what did they say? Did they leave a number?'

'Yes, yes. Hold your horses. And I'm sorry, okay. As I said, I was in a rush. I'm not sure where my head is at the moment. You and Garrick breaking up has affected me too, you know.'

Mia nudged Ella with her shoulder. 'I know it has. I'm sorry. What was the message?'

Ella smiled. 'It was from someone called Gill. Yes, as in a fish gill. It's short for Guillaume, he told me. Though who names their son Guillaume in this day and age is beyond me. The French, apparently. He's French by birth, he said, but he didn't sound French. Sounded as if he'd spent too much time in Oxford and got a punting pole stuck up his bum. Very prim and proper.'

Mia giggled. 'That's not nice. But what did he say about Mattie? And how did he get our number? It's ex-directory. Mattie made sure of that.'

Ella laughed. 'I'm getting to that. He told me that his grandfather had died recently and when they were going through his things they found letters from Mattie. They were friends and that's how Gill got the number. From the grandad's phone book. He was also called Guillaume, but Mattie called him Will. Don't ask. I foolishly did and got an entire spiel about how Guillaume is the French equivalent of William and that William is an ancient German name meaning Resolute Protector which is why Mattie called the grandad Will. That made no sense at all but I dared not ask him to explain. God, the guy is boring! I'd hate to meet him face to face. Anyway, long story short. He wants to have a chat with you about Mattie and his grandad and he left a number so that you could call him back.'

'Ella!' Mia turned back towards the cottage but Ella grabbed her and yanked her forwards.

'Not tonight. I told him you'd call him tomorrow. I knew that you'd use it as an excuse not to come to the fireworks, and that's probably why I didn't tell you, to be honest. Although I did write it on the notepad, as I said. But I knew you wouldn't look at that today. Oh look. There's Jet. And I think he's seen us. And there's Justin. I just want to have a quick word with him and then I'll come back.'

'Don't you dare leave me!' Mia demanded but Ella let go of Mia's arm and dashed away. There wasn't much Mia could do, unless she made it obvious and turned and ran. As tempting as that was, she stood her ground and watched Jet walk towards her. He was alone and didn't even have Mattie with him. Dressed casually, as always, he still looked drop-dead gorgeous. Damn him.

'Hello Mia,' he smiled.

'Hi. Where's Mattie?'

He raised his brows. 'At home. I thought a firework display might not be the best place for her. Pete hates fireworks too, so he's staying with her. You remember Pete?'

'Of course I do. The man who nearly made me several slices thinner.'

Jet laughed. 'Says the woman who nearly gave us both a heart attack.'

'Except you don't have a heart, so I can't.'

'Ouch. Where did that come from?'

'Sorry. That was uncalled for. I've been a bit upset. Not that you're in the least bit interested, of course.'

He furrowed his brows and looked her directly in the eyes. 'You of all people know that's not true.'

'Really? Then why are you the one person in the village who hasn't called round to see how I am? Or asked after me? Or sent me an email? Or anything?'

'Perhaps because I'm the one person in the village who thought you needed time to be alone. To think things through without distractions. To get over Garrick without me telling you he wasn't the right man for you anyway. But maybe I was wrong.'

She held his gaze for a moment before lowering hers and shaking her head. 'No. You're right. I suppose I should thank you for that.'

'Don't be ridiculous. I don't want your thanks.' He smiled. 'But now we're on the subject. How are you?'

She shrugged. 'I'm fine. I've been keeping myself busy. It hurt. I'm not pretending it didn't, but some things just aren't meant to be. We're still friends and always will be. I wish him every happiness. I really do. I wish them both happiness.' She let her voice trail off and they stood in silence for a few seconds, merely looking at one another.

He looked away towards the sea. 'Been swimming lately? I haven't seen you.'

'No. I haven't felt much like swimming and until yesterday, the weather's been appalling. Raining almost every day.' She smirked. 'Mind you, that sort of matched my mood.'

'And now the sun's returned and everything's going to be fine. Hot sunny days for a couple of weeks, so they say. Right into mid-October, possibly.'

'Great. At least if I decide to drown myself the water might be warm.'

His head shot round and he glared at her. 'Don't even joke about such things. And enough with the self-pity. Worse things happen than broken engagements.'

'Says the man who's never been engaged so wouldn't have a clue how it feels. And it's not self-pity. I'm feeling sad, that's all. I'll get over it.'

'I know you will. Shall we get closer to the action?'

'No thanks. I'd rather keep my distance. But don't let me stop you. How's Anna? Are you here with her?'

He gave her a confused look. 'Anna?'

'Dear God, Jet! Please don't tell me you've already forgotten who she is. The woman you met at the barbecue. Beautiful. Long black hair. The one you've been sleeping with.'

He grinned. 'Oh yes. The woman you seemed so determined to set me up with. I hate to break this to you but I haven't been sleeping with her. Or doing anything else with her either before you think of some sarcastic retort. We went our separate ways at your barbecue and I haven't seen her since.'

'But she was crazy about you.'

He looked her up and down and shook his head. 'Hmm. This may surprise you but I don't sleep with a woman just because she's crazy about me. The feeling has to be mutual.'

Mia tutted. 'Yeah right. You've never been crazy about a woman in your life.'

He sighed deeply and moved a little closer to her, looking down into her eyes. 'I've been crazy about a few women, actually. But I've never been in love.'

'Is there a difference?' Goose bumps crawled up her arms and her heart beat a little faster.

'I believe so. But I'm no expert, never having been in love.'

'So you're saying you can be crazy about someone but not actually love them.'

'Yes. When that passion dies, there's nothing left. That's not love. Love is about wanting to be with someone for the rest of your life, no matter what. I've never felt like that.'

'So what was wrong with Anna?'

He moved closer still and when the band struck up its pounding, pulsing drumbeat, he didn't flinch and he didn't turn around.

'Nothing was wrong with Anna. She simply wasn't you.'

'Me?' she croaked above the primal beat and the cheering crowd.

'You,' he said, his eyes alight with something she had only seen there once before.

Why she did it, she had no idea, but she reached out and grabbed the collars of his polo shirt, pulling him close and kissing him on the lips.

For one second it seemed that he might pull away. Instead, he wrapped his arms around her and pinned her to him, kissing her in a way she had never been kissed before. Not even by Garrick. It was as if her very essence, her heart and soul belonged to him, and his belonged to her.

The first firework zoomed into the night sky, hissing and banging and sending shards of sparkles through the air, followed by the second, third and fourth. It was only after the fifth that he suddenly let her go.

'Wow!' she said. Was she swaying? Was she actually swaying?

There was a strange look on his face. A mixture of surprise, delight and passion, followed quickly by something akin to doubt and confusion.

'Those fireworks weren't caused by me, in case you're wondering. I may be good, but I'm not that good.' He gave a little laugh but it sounded forced.

That was an odd thing to say. How could he be so blasé after a kiss like that? How could he make a joke of it? Perhaps he hadn't felt what she had. Perhaps to him, that was just another kiss from a woman who was clearly crazy about him.

'Now's not the time for jokes, Jet. Didn't you feel anything?'

He took a deep breath and shook his head. 'That kiss was incredible, Mia, but it wasn't a good idea.'

Her heart was breaking for a second time. Her ribs were cracking one by one and digging deep. 'Oh? Why not? We're both young, free and single, aren't we? And unless I misunderstood, didn't you just say you wanted me?'

He nodded. 'I did. But we both know it won't work. I'm not what you're looking for. I told you, I can't change. I don't want a relationship, Mia. And I definitely don't want to break your heart.'

'That's a bit arrogant of you, isn't it? Firstly, who says you'll break my heart? And secondly, who says I'm looking for a relationship with you? What if I just want to spend the night with you? Do you want me, Jet? No strings attached. Just a bit of fun. Do you want to spend the night with me?'

Fireworks whizzed and banged and crackled above them as they stared into each other's eyes. The sky lit up around them with reds and golds and greens but Mia hardly noticed.

He finally shook his head, let out a sigh as if all the troubles in the world had landed on his shoulders and shut his eyes tight for a moment or two and when he spoke, his voice sounded as if he were chewing one of those fireworks.

'You couldn't do it, Mia. You and I both know that. I care for you,' he said, something like sadness filling his eyes as he looked away. 'I want to be your friend. I couldn't bear to see you get hurt again.'

'Coo-ey!' It was Hettie's voice and she and Fred were closing in on Mia and Jet.

Mia ignored her. 'I can, Jet.' She could hear the desperation in her voice and tried to sound casual. 'After Garrick, I'm not looking for a relationship. I can promise you that.'

He looked briefly into her eyes and shook his head again. 'No you can't. I'm sorry, Mia, but no. I don't want to spend the night with you. It would be a mistake for both of us.'

'Jet?' She sounded like a pathetic mouse.

'I'm sorry,' Jet said. 'I really am.' And he turned and strode away.

End of Part Three

The Cottage on Lily Pond Lane

Part Four: Trick or treat

Chapter One

Mia stood on the beach and watched Jet walk away.

Was this all some extraordinary dream or had that really just happened?

Fireworks whooshed into the darkening sky, exploding like a cannon boom and sending crackling sparkles of red, gold, green and white through the warm night air.

Mia willed Jet to turn around, to at least glance back in her direction, but he disappeared into the crowd as Hettie and Fred bore down on her.

'Coo-ey!' Hettie waved again, looking surprised, no doubt because Jet had marched past her without returning her greeting or acknowledging Fred.

Mia wanted to run, but her legs wouldn't move. It was as if her feet were stuck in quicksand. A feeling she knew well.

She had made a complete and utter fool of herself.

Had she actually grabbed Jet's shirt collars, yanked him towards her and kissed him? Worse than that. Had she honestly asked the man to sleep with her? Even worse, had the bloody man truly said, 'No'?

What was wrong with her?

Was it because she was missing Garrick? His loving smile. His passionate kisses. Being held in his arms each night.

Or was it because she simply wanted Jet? Wanted him to kiss her. To hold her. To tell her he loved her.

Well, that was clearly never going to happen.

Although for one brief moment, she could have sworn he was enjoying that kiss. That he had even returned it.

'Deary me' Hettie said, the second she reached Mia's side. 'What's upset Jet? Oh goodness. The naughty boy hasn't tried to have his wicked way with you, has he, deary? Did you give him a flea in his ear? I've always had a soft spot for him, as you know, dear, but if he's tried to add you to his list after what you've just been through, I'll give him a clip around the ears, you mark my words.'

Mia sighed. 'No, Hettie. He didn't. Quite the opposite, in fact.'

Hettie glanced at Fred, who shrugged, smiled at Mia and turned to watch the rest of the fireworks.

'Quite the opposite, deary? Now what can that mean?'

Mia shook her head. 'Nothing, Hettie. It means nothing.'

Hettie gave her a curious look. 'Well never mind about that. How are you dear? We've all been very worried about you, you know. Prince Gustav hasn't been eating properly and Hector's delayed moving on to his next life until I can tell him you're as right as nine pence. Fred hasn't been able to concentrate on anything and as for me, deary, well, I've been a bag of nerves. Ella says you don't want to talk about it but I'm not sure that's wise. Not good to keep things pent up. Leads to all kinds of stress, that does. I was always saying to Hector, "You need to be more open, Hector. Keeping feelings pent up inside will be the death of you." I was wrong about that, of course. The car hitting him, tossing him in the air, and him landing on his head was the death of him. But if the car hadn't killed him, stress would have. Take my word for that. Oh deary me. There I go again. Talking ten chickens at a time. What was I saying? Oh yes. You need to talk about it. So how are you feeling, deary? Broken-hearted, I don't doubt. I thought that gorgeous Garrick was a lovely young man but it seems I was mistaken. To get another woman pregnant when he was engaged to you and to then run off with the trollop. Deary me. Of course you're heartbroken.'

'Hettie!' Mia glowered at her. 'That wasn't what happened at all and I truly hope you're not going around telling everyone it was. Fiona fell pregnant when she and Garrick were still together. She just didn't know she was until a couple of weeks ago. And yes, I am heartbroken, but so is Garrick. It wasn't easy for him to leave. It wasn't easy for me to let him go. It wasn't easy for any of us. And knowing that everyone in this damn village is gossiping about us, isn't making it any easier for me. We did what was best for all of us, but that doesn't mean it wasn't difficult. I'd be very grateful if, for once in your life, you could stop being such a nosy old woman, stop spreading gossip and keep your mouth shut.' She turned and stormed away but she didn't get very far before guilt hit her in the chest. When she turned back, Hettie was standing open-mouthed and Fred had wrapped his arm around her.

Mia took a deep breath as she stood in front of Hettie. 'I'm sorry, Hettie. I didn't mean that. I'm upset but I shouldn't take it out on you. Please forgive me. But I hope you'll understand that I would really rather not talk about it. Stress may kill me, but I'll take my chances.' She smiled apologetically.

Hettie sniffed and gave a little smile. Fred didn't say a word.

'I understand, deary. And you're right. I am nosy. I should mind my own business, shouldn't I? Nothing to forgive, my dear. We all say things we don't mean when we're upset. No harm done.' She leant a little closer. 'Is that why Jet looked so cross? Did you shout at him too? Oh deary me. There I go again.' She ran her forefinger and thumb across her mouth in a zipping motion. 'There, deary. My mouth is zipped shut. You won't hear another word from me tonight.' She smiled. 'What did you think of the fireworks? Aren't they gorgeous? Really gone to town they have. Mind you, it is a big celebration. Even if they have got the dates all mixed up. I don't know how many times I have to tell that vicar this village has been here long before his church and no foundation stone is ever going to convince me otherwise. I know you're friendly with the vicar, deary, so I don't suppose you'll take any notice, but I've always thought there's something not quite right with him. I told you that the day you came, I'm sure I did. Wouldn't get too friendly with him if I were you. Although I've heard a whisper that he'd quite like to step into young Garrick's shoes, deary. Oh I don't mean with Garrick's new – or old – sweetheart, of course. I mean with you, deary. The vicar would like to put his shoes beside your bed, if you get my drift.' She clasped her hands beneath her ample chest and pursed her lips. 'But my mouth is zipped shut so I won't say another word about it. Just be careful, deary. Heartbreak can make people do a lot of silly things they normally wouldn't.'

Mia was tempted to say Tom had told her himself he loved her. But there was no way she would tell Hettie. Neither would she tell Hettie that she knew heartbroken people did silly things because she'd done a really stupid thing herself by asking Jet Cross to sleep with her. Hettie would love to spread that news, especially if Mia added that Jet had turned her down. Instead she simply smiled and as Ella and Justin were heading towards them, she didn't need to respond.

'What's up with Jet?' Ella asked, glancing over her shoulder even though Jet was nowhere to be seen. 'He completely ignored us.'

'Mia told him she wasn't having any of his nonsense, deary,' Hettie said, before darting a look at Mia. 'But I'm minding my own business so I won't say another word.'

Mia almost laughed, except it wasn't really funny. Ella gave her a questioning look.

Oh God.

As much as she hated the thought, she would have to say something. She couldn't risk Hettie spreading that rumour, even if the truth meant Hettie would now, no doubt, consider Mia to be 'a trollop'.

She took a deep breath. 'Actually, Hettie, Jet didn't do a thing. It was me. All me. I kissed him. I asked him to spend the night with me. He said no and walked away.'

'Bloody Nora,' Ella said.

'Jet walked away?' Justin gave Mia a look of surprise and disbelief.

'Good heavens, dear.' Hettie's expression was similar to Justin's.

Fred merely smiled and shook his head. Mia had no idea what he was thinking.

'For obvious reasons,' Mia continued. 'I'd rather the entire village didn't hear about it. But I don't want anyone spreading lies about Jet either and that's the only reason I've trusted you all with the truth. Okay?'

'My lips are sealed, deary.'

Ella gave Hettie a doubtful look. 'I won't say anything and neither will Justin. Will you?' She nudged Justin's arm.

'No.' Justin shook his head. 'But may I just ask one thing? Jet honestly said no?'

'Yes. He definitely said no.' Now Mia did laugh. But it still wasn't funny.

'Mia!' Tom's voice rang out in the distance and Mia saw he was fast approaching.

Hettie glanced over her shoulder, pursed her lips and shook her head. 'It's high time we went home, Fred.' She tapped Mia lightly on the arm. 'We covered Prince Gustav's cage with a throw to lessen the sound of the fireworks but the little dear has probably tried to eat it. I'll see you bright and early in the morning, deary, and we can have a good old natter then. Nighty-night all.'

'Pleasant dreams,' Mia said.

Ella grinned as Hettie and Fred hurried away. 'She really doesn't like Tom, does she?'

'No. It's weird, especially considering she helps out in the church, and was friends with Grace.' Mia watched Tom stride purposefully towards them and couldn't help but smile. Did he ever wear any other colours but black and white? It suited him though, and now that he had a tan, even more so. When they'd first arrived in the village, he was pale and a little gaunt. Now he seemed to have put on a bit of muscle and she remembered how good he'd looked in just those swim shorts that day he'd come to her rescue at Rainbow's End. Tonight, he wore black trousers, a white T-shirt and a black V-neck sweater, despite the fact that it was a warm night.

'He's even better looking now than when we first came here,' Ella said, as if reading Mia's mind. She glanced at Justin. 'Not as gorgeous as you, of course.'

Justin gave her an odd look. 'He's looking better now, I'll give you that. He took Grace's death hard, but he seems to be getting over it.'

'It's such a shame we never got to meet his gran,' Mia said.

Justin frowned. 'She was a strange old bird. She and Mattie were really friendly at one time but that seemed to fade over the years. Grace hardly left her cottage for the last few years and Bear was always popping in to deal with various 'emergencies' that turned out to be nothing. Bit of a hypochondriac if you ask me.' He threw a sideways glance at Mia and Ella before greeting Tom with a friendly smile. 'Hi Tom. Excellent fireworks.'

'Thanks, Justin. Hello Ella. Mia, you're looking lovely this evening. I wonder, might I have a word?'

Mia glanced at Ella and Justin. 'Er. Yes of course.'

'We'll leave you to it,' Ella said. 'Mia. Don't go home without me. Tom. You make sure she doesn't. Okay?'

'I'm fine,' Mia said.

'I don't care.' Ella frowned at her. 'I promised Lori I wouldn't leave you alone in the cottage, especially after Garrick left, so don't think of going without us.'

'I'll happily walk Mia home and stay with her until you return,' Tom offered.

Ella hesitated but Mia reassured her. 'That's kind, Tom. There, Ella. I'll be fine. I know you two want to go to the pub, which I don't. You go and enjoy yourselves and I'll see you both at home later.'

Obviously satisfied, Ella smiled. 'Okay. We'll see you later.' Both she and Justin then headed in the direction of The Frog and Lily.

The band struck up its rhythmic beat and the crowd began to clap and cheer. The firework display had ended and now it seemed people were dancing on the sand. Mia was tempted to stay. It looked like fun. Instead, she turned and walked towards the cottage and Tom fell into step beside her.

Mia smiled at him. 'Since Garrick left, Ella's hardly left my side apart from a few hours during the day. She won't hear of me being alone in the cottage at night though.'

'Oh? Why's that? You're not still receiving those nasty little messages, are you?'

Mia shook her head. 'No. There's been nothing since before Mum left a month ago. But Mum insisted I mustn't be alone and obviously, now Garrick's gone, she's even more concerned, so Ella's simply obeying her instructions. Mum almost got on the first plane home, but I told her I'd be even more upset if she cut her time in Texas, short.'

'That's understandable.' He gave Mia a hopeful smile. 'You can always call me if you're scared, you know. Or if you want some company. Or anything at all. Just call me, Mia, and I'll be there.'

'Thanks, Tom. That's good to know.'

'I was sorry to hear about Garrick and the rather odd situation. I apologise. Odd isn't quite the right word.'

Mia laughed, but she couldn't hide the sadness in it, she knew that. 'Odd is precisely the right word, Tom. The whole thing was odd. And what is even more odd, is that a bloody fortune-teller predicted it all at the Summer Fête in August.'

'A fortune-teller? Are you saying that a fortune-teller told you that Garrick's ex-girlfriend was pregnant and that he would go back to Scotland with her?' There was a hint of concern in the laugh he gave.

'Not exactly. She was, annoyingly, rather cryptic with me. She warned me about a cold wind from the north but she told Ella more precisely. The woman said Ella would soon be an aunt. She also told Garrick she heard a child's heartbeat and something about his past love being present, and his present being past. Why the woman couldn't come right out and say it is beyond me. She was virtually spot on with everything she said. Why couldn't she simply use plain English? But I suppose it's all part of the mystical magic or whatever.' She glanced at Tom. 'It's pretty spooky though, isn't it? I mean, how *could* she know all those things? How could she be so right about so many different people?'

Tom looked thoughtful and slowly shook his head. 'I don't know, Mia. As a vicar, I don't believe in such things, but as a man, I've seen and heard some peculiar things in my life. Perhaps the reason she was slightly vague was so that, no matter what happened, you, and everyone else who had their fortunes told, would find some truth in her words.'

'Hmm. I see what you mean. But I can tell you, Tom, when I opened that front door and saw Fiona standing there, I felt a bitterly cold wind and a chill ran through me as that woman's words came flying back to me. I think I knew in that second that I had lost Garrick. I simply didn't want to accept it or admit it. I honestly hoped Fiona had come to say she was expecting a child with someone else.'

Tom stopped and took Mia's hand in his, looking her directly in the eyes. 'It must've been awful. I would give anything for you not to be going through this heartache, Mia. But your relationship with Garrick simply wasn't meant to be. And I know I shouldn't be saying this, but part of me can't help but be glad it's over. I'm sorry. But you know how I feel about you. I was dreading having to officiate at your wedding. I would've done it, obviously, but I completely understand what you're going through right now because I've been going through it since the moment you got engaged. Oh dear Lord. I'm sorry. I hadn't meant to say that.' He gave her a pleading look and shook his head in obvious despair.

'It's okay, Tom. I understand. Believe me.' She smiled at him as she eased her hand free. 'We all do and say things we realise immediately afterwards, we shouldn't have. I've done it myself tonight.'

'Oh?'

Mia ignored his inquiring stare and resumed walking towards Sunbeam Cottage. 'You're still getting over your gran's passing, and I'm so confused about everything I'm not even sure who I am these days.' She laughed. 'One minute I'm behaving like a sixteen-year-old, the next I see myself as some sort of super-sleuth, intent on unravelling the mystery of Mattie and her past. I'm not very good at either role. I'm yet to have a teenage tantrum – although I have come pretty close. And Mattie is still an enigma. Oh.' She instinctively placed her hand on his arm and he stopped in his tracks. 'But I may make some headway on that front tomorrow. Someone phoned this morning because his grandad's just died and he's discovered letters from Mattie to his grandad. Isn't that wonderful? I'll be speaking to him first thing in the morning. Oh God! Sorry. I didn't mean it's wonderful that his grandad has died.'

Tom smiled. 'I knew what you meant, don't worry. And before you say it, there's no need to apologise about my gran again either.'

Mia grinned. 'I was just about to.'

He grinned back. 'I know you were. I know you better than you may think.'

Mia quickly turned away and headed towards the dunes. 'Anyway. There's me going on about myself and Mattie and completely forgetting that you wanted to talk to me about something. What was it, Tom?'

He fell into step beside her but didn't respond until she looked at him again.

'Tom?'

He let out a meaningful sigh. 'It's not my place, I know, but I wanted to have a word with you about Jet.'

'Jet?' Mia came to an abrupt halt. 'A word about Jet? Why? Has he said something to you?'

He shook his head. 'No, no. Not in precise terms. It's simply that I know him so well. I know the way his mind works. I know the way *he* works.' He took a deep breath. 'Forgive me, Mia, but you're vulnerable at the moment. You're heartbroken and probably lonely. You miss Garrick and probably long to be held in someone's arms. Anyone's arms. Please don't let those arms be Jet's.'

'What?'

'I know. Don't be mad at me. I'm only saying this because I care about you so much. I couldn't bear to see you hurt again. Please just hear me out. Jet is hard-working, determined, ruthless even. He always gets what he wants, no matter what he has to do to get it. He wanted Little Pond Farm and he made sure he got it. He needed money. He got it. If he sees a woman he wants, he'll get her. He wants you, Mia, but it may not be for the reasons you think. Oh, I'm sure he's attracted to you. Who wouldn't be? You're a lovely young woman. We both know I've fallen in love with you myself. But you're also new to the village. And Jet likes that.

He's a good friend where men are concerned, although he'll happily steal a man's girlfriend and not think twice. All's fair in love and war as far as Jet's concerned. But he's not a good friend where women are concerned, Mia. He's just like his father.'

'Tom! Sorry. But I think you've said enough. It may be true that I don't really know him, but Jet has been nothing but kind, caring and friendly to me. Nothing. Okay, he has been flirting with me. But he's been the perfect gentleman, most of the time.'

Tom smirked. 'Oh, I'm sure he has. Jet has the patience of a saint when it comes to getting what he wants. But there's nothing saintly in his intentions, I assure you. You do know how 'friendly' he was with Mattie, don't you? You do know she gave him money to buy the farm. And I know you've been wondering who is named in Mattie's codicil. I believe Jet thinks it's him. Time will tell, of course. What I'm saying, Mia, is be careful. Jet's feelings for you may not be what you think they are.'

Mia stared at Tom in disbelief. And then the fortune-teller's words came back like a knife in her heart. "I also see someone who you think you can trust. You can't. Beware! Feelings may not be genuine." Had she meant Jet? Was he the one who'd left the toy frog, the dead flowers and the warning card? Was that why he'd said no to her tonight? Because he didn't really fancy her at all?

Was he simply leading her on as part of some sort of plan?

'I'm so sorry, Mia,' Tom continued. 'I know this probably wasn't what you wanted to hear. But I had to tell you. I had to stop you getting hurt again. I've got your best interests at heart although you may not think so at the moment. I'm here for you, Mia. I always will be. Just like I was there for you that day at Rainbow's End. The day Jet made sure he wasn't. I love you, Mia. You know that.'

As she stared at him, hurt, confusion and heartache collided in her heart and mind, and something else the fortune-teller said came back to her. "I see love that's black and white and surprising too."

Love that's black and white and surprising too. Tom always wore black and white. His first declaration of love had definitely been surprising. His continued love and loyalty was equally so. Had the woman meant Tom?

She'd also said, "I see happiness and joy beyond your wildest dreams. Choose love wisely. Love may not be where you are looking for it. You could so easily make a mistake. And Autumn will bring many changes and many opportunities."

Was Tom the wise choice? Was this an opportunity? Would he be the one to bring her happiness and joy beyond her wildest dreams?

'Mia? Are you okay? Have I overstepped the bounds of our friendship? Have I said too much?'

Mia gave him a wan smile. 'I'm fine, Tom. And no. I suppose I should be grateful to you. I was just thinking about that damn fortune-teller again.'

'Oh? Why? What else did she say?'

He looked genuinely concerned. Whether all that stuff he'd said about Jet was true or not, he clearly thought he should tell her. That meant he cared. Really cared. Wasn't he always around when she needed him?

And was he suggesting that Jet knew she would go to Rainbow's End even though Jet hadn't been the one who mentioned it? Had Jet effectively, set a trap by not being there himself for the first time, ever? Had she misjudged him so badly?

She seemed to be making a complete and utter mess of everything lately. But then, hadn't she always picked the wrong man? All her ex-boyfriends had been wrong, in one way or another. Even Garrick, as it turned out. Perhaps for once, she should listen to her head and not her heart. And hadn't the fortune-teller been right about everything else so far?

Damn the bloody woman.

She smiled again, albeit a little sadly.

'Come in and have a glass of wine, Tom and I'll tell you all about it.'

Chapter Two

Mia had a lot to think about. But the following morning, all she could think about was Jet. Was he really that much of a bastard? Tom was supposed to be his friend and yet he hadn't been very friendly towards Jet last night.

And could she really have got it so wrong about Jet? Surely if he wanted harm to come to her he wouldn't have thrown himself in front of the whirling, metal blades of that harvester, risking his own life to save hers. Or would he? He'd said there were signs on those chains but she hadn't seen any. Had he removed them on purpose?

Now she was being completely ridiculous. He hadn't known she was going to his farm that day. She was seeing drama where there wasn't any; declaring guilt without evidence. And that was because of what Tom had said.

But if Jet did like her, did care about her, why had he walked away last night? Surely they could've talked about it? That would've been the kind, friendly thing to do. He knew she was upset. He knew she might not be behaving in her own best interests. Couldn't he have been … more considerate? More understanding? Less grumpy and annoyed?

Oh God. She lowered her head onto the kitchen table and banged it against the wood, albeit gently.

'Are you impersonating a woodpecker?' Ella asked, coming in from the hall. 'Or are you trying to knock some sense into yourself? Because that's something you definitely need to do.'

Mia lifted her head and met Ella's grin. 'Why? Because I asked Jet to have sex with me?'

Ella raised her brows. 'No. I'd forgotten that, momentarily.' She grabbed a mug from the cupboard. 'I was referring to the doe-eyed looks you and the vicar were giving one another when Justin and I came home. Dear God, Mia. I know Alexia said she's dated every single man in this village but it's not a competition, you know.'

Mia glowered at her. 'What's that supposed to mean? And I hate to have to remind you, but Alexia hadn't managed to date Tom. She said she wanted to but Freda told her not to.'

'Silly me.' Ella threw her a sarcastic look and poured herself some coffee, topping up Mia's mug which sat empty on the table. 'All I'm saying is, we've only been here five months and you've dated Bear, Garrick, although he doesn't really count because he doesn't live here but even so.

Sorry. I shouldn't have brought up my stupid git of a brother.'

'Don't worry. I can hear his name without bursting into tears.'

'Yeah. But I can't,' Ella joked. 'I still can't believe he buggered off back over the border with little Miss Scotland.'

'Ella! That's not nice. Little Miss Scotland is the mother of your soon to be niece or nephew.'

'Yeah. And I've got to travel a million miles whenever I want to see the little brat … and my niece or nephew.' She grinned. 'Anyway, what was I saying? Oh yeah. In five months you've dated Bear and Garrick. You've tried to seduce poor, defenceless Jet.' She fluttered her eyelashes. 'And yes, I know you told me all that stuff Tom said, but I'm not sure I believe it. I think the vicar may be telling porkies. He's crazy about you and he knows you fancy Jet. What better way to remove his competition than to make you think the man is a would-be murderer? So anyway, Bear, Garrick, almost Jet, and now, unless I'm very much mistaken, you'll soon be arm in arm with a man of the cloth. Tell me I'm wrong. Please, please, tell me I'm wrong.' She got down on her knees and clasped her hands together in a prayer-like fashion.

Mia pushed her over. 'You're wrong. But would it be so bad if I did decide to date Tom? He's handsome, kind and thoughtful. He saved my life. He loves me. I could do worse.'

Ella grabbed the hand Mia offered and pulled herself to her feet, grinning. 'No. It wouldn't be bad, exactly. I just think you need to take a bit of time before you go rushing headlong into yet another relationship. Don't glower at me, miss. There's rebound, which is fair enough, but you seem to be bouncing from man to man faster than a tennis ball at Wimbledon. What's the rush? Take some time for you. Take a breather from *lurve* and smell the roses. Real roses, not romantic, metaphorical ones. Is that what I mean? God, I need coffee. Lots and lots of coffee. What time does Lori get home? She'll back me up.'

'You think I'm behaving like a tart? Is that what you're saying?'

'No. I'm saying that you're so confused, so mixed up that you're dashing around like a headless chicken trying to jump in the nearest pot without realising that all that will do is get you cooked. Slow down. Decide how you really feel. I know you're missing Garrick but don't jump into the nearest arms in the hope that they'll make you feel better.'

Mia sighed. 'Okay. I promise I won't rush into dating Tom. And Mum's flight landed at nine, as scheduled. I checked. Allowing for baggage reclaim and all that stuff, she should be home by noon. Oh. That's probably her calling now.'

Mia raced into the living room, grabbed the phone, putting it on handsfree and speaker at the same time, and immediately headed back towards the kitchen. 'Hi! I can't wait to see you. I'm so excited. I've got so much to tell you. How was your trip?'

'Oh. Gosh. I'm rather excited too. I assume I'm speaking with Mia.'

'Hold on. You're not my mum! Who is this?' Mia glared at the phone but all it showed on the caller display was 'international'. She glanced towards Ella sitting at the kitchen table, who shook her head and pulled a face, puffing out her cheeks, sticking her hands in her armpits and flapping her elbows.

'Your mum? Good heavens, no.' The man laughed and the sound made Mia smile, in spite of her surprise. 'I'm Gill,' the man said, at the same time as Ella.

'What was that?' Mia mouthed at Ella.

'A fish,' she said, loud enough for the caller to hear. 'You know, as in fish gill. I was trying to tell you it's the guy from yesterday.'

Mia rolled her eyes and Gill laughed down the phone.

'Fish gill. I've been called worse things,' he said.

'I bet you have,' Ella replied. 'I can think of a few myself.'

Gill laughed again. 'I do apologise for calling at just after nine on a Sunday. I telephoned yesterday and left a message, but I'm leaving here today and heading home via Paris where I'm dropping in on a friend, so I thought it best if I phoned again. I wondered if there might be a possibility of calling in on you on the way. I'm driving, you see, and Little Pondale isn't too far from the Channel tunnel. I live in Cambridge, so it is sort of on the way, with a slight detour. I'd relish the opportunity of discussing this in person. If it isn't an inconvenience, of course. You did receive my message yesterday, didn't you?'

'Yes. I was going to call you later. There's no need to apologise. We're early risers. Generally.' She grinned at Ella.

'So, Mia? What do you say? May I call on you? It'll be early evening tomorrow, I should think. I'll leave Paris after lunch. But if that's not convenient I can find somewhere local to stay and call on you on Tuesday morning. Either way, I shall stay somewhere overnight, I expect.'

'Either is fine. We don't have any plans, as such. I don't know anywhere local to stay, though. This village is about fifteen miles from the nearest town and that's not large. I suppose you could stay here. We've got a spare room.'

Ella shook her head and waved her arms in the air, mouthing 'No.'

Mia smiled. 'If you don't mind staying in a cottage with three women, that is.'

'Mind?' He laughed. 'That's without doubt the best offer I've had for a long time. But I don't want to be a nuisance.'

'You're not. I'm dying to hear anything you can tell me about my great-aunt. I never met her and believe it or not, no one seems to know much about her.'

'Oh. I hadn't realised that. That you never met her, I mean. Her letters contain quite a lot about you.'

'They do? Wow. But I shouldn't be surprised. She seemed to know everything about me and yet I know nothing of her. But it's not just me. It's almost as if she didn't want anyone to know of her existence. Who she really was, that is. Although we think she may have worked in the Intelligence Service, as bizarre as that my sound.'

'That's not at all bizarre. She did. So did my grandfather. That's how they met.'

'Really? That's really how they met?'

'Yes. But I'll explain all that when we meet. I'm looking forward to it, Mia.'

'So am I, Gill.'

Ella piped up. 'Oh, so am I. You have no idea how much.'

Gill laughed again. 'Why do I get the feeling that you mean the exact opposite of what you've just said? I'm definitely looking forward to meeting you … Ella, wasn't it?'

'Yes,' Mia said. 'Ella's my best friend and she's lovely really. She just has a bit of a wicked streak. You'll have to get used to it, I'm afraid.'

'A woman with a wicked streak,' he repeated. 'It sounds as if I'm in for a treat. Until tomorrow then, ladies. Enjoy your Sunday. Goodbye.'

'I'll give him a treat all right,' Ella said, the minute he rang off. 'Bloody moron.'

'Oh, I don't know. He sounded rather nice.'

Ella rolled her eyes. 'Bloody Nora, Mia. I swear if you decide you've got a crush on him tomorrow, I'm taking you up to Frog's Hollow and I'm drowning you in that pond. Even if it is on a Monday.'

Chapter Three

Franklin's car pulled onto the drive of Sunbeam Cottage shortly after noon and Mia was out the front door and down the drive before Lori had stepped out.

'Mum! You're home,' she shrieked, hugging Lori as if they hadn't seen each other for a year instead of merely one month.

Lori was equally excited. 'Mia, darling! Oh, I've missed you. Let me look at you.' She eased Mia away from her a little. 'Have you lost weight? Have you been eating properly? Who's been doing the cooking since …?'

'Since Garrick left?' Mia smiled. 'It's okay, Mum. You can say his name.'

'But not in front of me,' Ella joked, coming down the drive to join them. 'I'm more upset he's gone than Mia is. But it's only because neither of us can cook and we've been living on beans on toast, frozen pizza and ding-dinners for the last two weeks.' She winked. 'Although I've had a few meals in the pub without Mia knowing.'

'Hello, Ella. Ding-dinners?' Lori queried, smiling.

'Microwavable ready meals,' Ella replied. 'It's lovely to see you again.'

'You've been eating in the pub?' Mia asked Ella. 'I didn't know that.'

'I told you that you should've come with me.'

'It's good to be back, isn't it, Franklin?' Lori laughed, and Franklin grinned.

'Sorry,' Mia said, giving Lori another hug. 'Um. Are you staying here? Or at Franklin's?'

Lori smiled at Franklin and then at Mia. 'I'm going to stay here for a couple of nights, darling. Just until I'm sure you're really as okay with everything as you say you are. Don't give me that look. I'm your mother. I worry. Sue me.' She pulled Mia close again and kissed her face, her cheeks and her hair. 'I really have missed you so much. Let's get inside and catch up.'

'I'll bring the bags, honey,' Franklin said, with a genuine smile. 'Then if it's fine by y'all, I'll get along to see Jet.'

'Of course, sweetheart,' Lori said, glancing over her shoulder as she walked arm in arm with Mia towards the front door of Sunbeam Cottage. 'And take as long as you like. We've got a lot of catching up to do, haven't we darling?' She kissed the side of Mia's head.

'Absolutely.'

'I'll leave you to it,' Ella said.

'You don't have to,' Mia told her.

'I know. But it'll be good for you both to spend some alone time together, if you see what I mean. And besides, I can spend the entire afternoon with Justin without worrying about getting back. Oh. Not that it's been a burden or anything.' She grinned.

'Go away,' Mia said, laughing. 'I'll be safe with Mum.'

Ella blew Mia and Lori kisses, and Franklin too before racing off down the drive and across the village green to Justin's.

Lori watched her go before turning back towards the cottage. 'So everything's going well again with Ella and Justin then?'

Mia nodded. 'It seems to be. Although between you and me, he still doesn't seem quite as madly in love as he did. But I may be imagining that. I haven't said anything to Ella, so don't mention it, even though she'll be the first to agree it's not as great as it was.'

'Of course I won't. And you, darling? How are things really, with you? Are you honestly as over Garrick as you appear to be?'

Mia shrugged as they reached the front door and stepped into the hall. 'I think I am. I still miss him dreadfully, but I stopped crying myself to sleep after the first week. I've been doing a lot of thinking and I'm sure you were right when you said that it was a crush that got out of control, or something like that. I've sort of loved him all my life and spending so much time with him here, and being so physically attracted to him, made me think I was truly in love. I confused that, and the love of friendship with being 'in love', I think. All I know for sure is that it doesn't hurt much anymore.' They headed towards the kitchen. 'I honestly wish him and Fiona well, but I haven't been able to bring myself to talk to him via Skype or Facetime or anything and I've only spoken to him once on the phone. Ella's been passing messages between us. You know, checking if we're each okay and reporting back to the other one. I'm looking forward to the day when we can chat like we used to.'

'Don't try and rush things,' Lori advised, grabbing a bottle of wine from the rack whilst Mia got the glasses. 'Whether you were truly in love with him or not, doesn't matter now. You were engaged. You were planning to get married. You can't simply brush that under the carpet as if it didn't happen. And speaking of that. Have you taken the dress back?'

'My wedding dress? No.' Mia laughed as Lori poured the wine. 'Ella says I should hang on to it because knowing me, I'll find someone else I'll decide I'd like to marry before too long. Failing which, she says she might need it, if she can persuade Justin to get a move on.'

Franklin appeared in the doorway and grinned.

'I know.' Lori laughed, walking to him and kissing him. 'It's as if we haven't been away. The wine's already being poured and we've only been back five minutes.'

'Not a problem, honey.' He kissed her briefly, turned away, turned back and kissed her again, tipping her backwards and letting his Stetson fall to the floor.

Mia watched them and a tiny twinge of envy welled up inside her. She bent down and retrieved his hat, handing it to him when he finally let Lori go.

He winked at Mia as he took it. 'Well thank you kindly, ma'am.'

She grinned. 'Give my regards to Jet. Oh no, don't. I mean.' She coughed. 'Don't say anything to Jet, please.'

Franklin gave her an odd look. 'Somethin' happen while we were away?'

'Absolutely nothing,' Mia said, picking up her glass and taking several swigs of wine.

Well, it was sort of true. Nothing had happened.

The bloody man had said, 'No.'

Which was probably just as well if what Tom had said was true.

Chapter Four

Mia overslept. But it wasn't really surprising. She hadn't had a good night's sleep since Garrick had left and last night, she and Lori had sat up and talked until two a.m. When she finally fell asleep, curled up beside her mum, even a meteor colliding with Earth wouldn't have woken her. She didn't hear Lori get up, and Ella said it had taken at least five minutes to wake her, and Ella had shaken her, pulled off the duvet, shouted, sung along with the song blaring out from the radio, and finally, wafted two large, steaming mugs of coffee, under her nose.

'I was beginning to think you were dead,' Ella said, placing the mugs on the bedside table and clambering onto Mia's bed. 'Lori's gone for a run along the beach. She went out the back door five minutes after I came in the front. Apparently, she does that now. Runs every morning. Franklin likes to run.' She rolled her eyes and leant over and grabbed the mugs, handing one to Mia before propping herself up against the plush, purple headboard. 'Who knew?' She grinned. 'Remind me never to date a younger man. There's no way I'm going running when I'm sixty. Actually, there's no way I'm going running now. That Frog Hill Run nearly did me in. I'm never doing that again. Are you awake yet?'

Mia shook her head. 'Not really. And must you keep jabbering? My head hurts.'

'That's because we all drank too much wine with dinner, and you and Lori started at noon and carried on after I went over to Justin's. You do realise it's almost nine, don't you? Hettie'll be here any minute. Are you going to tell her about Gill coming to stay?'

'Nine?' Mia yawned. 'Is it really?' She glanced at the clock and groaned. 'I suppose I'd better get up. Did you say Mum's gone running?'

Ella nodded. 'Yep. She's meeting Franklin on the sand. They arranged it last night.'

Mia took a gulp of coffee and yawned again. 'She didn't mention it. I could've gone with her and gone swimming while they ran.'

Ella laughed. 'Yeah right. You can't even wake up, sleepy head. But I've got news. Want to hear it?'

Mia shifted position so that she could look Ella in the eye. 'Don't ask silly questions. Of course I do. News about what?'

Ella grinned, smugly. 'News about whom. I bumped into Fred at the bakery this morning. He was buying one of those extra special, scrummy blueberry muffins Justin bakes. You know the ones. With the lavender frosting and the edible Violet petals.' She beamed at Mia and drank her coffee.

'That's it? That's your news? Hold the press. Fred is buying muffins.'

'Not muffins. Just one muffin. A special muffin. Oh, for goodness sake, Mia. You really are asleep. Who loves Justin's blueberry muffins but says she only ever buys one on a very special occasion, like Prince Gustav's birthday?'

'Hettie. So?'

'So Fred bought her an extra special muffin. And he slipped an engagement ring among the petals.' Ella laughed. 'Fred's going to propose to Hettie. In fact, he's probably doing so right about now. Which is why you need to get up. I told Lori and she's going to be back by nine-thirty. Hettie'll want us all to see the ring.'

'Oh my God! Really?' Mia put down her mug and threw back the duvet. 'Why didn't you tell me right away?'

Ella shrugged. 'You could see if she wants to wear your wedding dress.'

'Oh, very funny.'

Mia dashed into the shower and was washed, dressed and downstairs in the kitchen shortly after nine-thirty, but there was no sign of Hettie.

'Do you think everything's all right?' Mia glanced at Ella who was making fresh coffee.

'Perhaps it's taking longer than expected,' Ella said. 'Or perhaps they're … you know. Having celebration sex.' She winked.

Mia shivered dramatically. 'Thanks. That's not a pleasant picture you've just put in my head. Should we call round? What if something's happened? What if she said no? What if—'

'There's the doorbell.' Ella nodded towards the front door. 'That can't be Hettie because I left the door unlocked and she always tries it before she rings the bell. I'd go, but I'm busy making coffee.'

Mia sighed. 'I'll get it. Whoever it is, is pretty impatient. I bet it's Hettie and she's doing this for dramatic effect.'

'Or Franklin. He probably forgot he was meeting Lori on the beach and he's so excited to see her, he can't stop ringing the bell.'

Mia strode along the hall. 'Okay. I'm coming.' She opened the door and her mouth fell open along with it. 'Jet!'

'Is Lori here?' He seemed anxious and his mouth was a firm hard line when he looked at her.

'No. She's with Franklin on the beach.'

He shook his head. 'She isn't. Franklin's at the farm. I've come to get her. Don't panic. It's not serious. But there's been an accident and Franklin's hurt. It's only cuts, bruises and possibly a broken wrist. Plus he'll have one hell of a headache, but Bear's with him and he says Franklin's fine. I've come to get Lori before she

224

hears it from someone else. She's on the beach, you said? May I take a short cut through here and go and get her?'

'Yes. Yes of course.' She stood aside to let him pass. 'Are you sure he's okay? God! It wasn't that harvester thing was it?'

'He's okay, considering,' he said, giving her an odd look. 'And no, it wasn't the harvester.' He marched along the hall.

She followed quickly behind him but he didn't give her another look.

'Jet?' Ella said, from the kitchen doorway. 'Did I hear you say there's been an accident?'

'Yes. I'll tell you about it later. I want to get Lori. Excuse me.'

He walked right past her and out onto the deck and then into the garden, dashing towards the beach as Mia and Ella exchanged worried looks.

'Coo-ey!' Hettie's cheery tone rang out from the open front door. 'May we come in, deary? We've got exciting news.'

Chapter Five

It had been a crazy day and by five p.m. all Mia wanted to do was soak in a hot bath and have an extremely early night. But Gill would be arriving any minute, so she couldn't. Instead, she and Ella made a large bowl of mixed salad, laid out a plate of ham, and another of cheese from Little Pond Farm together with a selection of bread and rolls from Justin's bakery. It wasn't much but it would have to do.

'He's just come from France,' Ella said, grinning. 'They live on bread and cheese in France. The salad and ham will be an added bonus.'

Mia grinned back. 'I'm sure he'll understand when we explain that, what with the drama over Franklin's accident and the excitement over Hettie and Fred's engagement, going to the shops was the last thing on our minds.'

'Yeah. If he doesn't like it, there's always the pub. And Justin did make a special cake for dessert, so it's not all bad.'

'Is Justin going to be joining us for supper?'

Ella shook her head. 'No. He says he's got some people he needs to meet tonight. Something to do with The Frog Hill Hounds. He can't cancel because it's important, apparently.'

'That sounds intriguing.'

Ella shrugged. 'He was a bit cagey about it. But he swears it's business and not another woman, so I suppose I'll have to trust him.'

Mia glanced up from laying the table. 'Don't you then? Trust him, I mean.'

'I do. I think. But sometimes it seems as if he's keeping something from me and to be honest, I'm getting a little tired of it. I told you. It hasn't really been the same since that bloody fortune-teller.'

'Oh God. Don't start with her again. I'm still trying to figure out what mine meant. Especially the bit about Tom. It's weird, but I can remember almost every word that woman said. I simply can't make sense of most of it.' She stepped back and inspected the table to see if she'd forgotten anything. She hadn't. 'I saw him briefly today.'

'Tom?' Ella got out wine glasses. 'When?'

'After Jet took Mum to Little Pond Farm and Hettie and Fred had left. He called round. You'd gone over to Justin's. Tom didn't seem himself either. I told him about Franklin's accident and he

227

was really shocked. And when I told him that Franklin was actually driving Jet's car at the time, so it could have been Jet, not Franklin who ended up crumpled against a tree, he almost looked cross. Anyone would think he's got a thing for Jet.' She grinned. 'But it was weird, wasn't it? The fact that it was Jet's car.'

'Why's that weird?' Ella poured them each a glass of wine. 'We need one after the day we've had.' She winked, before continuing: 'Brakes fail all the time. Well, maybe not all the time, but sometimes.'

Mia took the glass and sipped her wine. 'I suppose so. Jet clearly felt guilty though, didn't he? He said a couple of times that it was his fault because he'd asked Franklin to move the car for him and if he'd moved it himself, Franklin wouldn't have been hurt.'

'Yes, but Jet would've been, so that's just silly.'

'I know. And I shouldn't be saying this, but if Franklin had come to tell us that something had happened to Jet, I don't think I would've been as calm and controlled as Mum was. I would've been screaming and crying and behaving like an even bigger idiot than usual.' She sighed. 'I know all that stuff Tom said about Jet is probably true, but when I opened the front door and saw him standing there, my heart skipped a beat, I swear it did. I was so happy to see him I almost threw my arms around him and kissed the arrogant git.' She shook her head. 'And he was so concerned that Mum found out straight away that Franklin was okay, and that she didn't hear any horror stories via the village gossips. If he was really as bad as Tom says, he wouldn't have been so thoughtful, would he?'

Ella rolled her eyes. 'Are you now thinking that perhaps Tom did lie about some of those things he told you about Jet? I said he could've made them up to remove his competition.' She grinned. 'A vicar who lies. Well, there's a novelty. Not.'

Mia grinned back. 'But I can't believe Tom's like that either. Oh I don't know. I'm so confused about everything.' She flopped onto a chair and sighed. 'At least Franklin's fine. That's the main thing. And it was lucky he was simply moving the car so he wasn't going very fast. Jet races down that drive. I've been in the car with him so I know. Imagine that. He wouldn't have been able to stop and would've gone headlong onto Seaside Road, and been hit by oncoming traffic.'

Ella laughed. 'Sorry. It's not funny. But oncoming traffic? If more than three cars go along that road per day I'll be amazed. The chances of one being at that precise spot at that exact time is probably about a billion to one. He may've smashed into the hedge opposite the drive and possibly even got some broken bones, but I don't think anything too serious would've happened. There's no point in speculating anyway. It wasn't

Jet, it was Franklin, and he's fine, apart from the broken wrist and the cuts and bruises. Now what time did that guy say he'd be arriving?'

'Anytime now. He told me he thought he was about thirty minutes away when he phoned. That was thoughtful of him, wasn't it? To let us know he was almost here.'

'Perhaps he wanted to give us time to roll out the red carpet or something.'

Mia tutted. 'Don't be mean. Just because he's got a posh accent, it doesn't follow he'll be the pompous git you think he is.'

'I bet he looks like a nerd, with greasy hair, spots and glasses perched on the end of an exceedingly long, hooked nose.'

'And maybe a hunched back for good measure.' Mia gave Ella a sarcastic grin. 'I think he's got a lovely voice. And he seemed friendly. Anyway, I don't care what he looks like. All I'm interested in is what he can tell me about Mattie. Oh. That must be him now.' Mia put her glass on the table the moment she heard the doorbell, and turned towards the hall.

'Unless it's Jet, who's come to tell you he's decided he wants to sleep with you, after all.'

'Yeah right. The man hardly looked at me today and I think he said about five words to me in total. It definitely won't be Jet.'

It wasn't. But Mia was still surprised when she opened the front door. Gill was nothing like Ella had suggested, although he did have glasses.

Expensive glasses by the look of them and they sat perfectly on his slim, aquiline nose.

'Hello,' he said, beaming white teeth between shapely lips on a tanned face. 'You must be Mia. I'm pleased to meet you.' It was a handsome face, framed by lustrous, wild and wavy chestnut brown hair that shimmered in the late afternoon sunlight. His eyes were almost as intense as Jet's, but not quite as blue and he definitely took care of himself. He wore a red, white and green checked cotton, short-sleeved shirt, hanging loose over tailored khaki shorts and his long, athletic-looking legs were dark mahogany. He was clearly an 'outdoors' kind of man and, judging by the boat shoes he wore on otherwise bare feet, possibly one who liked messing about on boats. Although that didn't necessarily follow. Mia owned a pair of walking boots, but she didn't do much walking over rough terrain. Even his aftershave smelt divine as it wafted towards her on the warm breeze. 'Apologies for being a tad later than anticipated. I was stuck behind a tractor on Seaside Road.'

'Sorry?' Had she really been staring at him? 'Oh yes, that happens, but no apology is necessary. You must be Gill. Hello. You're only five minutes later than you said, and we hadn't expected you to be precise.' She gave a little laugh. 'Please come in. We've got a salad and some bread, cheese and ham but nothing more exciting, I'm afraid. It's been a bit of a mad day and we didn't get time to go shopping, especially as they're miles away.'

And now she was waffling. She stood aside to let him in and when she closed the door, he followed her along the hall.

'Bread and cheese sounds perfect. But you shouldn't have gone to any trouble. I had a rather large lunch with my friend in Paris, so I'm not very hungry. Thank you though. It was kind of you to think of me.'

'It wasn't just for you,' Ella called out from the kitchen. 'If you don't want it that leaves more for … Bloody Nora. You can't be Gill.' She blinked several times as Gill stepped into the kitchen. 'You're not at all what I expected.' She raked his body with disbelieving eyes.

Mia grinned as Gill scanned Ella from head to toe. It was like a moment from a movie.

Gill smiled broadly. 'Oh? You're exactly what I had imagined, Ella. I assume from the sarcastic tone, that you *are* Ella. I think I'd recognise your voice anywhere.'

Ella blushed. She actually blushed.

'Sit down, Gill,' Mia said, still grinning. 'Would you like a glass of wine? It's only cheap stuff, not vintage or anything, which you no doubt usually drink.'

He dragged his gaze from Ella and sat, and although he furrowed his brows a touch at Mia's comment, his smile somehow remained intact.

'What makes you think that?' He laughed. 'Vintage port, on occasion, yes. Although I'll admit my grandfather did have an extensive wine cellar and I have been drinking some particularly good 2005 Burgundy while we were sorting out his estate. In fact, I've got some in the car. I'll grab one for when we eat.'

'We're eating now,' Ella said, finally regaining her composure. 'We're starving.

'Now? But it's only ...' He glanced at his patently expensive watch and then his gaze shot from Ella to Mia and back again. 'Of course. I'll go and get it.'

'There's no need,' Mia said. 'Unless you really can't bear the thought of drinking cheap wine.'

'I'm happy to drink anything,' he said, smiling again. 'And price isn't always indicative of quality. I was going to give you a bottle or two for letting me stay, in any event. I simply didn't want to arrive on your doorstep with my bag in one hand and wine in the other. Not until I get to know you better, that is.' He winked. 'Oh. That was rather presumptive of me. I was assuming it is still all right for me to stay, but you said you'd had a rather hectic day. If it's not convenient, I'll stay elsewhere.'

'No! It's fine,' Mia assured him. 'Of course you can stay here.'

'Yeah. We won't get the wine if you don't,' Ella said. 'And we want the posh wine, believe me.'

He grinned. 'The wine is yours, regardless.'

Ella shrugged. 'Oh well. In that case, you might as well stay. I should warn you though. It gets a bit rowdy in the village at night.'

'It does?' His grin broadened. 'Now why don't I believe you?'

'Search me,' Ella said.

'I'd like that very much. But let me get the wine first.' He winked again and walked towards the front door.

Ella's mouth fell open. 'Did he just—'

'Yes, Ella,' Mia nodded. 'And I think Justin may be the one who needs to worry, not the other way around. I saw the way you two looked at one another. Be careful, or you'll find yourself in the same boat as I was. In love with two different men. And I've ended up with neither.'

Mia half expected Ella to protest and declare her undying love for Justin but instead she topped up her wine glass and knocked back the contents in a few gulps.

Less than a minute later, Gill reappeared, his overnight bag in one hand; two bottles of wine in the other.

'Leave your bag in the hall for now,' Mia instructed. 'Unless you'd like to freshen up before you eat. Sorry. I was forgetting you've had a long journey. I'm really not thinking straight this evening, and nor is Ella, but I'm sure she'll happily show you to your room. I need to quickly phone my mum, anyway. Her partner had an accident today.'

'I'm truly sorry to hear that. Is he – or she – okay? Are they both okay?'

'Yes thanks. And it's a 'he'. Franklin. It wasn't serious but he's sustained a broken wrist and some cuts and bruises, and naturally, Mum wants to stay with him. She would've been here otherwise. She was keen to meet you when I told her about our conversation.'

'Perhaps another time,' Gill said, casting a sideways glance at Ella. 'I wouldn't mind merely washing my face and hands, if that's okay?'

'Perfect,' Mia said. 'Ella, will you show Gill his room, and where everything is, while I call Mum?'

'Of course.' Ella gave Gill her sweetest smile but she glared at Mia as she passed by. 'Head for the stairs, Gill. It's the first door on the left at the top. I'm right behind you.' To Mia she whispered, 'So now you're throwing us together? Good plan, Mia. Excellent.' She shook her head and followed Gill.

Mia dashed into the living room, slumped on the sofa and called her mum on the landline.

'Hi, Mum. Just wanted to check Franklin's still okay and that there weren't any after effects from this morning. Gill's here and we're about to eat, so I can't talk for long. Hettie and Fred have decided to postpone their engagement celebration until Franklin's had a few days to recover. They suggested the weekend instead of tonight and asked me to tell you so that you could tell everyone at Little Pond Farm.'

'Thank you, darling. Franklin's fine and already complaining that everyone is making way too much fuss. Thanks for letting me know about Hettie. I'll tell everyone here.'

'Are you sure he's fine, Mum? You sound a little … anxious. You would tell me if it's more serious than they thought, wouldn't you?'

Lori sighed. 'Oh darling, it's not Franklin. He really is fine. It's Jet.'

'Jet?' Mia sat bolt upright. 'Has something happened to Jet? Is he okay?'

'Yes, yes. He's fine. The thing is, darling, a mechanic friend of his came to take the car away and, well, there's only one way to say this. The brakes had been tampered with, according to the mechanic. This wasn't simply an accident, Mia. Someone wanted those brakes to fail and whoever it was, obviously expected Jet to be driving the car when that happened. Isn't that dreadful? I'm not supposed to know but I overheard Jet and Franklin discussing it with the mechanic. Jet asked him twice if he was sure and the man was absolutely certain. "One brake hose splitting, can happen. The hoses to the front and back brakes splitting at exactly the same time? You've probably got more chance of winning the lottery." Those were his exact words. It was definitely foul play.'

Chapter Six

Mia couldn't believe what her mum had told her. Neither could Ella when Mia repeated almost word for word what Lori had said, while they waited for Gill to return to the kitchen.

'So someone tampered with Jet's brakes?' Ella queried.

'That's what the mechanic said.'

'But why? Oh! Perhaps it was one of the women he's dumped in the past. Or one of their dads.'

'It's not funny, Ella. Someone could've been seriously hurt.'

'Has something happened?' Gill stood in the doorway, a concerned expression on his face. 'Forgive me. I wasn't eavesdropping. I couldn't help but hear as I was coming along the hall.'

Mia explained about Franklin's so-called accident and how it now seemed it wasn't an accident at all, but an intentional act designed to cause harm, as Ella poured the wine Gill had brought, and they all sat down to eat.

'Do they have any idea who would do such a thing?' Gill asked, and Ella told him there could be a long line of likely suspects if the rumours about Jet's love-life were true.

'But why now?' Mia said, offering Gill the cheese plate. 'He hasn't dated anyone since we've been here. Why would someone from his past decide to take action after all this time?'

'It could be Tom.' Ella took a sip of wine and helped herself to one of Justin's crunchy, cheese-topped rolls. 'Wow. This wine's delicious.'

Gill grinned at her and Mia glowered.

'Tom? Do you honestly think Tom would go to Little Pond Farm and mess with Jet's brakes? Apart from the fact they're friends, he's a vicar, Ella. Okay, it's possible he hasn't been completely truthful about Jet, although we can't even be sure of that, but trying to kill the man is going a bit far, don't you think?'

Ella shrugged. 'People do all sorts of crazy things for Love.'

'The vicar loves Jet?' Gill asked, placing a few slices of cheese on a chunk of fig and hazelnut bread. He clearly couldn't follow the conversation at all.

'No!' Mia said.

Ella grinned. 'We're not completely sure about that, either. He says he loves Mia, but that could be a lie.' She looked excited. 'Ooh! Perhaps that's why he was so horrid about him. Perhaps Tom's been secretly in love with Jet all along and he's pretending to love you to get you away from '*his man*'. Didn't Hettie say the day we arrived that she thought Tom may be gay?'

Mia frowned. 'She did. But he's not. He kissed me, remember?'

'He could be Bi,' Gill suggested, and Mia and Ella both stared at him. 'Why not?'

Ella nodded. 'Yeah. I suppose so.'

'But isn't it more likely that he does love Mia?' Gill reasoned. 'That would make more sense if his intention was to get rid of Jet. Of course I'm only speculating here, never having met either man and not having full knowledge of the history or what's been said, I can't really give an informed opinion.'

Before she realised what she was doing, Mia had regaled Gill with a potted history of the last few months, with Ella jumping in and adding or correcting, as necessary. Mia hadn't intended to tell him as much as she did and definitely not the part about her asking Jet to have sex with her and his subsequent rejection. Ella added that part.

Gill listened intently and only when they had finished, some fifteen minutes later, did he comment.

'Has it occurred to you that Jet may have tampered with his own brakes? After everything you've told me, that's a possibility, isn't it? To throw suspicion from himself. If you believe he may be the person who inherits if you leave and that he has simply been stringing you along for all these months, that would make sense.'

'Bloody Nora.' Ella stared at Mia. 'We didn't think of that.'

Mia shook her head in disbelief. 'No. No he wouldn't.'

'But why ask someone else to move his car when he was perfectly capable of doing so himself?' Gill queried.

'He was probably busy, or something. I don't know. But I'm sure he wouldn't have done it. Besides, he wouldn't risk Franklin getting hurt. They're friends as well as work colleagues.'

'Didn't you say Jet and Tom are friends?' Gill said. 'And yet Tom told you Jet wasn't a nice man, didn't he? And that Jet had no heart. Psychopaths feel no empathy towards others.'

'Psychopaths?' Mia shrieked. 'Jet's not a psychopath!'

Ella sniggered. 'He could be. We thought Mattie was a sweet little old lady who had a bit of a shady past. She's turned out to be some sort of badass super spy who hacked into your computer. And Jet is Franklin's boss. Perhaps he's not really friends with anybody, he just pretends to be.'

'No! This is getting ridiculous. Jet's not a psychopath, and he's not cold and calculating, either. I'm sure he's not. Even Hettie likes him, and she doesn't like many people. Perhaps it was a business competitor of Jet's. Perhaps it's got nothing to do with me, or Tom, or Mattie's will. Speaking of which, you came here to discuss Mattie and your grandad, Gill, not to talk about us and our problematic love lives, or people trying to scare us away, or attempt to murder someone. It's almost seven already. Half the evening has gone. Sorry.'

Gill smiled. 'There's nothing to be sorry about, Mia. I've enjoyed discussing this mystery. I wish I could stay for longer and find out who the perpetrator was, and if it's the same person who's been trying to frighten you.'

'You can,' Mia said, without thinking. 'We've got room. Oh. Unless you have to get home and back to work.'

'What?' Ella looked astonished. 'I'm sure Gill didn't mean it, Mia. He was probably just being polite.'

Gill grinned. 'I never say anything I don't mean, Ella. As you'll find out when you get to know me better. I do always try to be polite, but I wasn't being insincere. I genuinely would like to stay for a day or two. But I don't want you to feel you need to extend your invitation, Mia. I may have placed you in an awkward situation. Sleep on it and see how you feel in the morning.'

'I don't need to sleep on it. You're welcome to stay for a few days, if you'd like to, isn't he, Ella?'

Ella shrugged. 'It's your cottage. I don't care either way.'

'Thanks.' Gill grinned at her.

'If you do stay,' Ella added. 'You can meet Tom, and maybe even Jet. Then you can give us your '*informed opinion*'.'

His grin broadened, despite Ella's obvious sarcasm. 'With pleasure.'

'You don't have a job to get back to then?' Ella buttered another roll and layered it with cheese, ham and salad as she spoke. 'Living on a trust fund, I suppose.' She squashed it down with the palm of her hand.

Gill watched her, grinning the entire time. 'No. I have a job, but not one I need to go home to do. I'm a freelance journalist. But I'm currently writing a book about the French Resistance during the Second World War.'

'A journalist?' Mia and Ella said, sounding equally worried.

Gill grinned again. 'Don't worry. I shan't be reporting on anything you've told me. My areas of speciality are business and politics. But as I said, I'm concentrating on the book. It's partly a biography of my grandfather, but it covers all aspects of the French Resistance, not just the part he played.'

'Your grandad was in the French Resistance?' Mia asked.

'Yes. Sorry. Didn't I make that clear? That's how he and Mattie met.'

'You did say they were both in the Intelligence Service and that's how they met, but I assumed you meant they worked in England.'

Gill shook his head. 'No. They met in Paris. My grandfather was originally in The Maquis. They were the rural guerrilla bands that later merged to form La Résistance. His brother was captured by the Nazis and Grandfather planned a rather daring rescue attempt. The Paris Resistance put him in touch with Mattie, who – and this may surprise you if you know nothing of her past – was already in Paris posing as the mistress of a fairly high ranking German officer, giving her access to anything from troop movements to prisoner movements and everything in between. She spoke fluent French, German and Italian, which was one of the reasons she was recruited.'

'What?' Mia nearly choked on a chunk of cheese she was eating.

'Bloody Nora,' Ella said, while Mia was clearing her throat. 'I always said she was someone's mistress, didn't I?'

'Yes,' Mia managed. 'But you thought a gangster's mistress, among other things. Was she really the mistress of a Nazi? Maybe that was why her family ostracised her? Although if they knew she was a British agent, surely they would've been proud?'

Gill looked suitably impressed. 'She was a bloody good agent. I can tell you that much. But I believe she was already cut off from her family.

My research, and speaking with Grandfather over the years, made it clear that she had no one to return home to, or so she said. When she agreed to help with the rescue – which wasn't actually what Grandfather had asked, he'd simply requested information, it was Mattie who said she could do more – he warned her there was a very strong possibility none of them would get out alive. He told me her precise words were, "I won't be missed. I have no one at home who cares." He assumed she meant her relatives were all deceased. It was only later he found out that wasn't the case at all.'

Now Ella looked impressed. 'So not just a super spy, but a heroine, too. Did you meet Mattie?'

Gill shook his head. 'Sadly no. I didn't know who she was until I found the letters last week. What I mean is, I didn't know Mattie Ward, who Grandfather had mentioned a few times, as 'a friend who lives in England' was the same woman he told me all the stories about. Her name was Margot Voss, you see. That was the name she was given when she was sent to France, no doubt by one of the many secret sections of SIS, the Secret Intelligence Service. She was recruited by SIS prior to becoming an SOE agent. Stories about covert operations are still coming to light today and few people know the true extent of it. SIS agents were bound by the Official Secrets Act and SOE records were dissolved after the war. All agents took their obligation of confidentiality extremely seriously even years after the war ended. Some – like Mattie, it seems – never spoke of it. Grandfather lied to me about Mattie though, and that was something he never did, so I was surprised when I discovered it and realised that Mattie and Margot were one and the same. He told me Margot Voss died in May, 1945, just a few days after the war in Europe ended. He said that she was in a car crash and died from her injuries. She didn't. The name may have, but Margot Voss returned to England and resumed her true identity as Miss Matilda Ward.'

Mia frowned. 'So … if your grandad never told you, and you say you only discovered it when you found Mattie's letters, how do you know Mattie was Margot?'

'Because in the letters, she calls him Will, and refers to him as her Resolute Protector, more than once. That's the meaning of William, which of course is the English equivalent of Guillaume, and RP was his code name during the war. And he frequently refers to her as his perfect Pearl. Margot Voss's code name was, you've guessed it, Pearl. It doesn't take a genius to figure it out. They were, in some small and romantic way, harking back to those years they spent together.'

'Spent together?' Ella asked. 'I thought she was the mistress of some German officer?'

'She was. But when he was killed – by them, as it happens. Don't look so shocked. This was war and neither Grandfather nor Margot thought twice about it if it needed to be done. They were trained to kill. She then joined Grandfather and worked for the SOE alongside the French Resistance. She and Grandfather became lovers soon after they met. She was caught in July 1943, but Grandfather and some of the others, rescued her from where she was being held, awaiting transport. She was one of the lucky ones. After being interrogated, she would've been sent to Ravensbrück. A few other female SOE agents were sent there and they weren't so lucky. After months of brutal treatment in appalling conditions, they were executed, shortly before liberation of the camp by the Allies.'

Ella slumped back in her chair, wine glass in hand. 'That's a cheery tale. Sorry. I know they went through hell and back, but would you mind if we discussed something a little bit more cheerful?'

'Sorry,' Gill said. 'Of course.'

'It's unbelievable what they went through,' Mia said, tears pricking at her eyes as she could picture the experience, from various films she'd seen over the years. But to know that Mattie, her great-aunt had gone through that, and kept it to herself, really brought it home to her. 'Ella and I think it's a disaster if we can't find the right nail varnish to go with an outfit we're wearing, but those women had—'

'Yes. Thank you!' Ella interrupted. 'I've seen the films. I don't need to be reminded.' She screwed up her face as if she could feel their pain.

Mia coughed and shifted in her seat. 'You're right. And yet we should be reminded, shouldn't we? We should all remember what those people did, especially what the women like Mattie did, in the name of freedom. Our freedom. You said you're writing a book, Gill? Are you writing about Mattie, too? Or Margot, or Pearl, or whatever she was called?'

He nodded. 'Yes. But I shan't reveal her true identity – unless you want me to, of course.'

'Oh. Um. I don't know. I'm not sure she would want that. I wish I could find her diaries. They might throw some light on what was going on in her head.'

Gill sat upright. 'Mattie kept diaries?' His excitement was obvious.

'Yes. But we don't know where they are.'

Ella sighed. 'Like everything else of Mattie's, they're hidden somewhere.'

'But you know for certain they exist? How?'

'We saw a photo of them on Mattie's laptop. And her laptop's another story. But I'll tell you that part later. The photo was in the wrong place, which was why we spotted it immediately. It should've been in the folder called 'Sunbeam Cottage' because it's a photo of the attic room upstairs. Instead she'd put it in the wrong folder. It

247

was in the folder containing lots of old photos of her.'

Gill leant forward. 'From what I've learnt about Margot, sorry, Mattie over the years, she wouldn't put anything in the wrong place. She was far too careful and intelligent for that. May I see the photo?'

'Yes of course. It's on the laptop, which is in the attic room. Come with me and I'll show you.'

He was on his feet in a split second. 'I think it may be a clue,' he said.

'A clue?' Ella asked. 'A clue to what?'

He beamed at her like a boy who had solved his very first puzzle. 'To where she's hidden the diaries.'

'Don't get your hopes up,' Ella said. 'We've searched that room from top to bottom and tested every floorboard to see if one is loose. They're all nailed down firmly and as Mattie was ninety-nine and the photo is relatively recent, there was no way even she could be nailing down floorboards at her age. And the diaries aren't in the 'secret room' we found, either. Or her safe.'

'Let's see,' he said, and they hurried from the kitchen as if the place had just caught fire.

Chapter Seven

'I can't believe it,' Mia said, beaming at Ella and Gill. 'I've been sitting on that window seat for the last five months and all this time, those diaries were right there, beneath me.'

Ella smiled at Gill. 'I can't believe you knew that's where they'd be, just by looking at a photo.'

'I can't believe you haven't found them sooner.' Gill grinned. 'That button was so loose I only had to touch it and it released. It should've popped open the first time you ran a duster over it.'

Ella laughed. 'That's easily explained. We haven't. Hettie, a neighbour comes to do the housework but Mattie never allowed her up here so neither does Mia. And Mia and I don't *do* housework until the dust is three feet thick. There's barely a centimetre up here.'

'That's because Garrick came up and gave the room a quick once over every other week,' Mia confessed. 'I haven't done anything since he left but he wouldn't have cleaned under the lip of the window seat anyway. Who goes to those extremes to keep a place clean?'

Gill pulled a face as if he were bemused. 'Anyway. You've found them now.'

'Maybe not,' Ella said, laughing. 'Just because it says "My diaries" on the top of that massive box, it doesn't mean that's what's in it. Knowing Mattie, it could be anything.'

'That's true.' Mia bent down to look. The window seat had popped up the moment Gill had pressed a hidden button beneath the lip, and the front panel had fallen open, nearly hitting Gill's feet, but he'd been standing to the side as if he knew what to expect. When they lifted the seat fully to an upright position, another large box had been revealed, with the inscription written in indelible ink on the lid. Mia removed the lid and gasped. The diaries were there, stacked in neat piles, each pile tied with red ribbon. But what immediately caught Mia's eye, was the note.

Ella burst out laughing once again. 'Is that really a note to you? The cunning old bag. Gill was right. Mattie expected you to see the clue in that photo and find them. Well, come on. What does it say?'

Mia stared at it. 'It says, "Only to be opened by Miss Mia Ward".'

Ella nudged her. 'Not the envelope, you daft cow. The note inside it.'

'Oh.' Mia picked up the envelope and opened it, reading the contents aloud. 'It says, "Dear Mia, I don't know how long it has taken you to find this note and my diaries, but I'm hoping that it has been a few months, at least, and that you have had sufficient time to get to know the locals. In particular, Jet Cross and Hettie Burnstall, but also Tom Tyburn and Alexia Bywater."' Mia looked up at Ella. 'Why them?'

'How the hell do I know? Is that all it says?'

Mia shook her head. 'There's more.'

Ella tutted. 'Then read the thing.'

Gill grinned and leant against the eaves.

'Okay. It goes on. "I'm also hoping that, as I have left you my estate, you will do me the courtesy of following these instructions to the letter."'

'What letter?' Ella asked.

'I think,' Gill said, 'she means Mia should follow the instructions precisely. She's not referring to another letter.'

'Thanks. We can't all be as smart as you.'

He merely grinned, but he didn't rise to the bait.

'Ella. Gill. Listen to this. "I want you to read my diaries in chronological order, leaving the most recent one until last. I understand how tempting it will be to skip to the year 2018, but if you do, you're not the woman I thought you were and that would be a pity. I rarely misjudge people. I sincerely hope I have not misjudged you. A man by the name of Guillaume De Fonteneau, whom I know as Will, or his grandson, Gill De Fonteneau may contact you.""

'De Fonteneau?' Ella stared at Gill. 'Is that your name?'

Gill laughed. 'Personally, I don't use the De bit, just Fonteneau. But yes. That's my name. From a very long line of De Fonteneaus, many of whom were named Guillaume.'

'And many of whom lost their heads to the Guillotine in the 1790s no doubt,' Ella said, sarcastically.

Gill shrugged and grinned. 'One or two, perhaps. Most of us got away.'

'Do you want to hear this or not?' Mia asked, but she was grinning too. 'Okay. "Please tell Will, I shall love him, always. I have told him myself, now that I know my days are numbered, but remind him, if he should get in touch. As for Gill. He's writing a book, I am led to believe. He will no doubt want my diaries from the war and possibly shortly after. It is entirely up to you whether you accede to his request. I have never met him but I loved his grandfather deeply and I am certain Gill is like him. I am not bothered either way. I shall be dead. The choice is yours." I assume that means you do want them?' Mia glanced at Gill, who nodded.

'Definitely. If you don't mind. I'll take excellent care of them and return them as soon as possible.'

252

'I don't mind. But I want to read them first. As Mattie has asked me to read them in order, it may take me some time to get around to them. So, either you can come back and get them when I've finished. Or you can stay here and read them and take notes or whatever until you're done. That way we can both read them.'

'What?' Ella said, an anxious look on her face. 'That might take weeks.'

'I couldn't possibly expect you to let me stay here for so long,' Gill said, but he looked keen to do just that.

Mia shrugged. 'Does it matter? There's plenty of room. Mum's going to be moving into the farm cottage with Franklin. She'll be there from today anyway because of what's happened. And it might be nice to have a man around the house again. We both miss Garrick.'

'Yeah but ...' Ella shot a look at Gill. 'Can you chop wood?'

He nodded. 'Yes.'

'Can you cook?'

'Yes. I'm quite good, even if I do say so myself.'

Ella sighed and shrugged. 'Okay. You can stay.'

'Are you sure?' He looked from Ella to Mia. 'You hardly know me.'

Mia nodded. 'I know. But I feel as if I do. That's weird, isn't it? But from the minute you arrived, we all got on and we told you all about us

253

within half an hour of you being here. You tell us all about you and we'll be fine. But tell us later. I want to finish this note first. Okay. "You're probably furious with me for planting Spyware on your laptop. My diaries will explain that too. They'll explain everything. But please, please, do read them in order, as I've asked. As to why I've left you my estate, that's simple. I have no other living relatives and frankly, you could do with some financial help."' Mia coughed before shrugging. 'She's not wrong about that. "I hope you are enjoying life in Sunbeam Cottage, Mia and that Little Pondale is finding a place in your heart. Should you feel the need to turn to someone for assistance, may I suggest Jet Cross? He may seem arrogant and a cad but the man has hidden depths. I hope you'll have discovered that for yourself, but if not, look for them, Mia. And if you have any sense at all, encourage a friendship to grow between you. I am hoping it already has, by the time you find this note."'

Ella and Mia simultaneously said, 'Bloody Nora.'

'Well,' said Gill. 'Mattie obviously had a high opinion of Jet. Which means the vicar may not have been telling you the truth.'

'Unless Mattie was wrong about Jet,' Ella said.

Gill shook his head, with a serious expression on his face. 'Margot Voss was never wrong about anyone. Even as Mattie, she wouldn't make a

254

mistake about someone's true character, I'm fairly certain of that.'

'Then I think we need to ask Tom why he lied,' Ella said. 'But I'm guessing it's because he's madly in love with you.' She smiled at Mia. 'What else does she say?'

Mia grinned and continued: '"I wish we could have met, but I think it's better that we didn't. I hope you make the right choices with your life. I believe I did, but as I reach my end, doubt is creeping in. Take this advice to heart. If you really love someone with every fibre of your being, and you know they love you in return, never give them up, no matter what. Take the risk. No matter how difficult the future may seem. Be happy, Mia. Live life to the full. Dance on the sand. Howl at the moon. I always did. And so did your beloved father, Ernest. But most of all, be true to yourself. I wish you every happiness." And it's signed, Mattie and beneath that it says, "Your great-aunt Matilda, who loved you from afar." Aw. Isn't that lovely?'

'Wonderful,' Ella said. 'Now can we please go back downstairs and open another bottle of wine while we discuss it? I'm gasping here.'

'That's a brilliant idea. I'll just grab the first diary so I can start reading that right away. But I also need to read this note at least three times to take it in.'

'You mean you're actually going to do as she says, and not read the latest diary? I'd go to that one without a moment's delay.'

'I'd like to. But she's right. She did leave me her cottage and everything else if I stay here for the year. Which I intend to do. So it's only fair that I honour her last wish, as much as it's killing me to do so.'

'I could read it for you and tell you what it says,' Ella offered. 'She didn't say no one else could read it.'

Mia tutted. 'I think it's implied, don't you? So keep your mitts off them, okay? I mean it, Ella. I'll be upset if you read it before I do. That goes for you too, Gill.'

He held his hands in the air. 'I'm only interested in the war years and perhaps the year or two before and after. But I'm happy to wait.'

'Okay.' Mia unwrapped the ribbon and grabbed the first diary from the first pile. It was dated 1931. She closed the lid and pushed the front flap up before shutting the window seat down on top of it and with a click, everything was back as it was. 'Let's go downstairs and pour some wine and you can continue telling us about yourself, Gill.'

He smiled as they headed towards the stairs. 'There's not much more to tell. I've told you what I do and about the book I'm writing. I'm thirty-five and single. No girlfriend, in case you're interested.' He glanced at Ella and stood aside to let her and Mia go down the stairs before him.

'We're not,' Ella said. 'What else?'

'My dad died when I was two and my mum, shortly after.'

'Oh. I'm sorry,' Ella said, glancing over her shoulder.

'Me too,' said Mia, doing the same.

Gill shook his head. 'No need. I don't remember either of them. Grandfather brought me up but he sent me to school in England when I was eleven, because that was my mother's wish. I live in Cambridge but I spend a great deal of my time in France. Grandfather lives in Meloisey, close to Beaune in eastern France. Or did. You'll have heard of Beaune, as you enjoy wine.'

'I've heard of it,' Mia said, as they reached the upstairs hall. 'But I don't know where it is. Perhaps you'll show us on a map. We're sorry about your grandad, too. I hadn't realised he meant so much to you but he clearly did.'

'Thanks. We were very close. He'd been ill for months, so it didn't come as a complete shock, and he was ninety-seven, so he'd had a good life. For the last six months though, he wasn't really with it. He had a stroke at the end of March and never recovered.'

'The end of March?' Mia queried. 'That's when Mattie died. Had someone told him about her death?'

Gill shook his head. 'I don't know. I was in the UK at the time and had to dash back. He couldn't talk or move, so I honestly have no idea what happened. His passing was a happy release for him.'

'How odd,' Ella said, walking down the stairs to the ground floor. 'They died within months of one another. Although considering their ages, I suppose it isn't odd at all. What happened with their romance? You said they were together throughout the war. Why did they break up?'

'I have no idea. As I said, I believed Margot, or Mattie as I now know she was, died in May 1945 and that's why it ended. He did tell me he had just proposed to her when she died. Perhaps she rejected his proposal and returned to England. Perhaps, in a way, Margot was therefore dead to him. And yet they obviously kept in touch through their letters. But I don't know if they ever saw one another again. I definitely never met her.'

'Perhaps her diaries will answer that question,' Mia said.

'And a lot more besides,' said Ella.

'So you'll stay then?' Mia asked.

Gill nodded as they entered the kitchen. He grabbed the second bottle of wine he'd brought and motioned with his hand for the corkscrew. Ella smiled as she passed it to him.

'If you're sure you don't mind. I would love to stay.' He filled the glasses they'd left on the table and sat down.

'Good,' Mia said. 'Then let's make a toast. To old friends and new. To Mattie slash Margot slash Pearl and Will slash Guillaume. To Ella, to you, Gill and to me. And most importantly, to the future.'

'Is that it?' Ella joked, raising her glass. 'I thought you were never going to end.'

Mia grinned. 'No wait! To howling at the moon and dancing on the sand. Now, shut up and drink.'

'You don't have to tell me twice,' Ella said. 'Cheers to all that.'

Gill raised his glass and smiled. 'Cheers to all that.' He took a swig, raised his brows and put his glass down on the table. 'I don't know what made me think of this. I suppose the dancing on the sand. But do you two like ballet?'

'Ballet?' Mia asked. 'Why?'

'I wondered if you'd like to go. It's a couple of months away. Not until early January, but tickets are selling fast. I was planning to get mine this week, so if you're interested, I'll happily pay for you both to accompany me. My cousin's a ballerina and she's touring the UK at present but it's at The Coliseum in London from the 3rd of January.'

'I've never been to a real ballet,' Mia said. 'I'd love to go.'

Ella shrugged. 'It could be fun I suppose, and an evening in London would be great, especially just after Christmas. We could go up for the day and hit the sales.' She glanced at Gill. 'Or not.'

He smiled. 'I'm happy with that plan. We could make a day and night of it. I'll book a hotel for us. Separate rooms, of course. It'll be a good way for me to say thank you for all this.'

'Okay then,' Mia said. 'That sounds wonderful. Thank you.'

'It's my pleasure,' Gill said, looking directly at Ella. 'My cousin, Isobel is incredible. But in addition to that, it's not only my favourite ballet, it was also the favourite of both Mattie and my grandfather. They speak of it often in their letters. So it'll definitely be the perfect treat.'

'Oh?' Ella leant forward. 'What is it? The Nutcracker is my favourite. For obvious reasons.' She sipped her wine somewhat provocatively.

Gill laughed and also leant forward, leaving very little space between them. 'Same composer. But it's Swan Lake.'

An arc of wine shot from Ella's mouth and cascaded down the front of Gill's checked shirt.

'Swan Lake?' Mia screeched, her eyes darting from Gill to Ella in astonishment. 'Did you just say, Swan Lake?'

Chapter Eight

'Oh. My. God,' Ella said, when Gill went upstairs to change his shirt. 'You know what this means, don't you?'

Mia nodded. 'It means that bloody fortune-teller is becoming a right pain in the proverbial.'

'It means a lot worse than that. It means that the Swan Lake bit had nothing whatsoever to do with me marrying Justin and becoming Mrs Swann-Lake. It means the fact that things have cooled off between us might have something to do with what that woman told him. And it means that meeting the man I'll marry whilst solving a mystery with my best friend, also wasn't about meeting Justin, because we hadn't solved the mystery until tonight. Oh God.' She lowered her head into her cupped hands and shook her head to and fro. 'It means that I'm going to see a ballet with a man who irritates the hell out of me. I don't even like Gill. And how can I marry a man with a pompous surname like De Fonteneau? Even without the De.'

'Well, you did like the idea of a double-barrelled surname and his comes ready-made. Ella De Fonteneau, sounds fabulous. And so does Ella Swann De Fonteneau. Or simply Ella Fonteneau. Plus he's gorgeous. I know Justin's gorgeous too and I like him a lot, but you said yourself things have changed between you two. It clearly wasn't meant to be. Like me and Garrick. And let's not forget, Gill may have a weird name, but his recently deceased grandfather has an extensive wine cellar.'

Ella lifted her head. 'Yeah. I suppose every cloud has a silver lining. And holidays in France might be nice.'

Their eyes met and they laughed.

'I know that damned woman's been right about most things so far, but your future is yours, Ella. If you don't like Gill, you don't have to date him, and you certainly don't have to think you've got to marry the guy just because some woman in a crimson tent tells you you will. But I saw the way you looked at one another. You're attracted to him, aren't you? Be honest.'

Ella sighed. 'Who wouldn't be? The irritating sod is bloody gorgeous. He's got the body of a god and the brain of a genius, plus he's got the sexiest grin I've ever seen. And a good sense of humour. Oh. Was that the doorbell? It's a bit late for someone to be coming round, isn't it?'

'Perhaps it's Mum.' Mia got to her feet and ran along the hall. 'Oh. Hello Justin. Ella and I were just talking about you. Come in.'

'Thanks,' he said, looking anxious. He lowered his voice. 'Is it possible to have a word with Ella alone, please Mia? I've got some news and I think it's best if I tell her privately, but I'd like you to be on hand if she doesn't take it well.'

'Oh my God, Justin. You're not dying or something, are you?'

He pulled a face. 'Dying? Why would I be dying?'

'I don't know. It's just that it sounds serious. Oh. Are you dumping her? Because if so, I have to say your timing is pretty unbelievable.'

'I'm not dumping her, exactly. Well, I suppose I am in a way. But not just yet. Unless she wants to end it now. But I've had an offer I simply can't refuse. Is she here?'

'Of course she's here. Ella! It's Justin. He wants to have a word in private.' She looked Justin in the eye. 'You can go in the living room. But whatever this is about, I hope you'll be kind. She's already had one shock tonight.'

'Oh? What was that?'

'It doesn't matter. Ah. Here she is. I'll leave you to it.'

Mia gave Ella a hopeful smile and returned to the kitchen. A minute or two later, Gill joined her.

'Is everything all right? I heard Ella's voice coming from the sitting room and she didn't sound happy.'

'I don't think she is. But it's a long story and you must be shattered. If you want to go to bed, that's fine by us.'

He grinned. 'Is that a polite way of telling me to make myself scarce?'

She grinned back. 'Yes. If you don't mind.'

'I don't mind. But I'm so hyped-up with excitement that I'm not ready for sleep. May I go for a walk in the garden? Or onto the beach. Can I get to that from your garden?'

Mia nodded. 'Yes. There's a gate at the end. Just go over the dunes onto the beach. You might want to take a torch. I know the moon's still almost full and there weren't any clouds earlier but you never know. It can get pretty dark out there. There's a torch in that drawer.' She pointed to a drawer near the end cupboard. 'I'm quite excited about what we've discovered today, myself, so I don't think I'll get much sleep either.'

Gill's grin broadened. 'Oh I wasn't only thinking about that. It's just a shame Ella has a boyfriend.'

Mia's mouth fell open but she quickly closed it and grinned again. 'Yes. Well. That may not be such an issue. Was that the front door slamming?' She stood up and turned towards the hall.

'I'll get out of the way. But shout if you need me.'

Ella stormed along the hall. 'You will never believe this,' she said. 'Oh. Where's Gill dashing off to?'

'The beach. To give us some privacy. What won't I believe?'

'That meeting Justin had tonight, wasn't a meeting at all. He was simply waiting for a phone call from his agent. I didn't even know he had an agent. Apparently, someone sent this agent a video of one of Justin's shows and the agent came to see another show live and offered to represent Justin. Can you believe that? He never said a word about it to me. Not one word.' She slumped down on her chair. 'Anyway, he's been offered a part in a film and he's agreed to take it. And you'll never guess what the bloody fortune-teller told him and why he's been backing off from me? Yep. She said he would be offered an opportunity that was far too good to miss and that he would see his name in lights within one year ... in Hollywood. Sodding Hollywood! But that he might feel torn over this chance, and a woman he cares for. He should start taking steps straight away to lessen the difficulty. And he should take the chance and forget the woman! I'm telling you now, if that damn fortune-teller ever shows her face here again, I'll kill her. But as she seems to know everyone's bloody future, she'll already know that, won't she?'

'Wow!' Mia said. 'So when did all this happen? And is the film in the UK, or in the States?'

Ella sighed. 'The agent contacted him the day after the Fête and a couple of days after that, Justin went up to London for an audition. Another thing he forgot to mention. He says he didn't tell me because if nothing came of it there was no point in rocking the boat. Rocking the Boat! I'm tempted to bloody well drown him. Now I know what that bloody woman meant when she told me that someone was leading me a bit of a dance. And the worst bit is, when the agent called tonight to confirm Justin got the part, he told him to be on a plane in two weeks' time and not to book a return, as there's a strong probability of another part. So much for him being such a nice guy.' She picked up her glass of wine from where she'd left it on the table and finished it in one long gulp.

'I'm so, so sorry, Ella. But why did he come and tell you this tonight? Surely it could've waited until tomorrow?'

Ella nodded. 'He said he was going to wait, but he started thinking about Franklin's accident and how lives can change in a split second and he decided he had to tell me right away. How bloody thoughtful of him? Not.' She sighed again. 'But once I got over the shock, the annoying thing was, do you know the first thing that popped into my head when he told me he was leaving?'

'Um. That Gill being here might be a good thing, after all?'

Ella smirked. 'Nope. Although I suppose it might be, now. But no. The first thing I thought was, no more delicious fresh bread and scrumptious buns, because who's going to bake them after Justin leaves?'

Ella looked at Mia and shrugged and then they both burst out laughing even though the prospect of no longer having Justin's buns, wasn't in the slightest bit funny.

Chapter Nine

News of Justin's imminent departure spread around the village in no time and, as much as everyone liked Justin, the same words, or very similar, were on everybody's lips: 'Who's going to bake our bread and cakes when Justin leaves?'

The good news was, even the man himself had thought of that. It seemed he had a plan in place. It was just a pity he hadn't thought to tell Ella he'd been making all these plans.

'A cousin of mine's coming to take over,' he told Mia, when she went to get fresh bread the morning after he'd broken the news to Ella. 'She trained in Florence and she's been working in a pasticceria there for the last two years. Her cakes and pastries are going to be even more delicious than mine.'

Mia, and one or two of his other customers, commented that Florence was better known for its art than its baking, but Justin pointed out that baking was an art if done correctly and neither Mia nor anyone else felt they could argue with that.

'By the time Justin actually leaves,' Mia said, during breakfast two days later, 'everyone will be so keen to try his cousin's buns, they won't even notice he's gone.'

'I'll notice,' Ella said.

In spite of his behaviour, Ella was still seeing him. She'd told Mia that it would give her time to get used to the idea that he wouldn't be around. Mia wasn't sure it was a wise decision but it was Ella's life and if that was her choice, Mia would support her no matter what. And be there for her if things turned really sour. Justin, of course, seemed more than happy with this arrangement.

'Just promise me you won't have 'Goodbye sex',' Mia had said, when Ella had told her, and they'd both laughed at that. They were getting rather good at laughing over bad, sad, or totally mad situations these days.

'Of course you'll notice. But you can read Mattie's diaries with me until you get another book to edit.'

'Oh joy,' Ella said. 'I'm hardly able to contain my excitement.'

'You can help with my research, if you'd like to,' Gill offered. 'That'll keep you busy.'

'My cup runneth over,' Ella replied, staring at the breakfast muffin on her plate as if that were a work of art.

Mia nudged her arm. 'It'll take time to get over him, but you'll be okay. You said yourself that things were cooling off anyway. And look at me. I felt as if the world had been taken from me when Garrick left, but I'm doing fine.'

Ella frowned. 'You've been sitting in the attic for the last two days, reading a dead woman's diaries, and taking them to bed with you at night. Forgive me for saying so, but that's not my idea of doing fine. It doesn't exactly scream, single, thirty-three-year-old woman having the time of her life, to me.'

Mia grinned. 'That's because you're thirty-four. We thirty-three-year-olds know how to have a good time.'

Ella pulled a face. 'That just makes it worse. So what have you discovered from the diaries so far? Do you know why Mattie was ostracised?'

'Not yet. The diaries haven't got to that bit yet. She started them from her twelfth birthday and so far it's been all about her friends, family and schooling. I've been reading about her family on her mother's side. I already knew quite a bit about her dad's side because of my dad, but her mum's side were fairly wealthy it seems from reading about their lifestyle, and so prim and proper that, to quote Mattie, "if one could capture in a bottle, the air they exhale during one conversation, the laundress would have starch enough to last a week."'

'Does that mean they had bad breath?' Ella asked.

'It means they were of the straight-back and stiff-upper lip generation,' Gill said.

Ella tutted. 'I know what it means. I was joking. What's up with you? I thought you got my humour the moment you arrived, but during the two days you've been here, you've gone all serious and nerdy and pole-up-your-bum-know-it-all-git, again.'

Mia gasped and Gill almost choked on his coffee.

'Again?' he queried. 'Is that what you think of me? That's good to know. I foolishly thought you rather liked me. It seems I was mistaken.'

'Like you?' Ella said, raising her voice and shoving back her chair as she got to her feet. 'I don't know what gave you that idea. Mia was the one who wanted you to stay, not me. I can't wait for you to leave. You're getting on my nerves.'

He raised his brows as well as his voice as he stood up. 'I sincerely apologise. If my presence annoys you so greatly, perhaps I should go now.'

'Please do!' Ella glared at him.

Mia banged her hand on the table. 'Please don't! Ella doesn't mean that, Gill. She's upset, that's all.'

'I do mean it,' Ella said, almost at shrieking pitch. 'And I'm telling you right now, there is no way I'll ever marry you so don't even bother asking.'

'Marry me?' His angry voice reflected the shock on his face and his eyes shot from Ella to Mia and back again. 'What in God's name makes you think I'd ask you to? I only met you three days ago. I'll admit I'm attracted to you. But marriage? … God … I haven't even asked you out.'

'No, you haven't.' Ella glared at him.

'Because you're still dating a man who's told you he's leaving.' Gill glared back. 'I have no intention of asking you out while you're chasing after him.'

'I'm not chasing after anyone. I'm still dating him because I like him. And because I like having sex. And because no one else has asked to date me. Okay?'

'Okay. But there's no need to shriek like a banshee. I like having sex too. You could date me.'

'Don't you dare call me a banshee. And I can't date you because you still haven't bloody well asked me.'

'Well I'm asking now. Will you go out on a date with me?'

Ella hesitated for a split second. 'Well, okay then.' Her voice came down an octave.

So did Gill's. 'Okay? You'll go out with me?'

'I might as well. It's better than reading Mattie's bloody diaries with Mia. And that's my only other option.'

'Fine. What about tonight?'

'Fine.' Ella sounded almost calm again.

'Okay. But you'd better tell Justin it's over. I'm not the kind of man who dates other people's girlfriends.' Gill even grinned. 'The pole up my bum won't let me.'

'Okay.' Ella grinned back. 'I'll go and tell him now. But as much as I like sex, I'm not the kind of girl who jumps into bed on a first date, so don't expect me to.'

'I don't expect anything.'

'Good.' Ella turned and marched along the hall. 'I'll see you later.'

'Good.' Gill marched out into the garden.

Mia sat at the table, blinking.

What on earth had just happened?

Chapter Ten

The Indian Summer was continuing just as Jet had said it would, that night of the firework display on the beach and, as neither Ella nor Gill had returned after an hour, Mia decided she'd take a break from the diaries and go for a morning swim. She didn't know why it was taking Ella so long to end things with Justin. Perhaps they were having 'Goodbye sex' after all.

A small part of her hoped she might see Jet but the only other person on the beach was Tom, and he hurried towards her the minute he caught sight of her. Where Gill had disappeared to, she had no idea. Perhaps he'd walked along the beach and up towards Frog Hill. He might return to the cottage via the village and she realised he didn't have a key. Ella might be back soon, so she could let him in. If not, he would simply have to wait.

'Hello, Mia,' Tom called out, seconds before he reached her. 'How are you, and how is Ella? I've been meaning to call but I've been so busy.

You didn't come to choir practice on Tuesday night.'

'Hi Tom. We're fine, thanks. Ella didn't go because she knew everyone would be looking at her and Justin, and I didn't go because we've found Mattie's diaries and I've been so engrossed in them that I've hardly thought of anything else.'

'Mattie's diaries?' His tanned face paled a fraction. 'Mattie kept diaries?'

'Yes. From the age of twelve. And you'll never guess what. Like everything else, they were hidden away where no one could find them. But she left a clue for us, and with Gill's help, we found them. Oh. I suppose you've heard that Gill is staying with us and that his grandad was a friend of Mattie's?'

Tom nodded. 'Yes. I heard. So you've got her diaries?'

Mia smiled. 'I knew the village gossips wouldn't let us down. This place could teach big business a thing or two about speedy delivery. Anyway, yes. We also found a note from Mattie to me. Isn't that amazing?'

'Amazing,' he repeated, stony-faced. 'What did it say?'

Mia smiled. 'She asked me to read her diaries in order and not to merely jump right to the one she wrote this year. So that's what I'm doing. But you wouldn't believe how tempted I am every single day to just take a little peek at this year's.'

'Oh I think I would.' He gave a small cough. 'So you haven't? Not at all?'

She shook her head and grinned. 'Nope. I've been really good. You might almost say, angelic.'

He grinned back but it looked as if it took effort. 'Has anyone else? Read this year's diary, I mean.'

'No. I've made it clear that no one, not even Mum or Ella can read them before me. You know what Ella's like. If it said something interesting or important she wouldn't be able to keep it to herself. And nor would Mum. Which reminds me. What did you think when you heard about Franklin's so-called accident and Jet's car?'

'Think?'

'Yes. About the fact that it wasn't an accident after all. That someone had tampered with the brakes, which meant they expected Jet to be the one who got hurt. Are you okay, Tom? You look as if your mind is miles away.'

'Sorry. Yes. I'm fine. Just got a lot on my mind at the moment. Is that what you believe? That someone wanted to cause Jet harm?' He shook his head. 'I expect that would give the police a long list of suspects.'

'I don't think they have any suspects. I'm not even sure they're taking it very seriously. According to Mum, the police officer who came said that while it may appear to be foul play, there are a number of other possibilities. No one knows what that means because it's clear to everyone except him that there's only one possibility. Anyway, he assured them that the police will continue to look into it and that any further incidents should be reported. Which basically means nothing will be done. Why did you say there will be a long list of suspects?'

Tom shrugged. 'There's a long list of broken-hearted women, many of whom have brothers and most of whom have fathers. Some no doubt, had husbands.'

'Tom! You really must stop saying horrible things about Jet. You're supposed to be his friend.'

Although to be fair, Ella had said almost the same thing.

Tom looked surprised. 'I am his friend. Friends should be honest about one another and to each other. Jet knows very well that I have never approved of his behaviour towards women and that I never shall. I lecture him about it, take my word for that. Not that it does any good, of course. Falls on deaf ears. Jet will do want Jet wants to do, regardless of what anyone may think.'

'Well, I think you're being unkind. And to be honest, Tom, I don't like it. I'd be grateful if you'd stop saying things about him behind his back. At least to me.'

He reached out and took her hand. 'Oh, Mia, I am so, so sorry. I have only ever had your best interests at heart. You know how I feel about you and I would do anything I can to save you from further heartbreak. I've known Jet for years and years. You've only known him for a few months. Surely you can see that I may know him a little better than you do. That I know – and have seen – the real Jet Cross. The one he keeps under wraps as much as possible.'

Mia snatched her hand away. 'You're doing it again, Tom. Saying horrid things. I mean it. I don't want to hear them. I like you, Tom, I really do, but if this continues, I'm not sure we can be friends.'

'Mia! Please don't say that. Your friendship means the world to me. You mean the world to me. Forgive me. Please, please forgive me. I promise I shan't say another word. Unless your life depends on it.'

'Unless my life depends on it? What does that mean?'

His expression was a mixture of anxiety and apology. 'I can't say. I promised not to say another unpleasant word against Jet, and I'll keep that promise. Until the time comes when I have to speak. Now let's change the subject and be friends again. Franklin is up and about, I hear and Ella is still seeing Justin in spite of the way he's treated her. That was a surprise to all of us. Justin has always been such a thoughtful man. But the promise of fame can turn a man's head. Just as can, the promise of money.'

Mia had a feeling there was more to that comment than met the eye, but she didn't pursue it.

'Ella may not be dating Justin for very much longer.' She glanced at her watch. 'In fact, I'd say by now she's not.'

'Oh? Does that mean she has ended things with him? Good for her if she has. No one likes to see a woman throwing herself at a man. Especially when the man clearly isn't interested.'

There was definitely more to that comment. Tom was beginning to get on her nerves. And to think. Just a few days ago, after the firework display, she had actually considered dating Tom. If she believed the things he kept saying, she probably would be dating him right now. But she didn't believe him. Something inside her kept telling her Jet Cross was not the man Tom wanted her to believe he was. Although of course, she could be making a big mistake. Tom was right about one thing. He had known Jet a lot, lot longer than she had.

Chapter Eleven

The water was wonderfully warm and Mia seemed to be the only person in it. She had lied to Tom and told him she was meeting Gill further along the beach towards Rainbow's End. He had offered to walk with her but she had said that, if he didn't mind, she would rather like to walk alone. With Ella and Gill in the cottage, she didn't get much me-time, she had fibbed but luckily Tom had believed it. She jogged to Rainbow's End and having checked that Tom had left the beach, she stripped off to her bikini. The tide was in and as she waded out to the rocky outcrop, she smiled at the memory of Tom saving her. To think, that was only three months ago. She wouldn't have believed that three months later, she would be swimming again and loving it.

Neither would she have believed that she would be swimming in the sea in October. Okay, it was only the 4th, but in Little Pondale, this was nearly the middle of Autumn.

She dived beneath the gently rippling waves and swam a few yards under water. It was so clear, she could see the sand, dotted with tiny shells, and small chunks of multi-coloured rock from Rainbow's End. She came up for air, felt the sun beaming on her face, took a deep breath and dived again, heading back towards the shore. When she resurfaced, she closed her eyes, tipped back her head and lay on her back, floating serenely as the salty water lapped against her body and her hair fanned out around her face.

She heard muffled sounds and splashes nearby and twisted round towards the shore.

'Jet!'

'Mia.'

His jeans were rolled up and he was ankle deep in the water. His dog, Mattie was beside him, racing in and out of the waves. Mia stayed low beneath the surface. If she stood, the sea would only come up to her waist and she felt embarrassed. Almost naked, somehow, even though the bikini covered everything it should. Just about.

'What are you doing here? It must be ten at least. Shouldn't you be working?'

'That's one of the many benefits of owning my own farm. I can do as I please.' He held her gaze and his voice grew cold. 'I can even try to kill off my employees if I choose. I suppose you've heard that I tried to do that. That I tampered with my own brakes and sent Franklin to his Fate.'

'Don't be so ridiculous. You did no such thing. You know it and so do I. And so does everyone else, so stop being so maudlin. Self-pity doesn't suit you and nor does playing the martyr.'

'You don't think I did it then?' He brightened visibly.

'I know you didn't.'

'Really?' Even from a few feet away she could see that his eyes seemed to dance in the sunlight. 'What makes you so sure?'

'I know you, Jet.'

'You may think you do. Perhaps you don't. Perhaps you only know the side of me I want you to.'

She studied his face. 'Has something happened? You seem … in an odd sort of mood.'

'Do I? I hear you have a new guest. A very handsome, very wealthy, very educated Frenchman, so I'm told.'

'I'm not sure if he's wealthy or not.'

'But you are sure he's handsome and well educated?'

'Yes. That's obvious the minute you meet him.'

'I haven't had that pleasure.'

'Come round for coffee one day and I'll introduce you.'

'Thanks. That's the first time you've invited me to your home, do you know that?' He frowned. 'Have you shrunk? Or are you kneeling down so that I can't see you in your bikini? You never did send me the photo you promised me.'

'The one you wanted to stick on the wall beside your bed?'

'The very one.'

She splashed her arms to and fro in the water. 'I didn't really think you wanted it.'

'I told you I did.'

'But I don't believe you. I mean, why would you want a photo of me beside your bed when you could've had the real-life me in it?'

He closed his eyes for a second and when he reopened them he shook his head. 'Let's not go there.'

'Go where? To your bed? There's not much chance of that, is there? You made it very clear you don't want me in it.'

'I didn't say I didn't want you in it. I said I didn't want to spend the night with you. I said it would be a mistake for both of us. I still think that. It doesn't mean I wish I didn't. It doesn't mean that I haven't been able to stop thinking about what it would be like. It doesn't mean that I haven't been going over and over that night in my head and wondering how I had the strength to say no and walk away.'

'Really? It looked pretty easy to me. You didn't seem to have any problem from where I was standing.'

'Then you definitely don't know me, Mia. Take it from me, walking away from you that night was one of the hardest things I've ever had to do.'

'You didn't have to do it. No one forced you to walk away.'

'You were heartbroken. You were vulnerable. You were feeling lonely. I couldn't take advantage of that.'

'Of course not. Because telling me you didn't want to sleep with me made me feel so much less heartbroken. Less vulnerable. Less lonely, didn't it? All I wanted was to be in your arms. To be held. To feel special. To feel wanted and desired. For a man with your reputation, I wouldn't have thought that was too much to ask.'

'That was half the problem. You didn't really want me. You just wanted a man to spend the night with. Or you thought you did. Anyone would've fit the bill. I didn't want to be your rebound guy and I definitely didn't want to spend one night with you and have you hate me the next day. And you would've, Mia. I told you then, you're not the kind of girl who can do casual relationships. And as much as I wish I could, I can't offer you anything more.'

God, he was making her mad. Really mad.

'That's crap and you know it.'

She stood up and for one moment was taken aback by the look on his face as he watched the water cascade down her body. His eyes opened wide and his mouth parted. She could hear the breath he sucked in and see his Adam's Apple rise and fall. It was as if he was watching Aphrodite, the goddess of love and beauty, arise out of the foam of the sea, not Mia Ward, the girl from London, with her okay body but a few lumps and bumps where they definitely shouldn't be.

And in that moment, she knew she was right about him.

She sauntered towards him, which wasn't as easy as she'd hoped, given that she was walking through water. Daniel Craig had made it look simple and ultra-sexy in the James Bond film. But then he didn't have Mattie darting around his legs, as she did. She did her best and from the way Jet coughed and bit his lower lip, she must've been doing something right. She stopped just inches from him and stared up into his eyes.

'I didn't want "just any man" and you wouldn't have been my rebound guy. Nor would I have hated you in the morning. And that's what really frightened you. I wanted you, Jet. You. And I'll admit, I may not be the kind of girl who can do casual relationships, but we never really know what we can do until we try. I didn't think I could ever get back in the sea. But look at me now. And Fiona didn't think she could ever want a child. But she wants her child more than she has ever wanted anything in her life. And Mum would've laughed if you'd told her just a few months ago that she would be head over heels in love again, let alone with a man almost half her age. And yet here she is, about to embark on a whole new life with him.' She grinned. 'Providing you don't kill him off, of course.' She saw that adorable twitch at the corner of his mouth but he didn't take his eyes off hers. 'And you, Jet. You keep telling me what you can't offer me. Perhaps it's about time you started thinking about what you can. And what you really want. Because until just now, even I wasn't sure what that was. But now I think I am.'

He swallowed and took a deep breath. 'You think you know what I really want?'

'Yes, Jet. I think I do.' She turned and walked back into the sea.

'Well perhaps you'd be kind enough to tell me, because I haven't got a clue,' he called after her.

She glanced back over her shoulder. 'You want me, Jet. And not just for one night. And that terrifies you to death.'

Without another word, she dived into the water and swam as far as she could before coming up for breath. He was still standing on the shore, scanning the water but a moment after he saw her emerge, he turned and marched back up the beach with Mattie, soaking wet and barking, running at his heels.

Chapter Twelve

Mia was feeling better than she had for a long time. Jet wanted her. She was absolutely certain of it. And she wanted him. More than she had ever wanted anyone in her life. More than she had wanted Garrick. But when she told Ella and Lori about this revelation, it wasn't met with quite as much optimism as Mia had hoped.

'That's lovely, darling,' Lori said, as they sat around the kitchen table shortly after eleven-thirty that morning, drinking coffee and eating chocolate digestives. 'It's good that you've finally accepted your true feelings for Jet and I'm sure the man has strong feelings for you too. You only have to see the way he looks at you, or the expression on his face when someone mentions your name. And let me tell you, he was none too pleased when I told him on Tuesday morning that Gill was here and was staying on indefinitely. I don't know how many times he's been taking Mattie to the beach since then. At least three times on Tuesday.

Several times yesterday and twice today. Perhaps now you've told him how you feel, the poor little dog may get to laze about all day and Jet may get back to work. Poor Pete has been rushed off his feet and, of course, my darling Franklin hasn't been able to do as much as he normally would. Although he's so much better now and he's sure his wrist will heal quickly. What was I saying? Oh yes. It's lovely. But Jet isn't the most easy-going of men, you know. And he does have a reputation.'

'I know, Mum. Has he really been going to the beach so often? In the hope of seeing me, you think?'

'Why else?' Ella asked. 'That's where you two usually seem to 'bump into' one another.'

Mia beamed. 'Then that proves my point even more. He was jealous. He wants me. He definitely wants me.' She did a little jig, seated on her chair.

'Of course he wants you,' Ella said. 'Anyone could've told you that. But the problem is, for how long? He told you himself that he doesn't want a relationship, or marriage, or anything people usually want. He doesn't want any woman living with him. Are you really prepared to get involved with a man who can't and won't promise to be with you forever?'

Mia shrugged. 'Can anyone ever promise that? Dad loved Mum with all his heart. But as much as he would've wanted to be, he isn't here now.'

Lori took Mia's hand. 'That's a different situation, darling. Your father died.'

'But that's my point. No matter how much we love someone, there are no guarantees. And people love each other when they get married and actually do promise to love and cherish one another till the day they die, but have you seen the divorce rate?'

'True,' Ella said. 'But they start out believing they will spend their lives together. It's only when they meet someone else, or fall out of love with their spouse that they leave.'

'Precisely. At least with Jet, he tells you up front it won't last. But what if it does? What if every day he gets up and thinks, I'll give this another day. And another and another. Suddenly, we might find we've been together longer than a lot of married couples.'

'Only not in the same house.' Ella grinned as she and Lori exchanged glances.

'That's true,' Lori said. 'That could happen. But what could also happen is that one day he could say, 'Right, that's it. Goodbye,' and you could be left with nothing. No family, no children, no partner. At least you would have your own roof over your head, so that's something, I suppose.'

'But that could happen whether I'm with Jet or not. What if I don't feel this way about anyone else? I thought I loved Garrick but I realised this morning that the way I felt for him was nothing compared to the way I feel about Jet. Sorry, Ella.'

Ella shrugged. 'That's okay. I completely understand. I thought I loved Justin but tonight I'm going on a date with Gill and I'm already feeling happier than I have been for ages. I never thought I'd be saying that. And certainly not about a nerd with glasses and a pompous French name that ties your tongue in knots just saying it. Although I will miss Justin's buns.' She winked.

'We'll all miss Justin's buns,' Mia said.

Lori nodded. 'Hettie was in tears. She was hoping he'd perform for her hen party and she said the W.I. don't know what they'll do without him. Although The Frog Hill Hounds will continue and they're looking for a replacement. Franklin said he's tempted to apply but I told him he could forget that right away.' She laughed. 'The only stripping that Texan hunk is going to do is in front of me.'

'Hettie's hen party, did you say?' Mia looked at Lori and Ella. 'I didn't know she'd set a date for the wedding. I thought the engagement party was this Saturday?'

Ella nodded. 'It is. She told me when she came to clean this morning. She was late because she and Fred were waiting for Tom at the church and he didn't get back until around ten, obviously because you kept him chatting.' She nudged Mia's arm. 'I was coming back from telling Justin, as Lori was arriving and Hettie and Fred were walking back from the church. She'd just left by the time you came bouncing in from the beach, all excited about Jet.'

'So when is it?' Mia asked, as Lori refilled their coffee mugs. 'What? Why are you two looking at one another like that? Oh God. She's getting married on the 27th, isn't she?'

Ella and Lori nodded.

'But I thought she said it was unlucky because it was a cancelled wedding? Surely with two cancelled weddings that makes it worse? And also because it's unlucky to marry so close to All Hallows whatsitsface?'

Ella laughed. 'According to Hettie, two wrongs make a right. Two cancelled weddings, sort of, cancel each other out, and that makes the date okay again. She was a bit concerned about the All Hallows Eve bit, but she said – and I quote, "I discussed it with Hector and he's going to have a word with the spirits and explain. Plus at our age, Fred and I can't afford to wait. We could be dead at any time. And we've already told the vicar that if one of us dies before the wedding, we can have the funeral on the date instead. We'll use all the same flowers and hymns." I've always said the woman is completely barmy and it seems Fred is just as bad. Oh, but I forgot. And that's your fault for charging in and jumping up and down and saying you had to tell us something right away. Hettie wants you and me and Lori to be her bridesmaids. And get this. She's going to ask Jet to be Fred's best man, because he doesn't have anyone else he can ask. Which is pretty sad. But she says at his age, all his friends are either dead or barely able to move, and he didn't have kids, or any siblings. And, of course, Hector's going to be giving her away.' Ella rolled her eyes. 'The fact that he's dead and no one will see him except her, didn't seem to bother her. She said she would've had Prince Gustav too, but as she'd said to you, he's got short legs and he might get trodden on.'

Mia grinned. 'It's a shame she won't fit into my dress. She could've had that. I wonder if she'd like my idea for Prince Gustav. Jet could hold the cage, or maybe one of us could. Shall I mention it to her?'

Lori laughed. 'Yes, darling. You do that.'

'Oh please tell her to insist Jet does it. I'd love to see his face. One love rat carrying a real rat. That's priceless.'

Mia grinned. 'Excuse me, Ella, but would you please not call the man I love, a love rat. It brings back memories of my ex in London.'

'Oh.' Ella laughed. 'I've just thought of something else she said.' She shook her head. 'I don't think she did much cleaning today, but I paid her anyway. She said that there's a cave the other side of Rainbow's End. The tide comes in, so you have to be careful, but if you go there on All Hallows Eve and call out the name of the man you love, and the name comes back to you, you'll live happily ever after with that man. But if the name doesn't come back, you won't. Obviously, we're all going to try it, aren't we?'

'Are we?' Mia said.

'What? Worried you'll say Jet's name and you'll be met by stony silence?'

Mia tutted. 'It's a cave. The echo will come back no matter what. I'm not in the least bit worried about that. I am, however, concerned about the tide. Being trapped in a cave on All Hallows Eve is not my idea of living happily ever after.'

Lori nodded. 'That's a good point, darling. We need to check the tides. We'll make sure we go when the tide is going out. That way we'll have plenty of time to get in and out and safely home.'

'So what's the plan for Jet?' Ella asked. 'How are you going to get him to realise he wants to spend his life with you? That is your plan, I assume.'

Mia shook her head. 'I don't have a plan. I'll just have to hope that he comes to that conclusion of his own accord.'

'Good luck with that,' Ella said. 'And by the way, have you seen Gill since he went out this morning? I hope he hasn't changed his mind and run away already. Oh, maybe that's him now.'

'I'll get it,' Lori said, getting up. 'I told Franklin I'd be home by lunchtime and it's almost twelve now.' She kissed Mia on the cheek and Ella on her head. 'Have fun you two.' She walked to the door and Mia and Ella could hear her voice and Gill's.

'I forgot they haven't met,' Mia said. Lori hadn't visited the cottage since Jet had come for her on Monday, and although they'd spoken frequently on the phone, it had slipped Mia's mind that they should meet, what with everything that had been going on.

'Your mum is lovely,' Gill said, when he joined them in the kitchen.

'Sorry. I should've introduced you,' Mia said. 'But you already feel like one of us and it completely slipped my mind.'

'We thought you'd got lost,' Ella said. 'We were about to send out a search party.'

He grinned. 'Sorry. I wasn't aware that this village has no phone signal and I'd walked halfway up Frog Hill, only to be told by a villager that I would have to go to the very top, or ask the vicar for access to the steeple.'

'Good thing it wasn't a Monday,' Ella told him. 'Although that would only matter if you went to Frog's Hollow, not the top of the hill.'

'No doubt you're going to explain that to me,' he said.

Ella did, but he shook his head and laughed when she'd finished. 'Superstitious nonsense.'

'You tell that to Hettie.' Mia got him a mug and poured him coffee without asking if he'd like some. 'The curse killed her husband. A car hit him, tossed him in the air and he landed on his head. Although she still talks to him.'

Gill laughed, taking the mug she handed him. 'Thanks. I'm beginning to wonder what I've got myself into. Anyway. I came back down and went to the church. I wanted to meet Tom after everything we discussed, and thought the phone was as good an excuse as any.'

'And?' Ella asked. 'What did you think of him?'

'He seemed friendly enough, especially when I mentioned that you and I were going on a date tonight. He asked where I was taking you and who would be staying with Mia while we were out. He told me to say that he would be extremely happy to pop round and spend the evening with you, Mia. Better to be safe than sorry, I believe he said.'

'I bet he did.' Ella smiled at Mia. 'If you'd rather we didn't go out, we can postpone it. Or have a date night at the cottage. Gill can cook me a four-course meal and you can hide yourself away in the attic with those diaries. We'll bring you up a tray.' She winked at Gill.

'I'm perfectly happy to cook something special,' Gill offered. 'But I wouldn't want Mia to shut herself away in the attic.'

'Don't be ridiculous.' Mia shook her head. 'You've cooked for the last two evenings, Gill. You both deserve to go out on a proper date. I'll be absolutely fine. I'm looking forward to a quiet night in and to read more of the diaries. You two go out and enjoy yourselves. I can call Hettie and Fred if I'm worried, or Mum and Franklin.' She grinned. 'Or maybe I'll call Jet.'

'From the look on your face,' Gill said, 'something more has happened with regard to Jet. Am I allowed to enquire what?'

Ella told him briefly and he smiled. 'I'm looking forward to meeting him.'

'He wants to meet you,' Mia said. 'You'll see him at Hettie's engagement party on Saturday.'

'The woman who talks to her dead husband is getting married?'

'Yep.' Ella grinned. 'And he's giving her away. Plus Prince Gustav will also walk down the aisle with her. But he'll be in a tiny, ornate cage.'

'Prince Gustav? I'm utterly confused,' Gill said.

'Welcome to our world,' said Ella.

Chapter Thirteen

After discussing the matter with Mia, Gill had decided to take Ella to the nearest town for dinner, rather than The Frog and Lily or one of the nearby villages. But he left Mia the number of the restaurant and both he and Ella said she should call them if she was in the least bit worried and they would come back home immediately. She had assured them she would be fine and that she would lock all the doors and windows but by the time she'd lingered in the bath, she was feeling far too warm to have the doors and windows closed. It was another balmy night and there was hardly any breeze. She wanted to continue reading Mattie's diaries, so she grabbed the next one from the hidden box and took it to her bedroom. She opened the French windows to allow what breeze there was to have greater access and propped herself against the pillows to read more about Mattie's life. She hadn't realised how tired she was after all the excitement of the day and before she knew it, she had drifted off to sleep.

When she first heard the rattle of the kitchen door, she thought she must still be dreaming but when she heard the smash of glass, she knew that she was not.

Reaching instinctively for the bedside light, she flicked the switch, but nothing happened. She tried it again. Still no joy. She felt in the darkness for the landline phone beside her bed and breathed a small sigh of relief when her fingers touched it. Thankfully, the dial was backlit so she would be able to see the numbers.

Except it wasn't and she couldn't.

Not only had the power gone out, but so had the telephone line. It was completely dead. Not even a dial tone. Her mobile phone was useless. There was no way she could make a call.

The stairs creaked as someone made their way up them. Mia pulled her legs against her chest for comfort and glanced around not knowing what to do. Should she call out? It could be Ella and Gill. But the footsteps sounded slow and careful. Ella always ran up the stairs, no matter what time of day or night it was. And they wouldn't have smashed glass. Or if they had, they would have called out to her and told her it was them and there was no need for concern.

And Mia was concerned. She was trapped in her bedroom with no lights, no phone and no way out. Her eyes frantically searched the room.

There was a way out. Not an easy one, but it was a way out. She scrambled off the bed, and raced to the French windows as quietly as she could. Because they were wide open, she didn't have to make a sound and she went out onto the balcony and climbed over the top. The glass roof covering the decking was beneath her but if she moved to the very edge of the balcony, she should be able to drop into the garden below, avoiding the roof. It was a long way down, but it was her only way of escape.

She inched her way along and spotted the drainpipe. If she stretched out fully, she may be able to reach it. It was old and solid, and clearly made of lead, not the new plastic variety and she managed with a little effort to get her fingers around it. Somehow, she got her feet against the wall and climbed down the wall and pipe a bit like one of the old-fashioned toy monkeys on a stick her dad had kept from his childhood, dropping to the ground when she felt she could without causing herself an injury.

The moment her feet hit the ground, she moved as fast as her legs would carry her. She ran around the side of the cottage, down the drive and to Hettie's cottage and banged on the door and rang the bell until Fred came and opened it. She fell into his arms, half screaming, half crying.

'Someone's in the cottage. The lights are out and the phone won't work. Please call the police. And Mum. And Jet. Please call Jet.'

Fred led her towards the living room but Hettie met her in the hall and wrapped her arms around her.

'You're safe now,' Fred said.

'Oh good heavens, deary. You come and sit with me. Fred will make the calls. I'll get you a brandy. Here sit down and tell me what happened. Are you hurt?'

Mia shook her head. 'I'm fine. I climbed down a drainpipe. Just scared, that's all. Who would break in, Hettie? And why? Is this connected to the threats? Or is it just a burglar taking a chance?'

Hettie poured her a drink and had one herself.

'I don't know dear,' she said, pouring them both a second. 'But Fred will go and see what he can see.'

'No! Please don't go, Fred.' Mia's eyes shot towards the hall. 'Whoever it is may be dangerous. Wait for the police. Wait for Jet.'

'I'll just take a look outside,' he said. 'I've spoken to the police and they'll be here any second. There was no reply from Jet's, but I left a brief message on his answerphone. And your mum is on her way with Franklin. You stay here with Hettie and you'll be fine.'

He was only gone a few minutes before sirens screeched down the lane and as Mia and Hettie made their way to the window to look out, two police cars pulled up outside Sunbeam Cottage.

Fred spoke to the officers and they ran towards the cottage.

'Let's sit back down,' Hettie said, 'and wait until they come and tell us what they've found.'

Mia allowed Hettie to lead her back to the sofa and they sat huddled together until Fred appeared, smiling, followed by Lori who raced to Mia's side and threw her arms around her.

'Are you all right, darling? Are you hurt? What happened? Why were you in the cottage on your own?'

'I'm fine, Mum. Ella and Gill are on their date. Don't be cross. I told them to go. I wanted a night on my own. I didn't think for one minute that something like this would happen.'

Franklin joined them. 'You okay, honey? What happened?'

Mia nodded. 'I'm fine. Someone smashed the glass in the kitchen door, I think, and broke in. I heard footsteps on the stairs and I ran. I didn't see who it was. Have you seen Jet?'

'Jet? Why no, honey. I haven't.' He gave her a curious look.

'It's silly,' she said. 'I just wanted him to know.' She shot a look at Lori. 'Fred called him but there was no reply.'

'He's probably in The Frog and Lily,' Lori said. 'Franklin, sweetheart, would you go and see?'

He nodded and disappeared as quickly as he arrived.

'Should Franklin be out?' Mia asked. 'Sorry. I wasn't thinking. I probably shouldn't have asked Fred to call and worry you all.'

'Don't be silly. I would've been furious if you hadn't. Franklin's fine. Don't worry about him. It's you we need to be concerned about. Thank you for taking care of her, Hettie. And you, Fred. Thank you so much.'

'No thanks necessary,' they replied, smiling.

'I'm fine now, Mum. I was frightened. Really scared. But I'm safe and sound. And now I'm more angry than anything else.'

'You're still in shock, darling. You'll experience a gamut of emotions, I'm sure. Let's get you home to our place. Can you walk?'

'Mia? Mia?' It was Jet's voice and he came charging into the living room with an expression on his face of fear and concern. 'My God. Are you okay?' He crouched in front of her and took her hand in his.

She nodded. 'I'm fine. Oh. You've cut yourself. Your hand is covered in blood.'

He glanced at his hand and the thick red line running down it and wiped it against his jacket. 'Now it's not.'

A terrible thought ran through her head. She'd heard smashing glass. Jet had blood on his hand. Could it have been him who had broken in? Was that why there was no answer on his landline?

'Jet? How did you cut your hand?'

He held her horrified gaze for just a second or two, and sighed. 'Not by smashing my way into your cottage if that's what you're thinking.'

'How did you know the glass was smashed?'

'Seriously, Mia? You think I did this?'

Lori glared at him. 'It's a simple question, Jet. And I believe it deserves an answer.'

Hettie poked him on the arm. 'You haven't been up to your old tricks again have you, young man? I remember what a tearaway you were when you were a very young lad.'

His eyes narrowed and he looked directly at Mia. 'So much for believing me,' he said, getting to his feet. 'I don't know where or how I cut my hand. I was in such a rush to get to you when I heard Fred's message that I knocked a vase over. Maybe it was that. Or maybe it was a nail on the gate when I yanked it open. I have no idea. But I definitely didn't get it from your cottage, Mia. And I'll willingly let the police take my fingerprints to prove it.'

'You may've worn gloves,' Hettie said.

'Then I probably wouldn't have cut my hand on the glass'

'I told him what happened,' Franklin said, from the doorway, pointing his thumb over his shoulder to indicate he'd met Jet outside.

'I'm sorry, Jet,' Mia said, looking up into his eyes. 'I'm not thinking straight. Of course it wasn't you. I know it wasn't you. I'm sorry.'

'I'm afraid I'm not so convinced,' Lori said.

'Neither am I, deary.' Hettie poked him in the leg. 'Even though you're my favourite. If you had anything to do with this, you'll have me to answer to.'

'I didn't. I swear to that. But frankly, I don't really care what you think. Or you, for that matter, Lori. All I care about is that Mia believes me.'

'I do,' she said. 'I'm sorry I doubted you.'

He smiled, knelt down again and ignoring the huffs and puffs of Hettie and Lori, he took Mia's hand in his once more. 'There's nothing for you to apologise for. I'm sorry for behaving like a jerk. You're in shock, and by the smell of it, you've had a brandy or two. You're entitled to suspect me. I would probably suspect me if I were you. Except I know I didn't do it. Where are Ella and Gill?'

'Out on a date.'

'Then once we get the all clear from the police, I'm coming to stay with you. Or if we can't go back inside, you're coming to stay with me.'

'I'm sure you mean well, Jet,' Lori said, a little curtly. 'But I'm her mother. If anyone is staying with her it's me. Or she's coming back to ours.'

'Forgive me, Lori, but if someone is trying to harm her, you won't be able to stop them, and nor might Franklin at the moment, although I know you'd both try.'

'We surely would,' Franklin said. 'He's right though, honey.'

'Besides, your cottage only has one bedroom. My house has several. You're welcome to stay with Mia at my house. And of course I know you'll stay with her if she returns to the cottage. What I meant was, I'm coming too. I apologise for being rude. I'm sure you understand, because I know you're feeling it too. I'm half out of my mind with worry. But that's no excuse for being rude. I'm sorry. Now I'm going to speak to the officers. I'll be back in a moment.'

He raised Mia's hand to his lips and kissed it. It was such an old-fashioned gesture but it sent a burst of adrenaline rushing through her body and as she watched him walk away and turn and glance back at her and smile reassuringly, she knew how foolish she had been for even thinking for one moment that he could have been her would-be attacker.

Chapter Fourteen

Mia was still furious on Saturday evening as she, Ella and Gill walked into The Frog and Lily for Hettie and Fred's engagement party, and the place went quiet as everyone turned to look at her.

'Why doesn't anyone believe me?' She glanced at Ella and Gill and shook her head.

'We believe you,' Ella said. 'And so do Lori and Franklin, Hettie and Fred, and Jet, of course. That's all that matters. Oh God. Here comes Tom. I swear he's like a heat-seeking missile as far as you're concerned. Gill will get drinks. We'll go and sit at that vacant table. That way, you can avoid the inevitable questions at the bar.'

Mia sighed. 'But not Tom.'

Ella rolled her eyes. 'He'd find you on Mars. Oh, hi Tom.'

'How are you, Mia?' He gave Ella a brief smile.

'Fine thanks. Just wishing people didn't think I was an attention-seeking nutter with a drink problem.'

'No one thinks that.'

'Yes they do,' Ella said. 'Mia heard someone say it yesterday morning when she was in Justin's bakery.'

Tom glared at her before smiling at Mia. 'I'm sure Justin set them straight.'

Mia sighed. 'If telling the silly cow that "Mia doesn't drink that much, considering they all come from London," is setting her straight, then yes, he did a bang-up job. I only went in there because Ella's not entirely flavour of the month for Justin and having dumped him for Gill, Gill is persona non grata as far as almost everyone in the village is concerned.'

'Oh good heavens. Well, not to me. And you can understand Justin being upset, although I suppose as he's leaving next week anyway, he shouldn't be. But Love makes us all behave strangely at times.' He threw Ella another brief smile and squeezed Mia gently on her arm. 'Anyway, I'm sure everyone else believes that Thursday night happened exactly as you said it did.'

She raised her brows. 'Yes. That's why silence descended the minute I walked in. I'm not even sure Jet believes me. I haven't seen him since, so he's clearly not worried about my safety and I saw the look on his face when he came back inside after talking to the police. And they definitely thought I'd had too much to drink, fallen asleep and dreamt the whole thing, even though Hettie told them she had plied me with brandy for the shock.' She sighed again. 'Sorry. I didn't mean to rant. I'm angry, that's all.'

'The silent treatment could've been meant for me and Gill,' Ella said. 'As you just said, they're not happy. They seem to have forgotten that it was Justin who effectively broke up with me first by taking the film role. I think they're now all blaming me for him leaving.'

'Do you honestly think Jet doesn't believe you?' Tom asked, ignoring Ella.

'He says he does, but I suppose I can see why he and others wouldn't. Only Ella, me, Mum, and now Gill, has keys to the front and back doors. There was no sign of forced entry. No smashed glass in the door, or any of the windows. The only smashed glass was my wine glass and the empty wine bottle that I'd left on the worktop because I couldn't be bothered washing them before I went upstairs. But how they could've fallen to the floor and smashed is a mystery. The police seem to think I'd put them too near the edge, in my so-called 'state of inebriation' and they'd toppled over. But I wasn't drunk and I would've noticed if they'd fallen. And there was no way a cat could've got in and knocked them down, as the police also suggested as a possibility. The doors and windows were shut down stairs. And I know I locked that kitchen door before I went to bed, even though they said it was unlocked. But a cat turning the door knob, coming in, knocking a glass and a bottle to the floor and then closing the door behind itself, seems as ludicrous to me as the truth seems to be to them. And there was hardly a breeze, let alone the wind it would've taken to blow that kitchen door open and shut again. I think whoever came in, didn't see the glass and bottle and knocked them over. I didn't dream it, Tom. Someone was coming up the stairs. I heard them. I hope Jet believes me.'

'Well, I believe you, Mia. But why does it bother you so what Jet thinks?' He studied her face for a second or two and his entire body visibly stiffened. 'Or need I ask? I suppose I should've guessed Jet would win. He always does. Enjoy your evening, ladies.'

Mia and Ella glanced at one another as Tom marched off.

'That was weird,' Ella said, heading towards the vacant table. 'Tom's clearly in a strop because you prefer Jet to him.'

'He'll get over it. Can you see Jet?'

'Not yet. But he'll be here. He wouldn't miss Hettie's engagement party. Especially as he's agreed to be Fred's best man.'

'She loved the cage and jacket I gave her for Prince Gustav. And she also loved the idea of him going down the aisle. But she asked me if I'll carry the cage and walk in front of her.'

Ella frowned. 'When was this?'

Mia grinned and sat down. 'This evening. I popped round while you and Gill were in the shower. Together, if I'm not mistaken.' Mia raised her brows and gave Ella a pretend look of disapproval.

Ella blushed and laughed. 'Well tonight is officially our third date. Even though we spent last night in, with you, we still counted it as a date.' She winked. 'You didn't mention visiting Hettie.'

'Because both of you would've lectured me, so I thought I'd wait till now. Anyway, she says she doesn't want everyone staring at her as she walks down the aisle and it's just as much Hector and Prince Gustav's day as hers and Fred's, so Prince Gustav and I are going several paces ahead, followed by her and the invisible Hector then you and Mum. I didn't want to at first, because it was supposed to be my wedding day and walking down the aisle like that might be too close to the day I had planned, but I realised it's important to her and besides, I'm over Garrick, so it would've been churlish to say no.'

'I wasn't going to tell you this but he almost got in his van and drove down here when I told him about the break-in. He was going crazy. I managed to calm him down and get it through to him that turning up back here wouldn't be his wisest move. The last thing any of us wants is for you two to decide you've missed each other and fall back into one another's arms. Not that you would, of course, now that you've realised you're in love with Jet. Still not wise to tempt Fate though, in my opinion.'

Mia was astonished. 'Was he really worried? So he believes it then?'

'Of course he believes it. He knows you wouldn't make it up. And he saw the warnings, remember? He was furious the police aren't taking it seriously and said that on top of the toy frog, dead flowers and the card, they should be giving you the benefit of the doubt. He's glad Gill's here though. I didn't mention anything about Jet. I'm not as convinced Garrick's over you, as much as you're over him. That's not a dig at you. That's just a fact.'

Mia linked her arm through Ella's. 'I know. That's why I still can't speak to him yet. It'll stir things up for both of us and we need more time and space until either of us is ready for that.'

Ella smiled as she stretched her back and neck and scanned the pub. 'Where's Gill with those drinks? Oh. Finally. And he's talking to Jet. Look.'

He was. He and Jet were ambling towards the table, deep in conversation. A serious conversation judging by the expressions on their faces.

'Hi Jet,' Mia said, when they arrived.

He cast a quick glance over her. It was like being kissed by moonlight.

'Hi. How are you?'

She grinned at him. 'Still alive. No thanks to you.'

He frowned and stared her in the eye.

Ella gave a little cough, got to her feet and grabbed Gill with one hand and the drink he'd placed on the table for her, with the other. 'Time to mingle,' she said, dragging Gill away, his pint of beer slopping over the rim of his glass as she did so.

'Was that sarcasm?' Jet asked, the furrow in his brows growing deeper by the second.

'Merely an observation. For someone who was so worried about me on Thursday – before you thought I'd imagined the whole thing of course – you've hardly been concerned for my welfare since, have you?'

'I've been concerned, believe me. But you were so cross about what the police said and then flatly refused to come home with me, or to let me stay, accusing me of not believing you either, that frankly, I didn't think I'd be that welcome. Besides, Lori, Gill and Ella have all been at your side virtually every minute, not to mention Hettie and Fred. I think you've been in safe hands, and so do you, so why are you still spoiling for a fight with me? If I'd thought you were in danger, you would've needed a crow bar to prise me from your side.'

'So you do think I imagined it?'

'No. But there was no sign of a break-in, so it does seem odd. I don't think whoever it was, will try anything again so soon after. The police may be sceptical at the moment, but added to the things left on your doorstep and the business with my car, if something else happened now, the police would intensify their investigations. What I'm trying to figure out is why I was targeted. I don't benefit from Mattie's will and if that's what the threats on you are about – and I can't see what else they could be – then was someone sending me a warning to stay clear?' He smirked. 'As if that would work.'

'Well, it sort of has. You've haven't been near since Thursday.'

'I told you, I didn't think I'd be welcome. I thought you needed time. But just because you haven't seen me, it doesn't mean I haven't been near.' He grinned. 'You see. I've even got on board with the whole Mattie being a spy, thing. I've been keeping an eye on you, I can assure you. And now you'll probably shout at me for that.'

Mia grinned up at him. 'Are you going to sit down? I'm getting a crick in my neck looking up at you.'

He sat, but he kept his distance and neither of them spoke for several seconds. Mia sipped the wine Gill had bought her and Jet sipped his pint. When they finally did speak, they both did so at the same time.

Jet grinned. 'You first.'

'No, no. You go ahead.'

'I was just going to say how great it is to see Hettie so happy. I know she's a gossip and doesn't understand the concept of privacy but her heart's in the right place and Fred seems like a really good guy.'

'Yes. And both Hector and Prince Gustav have given their blessings, so Hettie's over the moon. Although what she would've done if either of them had been against the match is beyond me.'

A huge grin spread across Jet's face. 'You don't believe they actually do talk to her, do you?'

She grinned back. 'I believe she believes it, and that's good enough for me. She also believes in Destiny. All this was meant to be. Mattie leaving me the cottage, Mum coming to stay and starting the book club, which is where Hettie met Fred.'

'Do you believe in Destiny?'

She tipped her head to one side. 'Yes. I also now believe in fortune-tellers. Because so far that fortune-teller at the Fête has been virtually spot on.'

'Oh? I know she was right about Tiff and the engagement. What else has she been right about?'

Mia shrugged. 'Everything. About Ella meeting Gill. About Mum and Franklin. About Justin. And definitely about Garrick and the baby.' She took a quick breath. 'Oh, and several bits about me. But not all of it has come true yet.'

'Yet? So what has and what hasn't?'

'Um. The bits that have are, me overcoming a fear. She saw water. And I've overcome my fear of that. Someone leaving and something not meant to be. That's Garrick, obviously. Autumn bringing

314

many changes. It has. Mum and Franklin, Garrick leaving. Gill arriving. Ella and Gill. Hettie getting engaged, etc. Um. About love not being where I was looking for it. That's Garrick again. I thought at first it might be … someone else, but I'm pretty sure it's him. She said I had to choose Love wisely and that I'd have happiness and joy behind my wildest dreams. Oh and a love that's black and white. That's not Garrick, that's Tom, of course. And I also think Tom's the one …' she leant forward and was about to continue in a whisper but she didn't get a chance.

'Tom? You're in love with Tom? Since when?' He glared at her and got to his feet. 'Was what you said at the beach a lie? Just a game to get back at me for rejecting you?'

'What? No. I'm not in love with Tom. I'll admit I thought I could be after that night of the fireworks when he came back to the cottage with me.'

'Tom? You spent that night with Tom. You never mentioned that. You asked me and I said no so you slept with him instead? So all that stuff on the beach definitely was a lie. Jesus, Mia. First Bear, then Garrick then me and now Tom. Exactly how many men have you got to fall in love with you in five months? And you have the nerve to criticise me.' He thumped his glass on the table and stormed off.

What the hell had just happened?

Mia watched Jet shove his way through the crowded bar, going over in her head how he could've possibly thought she'd said she was in love with Tom. And then it hit her. He'd only heard her say Tom was the one. He hadn't let her finish and say the one she thought she couldn't trust. And when she'd mentioned him coming back to the cottage, Jet had put two and two together and made sex. He'd thought she was so lonely and sad that she'd have sex with anyone that night. He'd said that on the beach. How dare he?

She banged her glass down on the table, got up and went after him, edging her way in the same direction he had gone and out of the door into the lane.

'Jet!' He didn't stop. The lane outside was silent save for the sounds coming from the pub. 'Jet. Stop. Jet! You're behaving like a child. Stop and listen to me.' To her surprise, he did.

She hurried to him and looked up into his face.

'What's on earth's got into you? I'm not in love with Tom and never have been. And I didn't sleep with him that night. Or any other night before you ask. Not that it should matter if I did. You've slept with half the county, so I heard.'

'But I've never told anyone I loved them. Ever. I never led any of them on and made them believe there was even the slightest bit of hope that we might be able to have some sort of future together.'

'And you think I have?'

'Let me see. Bear was crazy about you after your first date. You were engaged to Garrick and had a wedding date set. I don't know what's gone on with you and Tom, but clearly something has if you thought he might be The One, and as for me. Well, we both know what you've been trying to do with me, don't we?'

'Do we? Because I think you and I have very different ideas of what I've been trying to do with you. And if you'd let me finish my sentence in the pub before acting like a crazy person, you would've realised that nothing has been going on with Tom and me. And I have never seriously considered a future with Tom. And, not that it matters, but I didn't have sex with Bear either. In the last five months, the only man I've had sex with or said to their face that I was in love with, is Garrick. And if you're the sort of man who has double standards, then I've been wrong about you. If you think it's okay for a man to sleep with lots of women in his lifetime, but not for a woman to sleep with more than one man in hers, then you're a pillock from the dark ages. And not merely a pillock, but a prize pillock with gold knobs on.'

He raised his brows and the tiniest twitch tugged at his mouth. 'I'm not a pillock, of any sort. I don't care how many men you've slept with, but I do care if you sleep with men, string them along with looks and words and promises and then move on to the next one. That's fine if you tell them at the start, that's your intention. It's not fine if you lead them to believe you're the kind of girl who is. looking for the love of her life. The kind of girl who wants a long-term relationship. The kind of girl a man can trust. If all you want is sex, then be honest and say so.'

She burst out laughing.

'You find that funny?' He glared at her.

'No. Well, yes.' She reached for his hand as he turned away. 'Don't you dare walk away from me again, Jet Cross. Not until I say this anyway.'

He glanced at her hand on his and turned back to face her.

She took a deep breath. 'First let me say what I was going to about Tom. And don't interrupt. I was going to say that I think Tom might be the one the fortune-teller said I think I can trust, but can't. She also said someone's feelings may not be genuine. I'm not sure who that is but it may be Tom. Or it may be you.'

'Me?'

'Yes, you. One minute you look at me as if I'm some sort of goddess, the next you're walking away and I don't see or hear from you for days. I have no idea quite where I stand with you. But we'll get to that. The reason I burst out laughing was because you said that if all I wanted was sex, I should be honest and say so. I asked you for sex. You said no and walked away. You've got to see why that was funny.'

He frowned. 'Not really. I walked away because I thought it would've been a mistake not to. Because I thought you wouldn't be able to handle a one-night stand. And that was all I could offer. Okay, maybe not just one night, but nothing long-term.'

'So you keep saying. But I think you're wrong. I think you hated the way your dad treated you and your mum and you've let it affect your judgment. Your opinion of yourself.'

'Mia. Stop right there.'

'No, Jet. This needs to be said and I'm going to say it. Everyone tells you you're like your dad. And you believe it. Women are attracted to you but you've only seen one way to treat them, so that's the way you do. You know it's not right, but you do it anyway. You're a man. You can't take after your mum and be loving and kind and gentle and giving because look what happened to her? Your dad betrayed her. Used her. Tossed her aside. So you decided you'll be like him. You'll be the one who walks away, not the one who gets walked on.'

'Mia! I don't want to hear this.'

'Well, you're going to. So shut up and listen.'

He blinked, open-mouthed, as she continued.

'Deep down, I don't think you're like your dad at all. I think deep down you're like your mum. And that when you fall in love, you'll fall deeply and forever. And I think it'll be your mum you take after, not your dad. You'll do everything in your power to love and nurture and respect your wife, and your children, if you have them. And I think you'll be passionate and caring, kind and giving. And whoever that woman is, she'll be the luckiest woman in the world. And I may be wrong, Jet. But I think that woman could be me.'

There was sadness in his eyes, but there was something else. Something she'd seen there twice before. 'Not even you can change me, Mia.'

'No, I can't. The only person who can change you, is you. No one could change me. I changed myself. I was terrified of water because it nearly drowned me. Now I love being in the sea. I had convinced myself I couldn't go in because if I did, I'd drown. But when I saw that little girl, I forgot my fear and in I ran. And look at me now. I go swimming every day – unless it's really rough. I'm not a complete idiot. It may be harder for you, but I believe you like the idea of a relationship. And I believe you want a relationship with me. You're just terrified to try it. You say you only want to have fun. But have you had any fun since I've been here? And don't brush this off with some sarcastic remark about me not doing myself any favours with that comment. I meant, you haven't been with a woman since I arrived. Not one. And yet I've seen women look at you. I've seen you look away. Anna, for example. And I've seen the way you look at me sometimes. The way you looked at me the other day on the beach.'

'I want you. I admit that. I've never denied it. And sometimes I look at you and I can't breathe.

Sometimes I want you so much it hurts. But I know myself, Mia. Maybe once I get you into bed, the thrill of the chase will be over and I won't want you anymore.'

'Perhaps. But I'm willing to take that chance.'

'Why? Do you honestly think you're the one woman on this planet who can make me feel what no other woman I've met before has ever been able to? The one woman who can make me fall in love? Deeply and irrevocably in love. So in love that I'll be faithful for the rest of my life? In spite of my genes.'

She shrugged. 'I think perhaps I am. But what is more important is that I think that's what you think. And that's why you're so terrified to go to bed with me. Because the idea of being that much in love scares the living daylights out of you. And I think that's why you blow hot and cold. You make yourself stay away from me. You tell yourself you don't care. You convince yourself I don't mean that much to you. But I think I do, Jet. I really think I do.'

His breathing had increased, his expression flashed from glad to sad to bad and back again. She had never seen him look so unsure, so torn, so cross.

He took a deep breath and pulled his hand from hers. 'And I've told you before, Mia. You think too much.'

And once again, he turned and walked away and once again, she watched him go.

Someone needed to hit the man over the head with a very heavy object because clearly there was no other way to get through his thick skull.

Chapter Fifteen

Mia was feeling miserable. Having the hangover from hell wasn't helping and neither was the weather. So much for the forecasters predicting the Indian Summer would go on until mid- October. The heavens opened shortly after dawn on Sunday morning and it bucketed with rain all day.

Of course, the reason for her sombre mood was Jet. Had she been completely wrong about him? She had been so certain he was falling in love with her but that he simply wouldn't admit it. Not to himself, and certainly not to her. But the look he had given her when he walked away last night, made her wonder if, in fact, he was more like his dad than she realised. Not that she knew what his dad was like, having never met him. And perhaps that was the problem. She didn't really know Jet either. She just thought she did. She had convinced herself she did.

And her dreams on Saturday night hadn't helped. She'd dreamt she was in the steeple of St

Michael and All Angels and the stairs were going on forever. She couldn't reach the top. She couldn't get out. A bell was tolling – just like the fortune-teller had said it would – and it was a mellifluous sound at first, turning to a doom-like warning bell the more she ran. And suddenly, she was falling and falling and calling for Jet. But he was nowhere to be seen. And when she woke up, she couldn't shake the feeling that something bad was going to happen.

'You look like death,' Ella said at breakfast.

'I feel even worse,' Mia replied. 'I'm not setting foot outside today. I'm going to the attic and I'm not coming out till bedtime.'

'What happened with Jet? You wouldn't talk about it last night. Ready to today?'

'Nope. I don't want to talk about Jet today, or for the foreseeable future, in fact. I thought Mattie had secrets and liked to keep things hidden but Jet beats her hands down. That man has hidden his true feelings so deep inside he may never find them again.'

'He walked away again, didn't he?'

'Yep. It seems to be his thing.'

She made herself coffee, grabbed a banana from the bowl and a bottle of water from the fridge, and padded upstairs to the attic, only returning to the kitchen at seven that evening when Gill said he had made dinner and insisted she come down and eat.

'It gets a bit much when I can't do what I want in my own cottage,' she moaned, but she grinned at him as he poured her a glass of wine and put a huge bowl of Thai Green, chicken curry in front of her. It was her favourite dish, as Ella had probably told him.

'Good day in the attic, dear?' Ella joked.

'Yes, actually. I now know why Mattie was chucked out, and how she got involved with SIS.'

Ella gasped. 'And when were you going to tell us?'

Mia grinned. 'I'll tell you now. I didn't want to tell you anything until I'd found out something important and although I've been reading the diaries for a few days now and finding out horrid stuff, there was nothing really exciting until today. Anyway, as you know, they start when she was twelve and it's clear she had a rebellious streak. There are lots of mentions of her getting into trouble and her mum – who sounds a bit of a witch, and not in a good way – actually had her beaten. Can you believe that? She was beaten with a cane. She says she cried the first time but that seemed to please her mother so she never cried again.'

'What a cow. But that generation believed in punishment, not nurture. I remember my mum saying that even in her day her teachers often gave her a rap across the knuckles with a cane.'

'They believed it was character-building,' Gill said, pulling a face that made it clear he found it as distasteful as they did and then he smiled. 'But in Mattie's case it probably was. She learnt at a young age how to take pain and not show it.'

'Hmm. I'm not sure that's good. She then says "Mother found my new diary. She threw it on the fire. I lied and told her it was my first. I got six lashes. She will not find the others. No one will ever find the others." So that's when she started hiding things. She was fourteen at the time and it was January, so she'd started a new year.'

'Learning life skills along the way,' Ella said, sarcastically. 'Did her dad know what her mum was like?'

'I'll get to that. You wait until you hear that bit. I couldn't believe it.'

'Well, get on with it,' Ella said.

'Shouldn't we eat first?' Gill suggested.

'Okay. But hurry up. And Mia can still talk. Just not with her mouth full or I'll rap her across the knuckles.'

'Try it and see how long you live,' Mia joked. She took a mouthful of curry, ate it quickly, swallowed and continued: 'So. She's always getting caught for doing stuff she shouldn't. She gives a maid a dress that no longer fits and her mum finds out, burns the dress, sacks the maid, and, yep, more lashes for Mattie. She climbs a tree with her brother. He gets off scot-free, she gets lashes. She's seen walking in the stable yard, chatting to a groom and yep, more lashes, more sackings. They were wealthy, remember. They had stables, horses, a massive house. Anyway. There are pages of stuff like that. Up until then, she's had a governess but now she gets packed off to boarding school. She says she realises the importance of not being seen doing things someone may disapprove of, so she's more careful after that. She's happier at school but comes home for the holidays. She's still doing stuff but she's no longer getting caught and it seems she's doing more and more outrageous things almost to see what she can get away with. But she's also watching people to see who she can trust and who she can't. Then, when she's seventeen, her mum says they've arranged a marriage for her. Rich people still did in those days, but she's not having it and flatly refuses. She's locked in a room in the attic for three weeks with only one meal a day.'

'Bloody Nora. But what about the dad?'

'Patience. He's hardly ever at home. Except at Christmas and other holidays. The next big thing is one month after she's released from the attic. Her mum's still trying to force her into this marriage but it's now her brother's twenty-first birthday and there's a shindig at the house. Lots of people coming to stay for the weekend. You know, like those house parties we've seen on TV shows set in the 1930s. So, her dad's home and he's got lots of important friends staying. She's following them about, hiding in corridors, listening to conversations, basically having fun. Then when the party's in full swing, she goes up to that room in the attic, which is where she hides her diaries in a box, hidden beneath a type of window seat that's never used. Yep. That's obviously where the idea for the window seat upstairs came from. There's other stuff up there, including a bed, because this is the room she was locked in for three weeks, don't forget. But anyway. What does she see?' Mia took a mouthful of food. 'Oh, Gill, this curry is so delicious. Thank you.'

'What?' Ella shrieked, slapping her on the arm.

Mia pulled a face and chewed her bottom lip. 'She sees her dad, having "intimate relations" she calls it … with one of her brother's best friends! A male, friend. And what's more, he's the very same man that her parents are trying to get her to marry!'

'Bloody Nora!'

'I know!'

'Being gay was illegal in the 1930s,' Gill said, as nonchalantly as if they were discussing the weather. 'It could mean a life sentence.'

Mia nodded. 'Yes. But her dad's having an affair with her brother's best friend and the man they wanted her to marry! That's even more shocking, isn't it?'

Gill shrugged. 'To her, I suppose it would've been.'

Mia tutted. 'To any woman. Anyway. She goes berserk. Completely berserk. Rushes downstairs and tells her brother, who tells the mum, who goes equally berserk – but not with the dad – with Mattie. For making such a fuss and causing possible embarrassment to the family! Her dad, obviously worried and trying to keep the whole thing quiet, agrees she doesn't have to marry and also agrees she can go off to finishing school in Switzerland, which is what she wants. She says she learnt the importance of knowing other people's secrets and using that knowledge to good purpose. Which is sort of blackmail to you and me.'

'You can't blame her though, can you? What a horrid family!' Ella said.

'Yeah. The sad part is, less than two years later, her dad shoots himself. He can't live with the fear of people finding out and her mum, of course, blames Mattie, and so does her brother, even though Mattie says she swore to her dad that she would never speak of it again. So that's when her mum tells her she's no longer welcome at the house and basically that if they never hear from her again, it will be too soon.'

'Does she have any money or means to support herself?' Gill asked.

'Nope. But at that weekend party, Mattie had met a friend of her dad's who works for SIS although she didn't know that, simply that he was something to do with the government and intelligence. They got on well that weekend – before the business with her dad – so when, almost two years later, she's kicked out, she goes to him to see if he can help her find a job. Anything really because she's broke. When she tells him she can speak fluent French, German and Italian, has no interest in marriage or having children, he sees her potential. I think her mum and dad's relationship, plus her almost-fiancé, have put her off marriage for life. Anyway, she's nineteen, and by the age of twenty, she's in Paris working as a spy. And then when war breaks out, she stays and after Paris is occupied by the Germans in 1940, she catches the eye of a certain German officer, and we know where that's going, don't we? That's all I've read so far. I can't wait to find out more.'

Ella sighed. 'It's hard to believe that by twenty, she'd had more excitement and adventure, pain and suffering than I've had in thirty-four years.'

'Different times,' Gill said.

'Rich people were different in those days too,' said Mia. 'I think. But she does actually say that she has her family, and particularly her mother, to thank for teaching her so many lessons in life that would prove useful in her future. But I don't think she meant it as a compliment. It makes me even more sad that I never met her.'

Chapter Sixteen

It rained all the following week, although it remained warm for the time of year, but the winds picked up and the sea was choppy. Mia had regained her confidence but swimming in rough waters wasn't something she was keen to try. Instead, she stayed indoors and read more of Mattie's diaries.

'You're becoming a hermit,' Ella said, but as she stayed in most days as well, either reading the diaries Mia had already read, or helping Gill with his research for his book, she could hardly talk.

Hettie still came to clean on Monday and Thursday, despite no longer needing the money now that Fred had moved in permanently and, having sold his own house within a matter of days, followed by a speedy exchange and completion date, they would soon have ample funds to live on.

'I enjoy the company of you youngsters, deary,' Hettie said, when Mia told her they would be happy to do the cleaning themselves. 'Besides, you wouldn't get the duster out for a month and goodness knows what the place will look like come Christmas. No. We'll carry on as we are, deary.'

Lori popped in regularly for coffee and she and Franklin came for dinner one evening in the week. Mia told them all about Mattie's upbringing and as she was now reading the war years, she regaled them with tales of secret codes and secret missions but the diaries were scarce on detail.

'It's because writing a diary in an enemy occupied country, was not a wise way to spend one's time,' Gill said. 'Most of it was probably written after the war, from memory.'

He knew more details, having had the benefit of hearing the stories from his grandfather, but even so, there was a lot that was probably left out.

'Mattie was now working for the SOE,' Mia said. 'Her duties were sabotage and subversion. Winston Churchill's orders were to "set Europe ablaze" and that's what Mattie and Will, Gill's grandfather tried to do, by blowing up bridges, buildings, factories and even trains.'

Lori shook her head. 'It's so difficult to comprehend what life was like for her. From what you've both told us, she would go for days without food, have to move at a moment's notice, be constantly on her guard, risk her life on a daily, if not hourly basis and all that from the age of just twenty until the war ended when she was twenty-six. It's astonishing. Truly astonishing.'

'And don't forget,' Gill said, 'she was captured and interrogated. We won't tell you what she endured because it's pretty grim reading, but at least she was rescued from an even worse Fate by Grandfather and some of the group.'

'And your grandad told you that his lover, Margot Voss died in 1945?' Lori queried. 'Do Mattie's diaries say what really happened?'

Mia nodded. 'But not in great detail. She says he proposed and she was torn. She loved him but hated the idea of marriage and unlike him, she didn't want kids.'

'A bit like Fiona,' Ella joked. 'Sorry.'

'Don't worry,' Mia said. 'But yes, she was adamant about that. Will wanted a family but he said he'd give that up for Mattie. She wouldn't let him do that, so she lied and said she didn't think their love would last. That without the excitement and thrill of completing their missions, and the fear of death each day, their passion would peter out. He assured her his wouldn't. She said she knew hers would. Another lie because she said in the note she left that she loved him still and always had. But he was only twenty-four at the time, because he was two years her junior, and she thought he'd get over her. That they'd get over each other. I think she realised many years later that she should've taken the risk and married him. She says that Will loved her so much that the only way he could move on with his life was to act as if the woman he adored, was dead. And in a way, she was. Margot Voss no longer existed.'

'I can't wait to hear more,' Lori said.

Mia grinned. 'I can't wait to read more. I'm hoping the rain keeps up next week as well so that I've got an excuse to stay indoors and read.'

It did. And the wind increased even more and the temperature dropped, so much so that Gill lit the fire in the living room each evening. It wasn't really cold enough to have the heating on all day but the evenings did get chilly and the fire warmed them until they went to bed. They had got into a habit now of having dinner at seven-thirty, then curling up on the sofa or the chairs, with a glass or two of wine while Mia read from the 'latest' diary. By the end of that week, they had got to 1992, the year before Mattie moved to Little Pondale and on Monday, Mia started reading 1993.

'What did Mattie do in the intervening years?' Lori asked, on Monday morning when she popped round for coffee.

Hettie was there too, Monday being one of her mornings to clean and they were sitting in the kitchen as they always did when Hettie had finished for the day.

'When she returned to England, she worked for MI6. Oddly enough, her diary-keeping dwindled even more. There're loads more blank pages between 1945 and 1955. She had a couple of lovers, but no one special, that's obvious from the way she writes about them. She and Will are in contact, but he's married now, believing of course that Mattie didn't really love him. Gill says that his grandad made it clear to him that even though Margot Voss was dead, he still adored her and had never got over her. Gill, of course, had no idea that Mattie was Margot, and she was alive and well in England. He now thinks that if Mattie had said the word, Will would've left his wife and kids for her. That's kind of sad, isn't it?'

'Men shouldn't leave their wives and children for another woman, deary, no matter who she is,' Hettie said. 'Look what it did to Sarah Cross, and to Jet. Mind you, that's not a good example because they were better off without that man, deary. They just didn't know it at the time. And Sarah, poor dear, never stopped loving him. Not even on the day she died.'

'I think that's why Jet's so anti-relationships. He saw how it destroyed his mum. But I'm not going to start thinking about Jet. Needless to say, I haven't seen or heard from the man since your engagement party.'

Hettie puffed out her cheeks and clasped her hands beneath her chest. 'Haven't you, deary? Why he's been popping in and out all the time. He always asks after you. But he does ask me not to mention it, now that I think about it. Oh dear. I just have. Forget you heard that, deary. Tell us more about dear Matilda.'

Mia had to force herself not to ask Hettie to elaborate. Jet had been asking about her? That was a good sign, wasn't it? She and Ella hadn't been to choir practice for the last few weeks, in fact Mia hadn't been since before Garrick left, and they hadn't been to The Frog and Lily since Hettie's party either. Reading Mattie's diaries was beginning to take over all their lives.

'Okay. Where was I? Oh. 1955. She goes to the launch of The Fountain restaurant at Fortnum & Mason in Piccadilly and amazingly, bumps into someone she helped rescue in the war but she doesn't give any details of how, merely that she hadn't seen her since the day they helped her get out of France. The woman's name is Esther, and she's in London on vacation. And this is the best bit. It seems Esther has also gone into the intelligence business, but as an independent and in the States. They get talking and the following year, Mattie leaves MI6 and she and Esther start a business together. They call it Durieux Ward Associates, because Esther's surname is Durieux and Mattie's is Ward. Mattie runs the London office and Esther runs the one in Washington. All she says about it is that they're in the business of intelligence. I can only assume it means they're spies for hire and it's anyone's guess exactly what that entails. She also mentions Dad a few times over the years, Mum, and I'll give you the diaries where she does, because it's clear she loved him, even if she never knew him. She also mentions her brother – my grandad, and the fact that, despite being ostracised, when her mum dies, she's left

336

some of the family jewellery. It seems the family solicitor still knows how to get in contact with her even though the family wants nothing to do with her, not even her own brother. Which is very sad, I think. I didn't realise Grandad was like that. She also mentions me a few times too in the later diaries, but I'm really young, of course. Anyway, the business clearly had a lot of clients, or whatever over the years, because at the end of 1992, when Esther dies, Mattie, along with Esther's children, sell the business for a fortune. Annoyingly, she doesn't give details of who to, but I suppose if you're dealing in secrets, you keep stuff about your business secret too.'

'And I had no idea about any of this, deary,' Hettie said, shaking her head. 'Matilda never said one word about it. Any of it.'

'Good heavens, darling,' Lori said. 'What a pity we can't find out what she did for all those years.'

Mia smiled. 'That's exactly what I said when I was reading it to Ella and Gill. Naturally, Ella was over the moon because she always knew Mattie's money came from nefarious activities and she said you can't get much more nefarious than being a spy for hire. But Gill said it would make a good plot for a novel and Ella said it would be a very sexy novel if two women are the heads of an international spy organisation, and the next thing we know, we're agreeing we should write one. So guess what? Me, Gill and Ella are going to use the pseudonym, M.E.G. Ward, get it? Mia, Ella and Gill and Ward for Mattie. It may come to nothing, but it'll be a lot of fun.'

'Oh deary!' Hettie said. 'That's so exciting. And it'll give you something to do when you're in this cottage on the long cold winter nights, especially as you haven't got a man to cuddle up to.'

Lori grimaced and shook her head. 'Thank you for pointing that out, Hettie. I think it's wonderful, darling. I really do.'

Mia grinned. 'Yes, Hettie. Thanks for reminding me. And guess what we're going to call the male hero? The one the female spies keep saving.'

'What, darling?' Lori looked anxious.

Mia grinned. 'Jet. Jet De Fonteneau.'

'Good gracious, deary!' Hettie said. 'Are you sure that's wise?'

Chapter Seventeen

Mia didn't have quite as much time for reading that week, but she still managed to cover several years. Again, there were lots of blank pages. A diary wasn't top of Mattie's to do list, obviously. Mia had reached 2005 and Little Pondale was as lively then as it was now. Basically, nothing much was happening. But Mattie did write about Hettie and all the others in the village. And she wrote quite a bit about two people in particular. One was Grace Tyburn, Tom's gran; the other was a cheeky child, growing up over the years, called Jet Cross and it was clear that both of them had found a place in Mattie's heart, but for very different reasons.

On Tuesday, Mia, Ella and Lori went with Hettie to have their final fittings. Hettie's long, silk chiffon gown was pale lavender with a silk, one-button coat of lavender with purple flowers embroidered here and there. The bridesmaid dresses were full-length, purple silk chiffon with lavender lace, bolero jackets. Prince Gustav would be wearing his purple jacket and Jet and Fred would wear grey morning suits and matching top hats with a pale lavender band, and purple waistcoats.

'You look stunning, Hettie,' Mia said. And she meant it.

The gown was empire style, as were the bridesmaid dresses, and the one button on the coat was set just below Hettie's ample chest. The sweep of the outfit gave her a streamlined figure.

'Fred said I could have whatever I want, deary, and this is it.' There were tears of pure joy in her eyes but she sniffed and wiped them away with the back of her hands. 'What a silly old fool I am, getting all emotional.'

'You should be emotional,' Ella said. 'It's your wedding day on Saturday and Fred's a

lucky man. You look beautiful.'

'Get away with you, deary. I look like an old woman.'

Lori hugged her. 'You look like a woman in love, Hettie, and the girls are right. You look incredible.'

On Wednesday, Gill and Ella went shopping and Gill informed Mia that she had to go with them.

'I promised Jet, at Hettie's engagement party, on pain of … I'm not sure what exactly, but something very unpleasant if the look on his face at the time was anything to go by, that I would never leave you alone in the cottage.'

'But it's the middle of the day and I'll be fine.'

'Yes you will, because you're coming with us,' Ella said. 'Don't argue. I promised Jet too.'

'Well, I didn't. Oh okay. Don't look at me like that. I'm coming. But I'm bringing one of the diaries with me and I'll read it every chance I get.'

Hettie came to clean on Thursday and stayed all morning showing Mia and Ella the cruise she and Fred were going on for their honeymoon.

'I need to ask you a favour, deary. Will you look after Prince Gustav while we're gone?'

'Of course, we will. Gill will bring his cage round here just like Garrick did when you stayed with us.' That memory sent a pang of sadness through Mia's heart, especially as it was getting close to what would have been her and Garrick's wedding day.

On Friday, she, Ella, Lori and Hettie went into town for manicures, pedicures and to have their hair done and Friday night, when Fred was having a stag night in the pub, the 'girls' had Hettie's hen night in Little Whitingdale, watching The New Frog Hill Hounds, but they weren't the same without Justin.

'I still can't believe he left without saying goodbye,' Ella said.

'He didn't say a proper goodbye to anyone, deary. Didn't want a fuss, he told me. Fuss indeed.

After all the years he's lived in Little Pondale. But he wasn't having it. Jet was the only one he spent any real time with before he jumped on that plane. But I can't believe we still haven't got fresh bread, deary. That cousin of his should be over here by now. Once you close a bakery, people will start looking elsewhere.'

'Gill's been baking bread for us,' Ella said. 'It's not as good as Justin's but it's better than that plastic stuff, or a long journey to town to get some. Sorry, Hettie. I'll get him to bake you a loaf or two.'

'Well it's a bit late now, deary. I'm getting married tomorrow and then we're off on our cruise. By the time we get back, the bakery should be up and running, or so the note said on the door.'

On Saturday, Mia just about had time to read the start of the diary for the year 2010 and what she read almost made her late to Hettie's wedding. She was sitting on the window seat in the attic when Ella came thumping up the stairs.

'I've been looking everywhere for you. We've got precisely an hour before the wedding and we've got to get to Hettie's to help her. You're not even showered!'

'Oh my God. I lost track of time. Why didn't you call me sooner?'

'I thought you were getting ready. I called you two hours ago and told you you were cutting it fine. You said you'd come right down.'

'I got to the bit where Mattie decides to start watching me. She doesn't mention her will, she just says she got an interesting idea and needs to get to know me to see if it will work. And I've only just found out what that idea was. You'll never believe it, Ella. Not in a million years.'

'I'll believe it, but you'll have to tell me later. We've got a wedding to get to.'

She grabbed Mia's arm and virtually dragged her down the stairs and threw her in the shower. She laid out her clothes, did her hair while Mia did her own make-up and Mia was still putting on her jacket as she was being dragged along the hall.

They made it in time to help Hettie and by the time they arrived at the church, even the clouds that had been threatening rain all morning, lifted to reveal the sun.

'That's Hector,' a tearful Hettie said. 'He's arranged for the sun to shine for me and Fred.'

'I think you'll find ... Oh never mind,' said Ella. 'Let's get you married. Where's Prince Gustav?'

'I've got him,' Mia said, holding up the Cinderella carriage-like cage. It had a pale lavender cushion for him to sit on and he looked every bit the prince in his purple jacket.

'Off you go then,' said Ella.

Mia grinned. 'When did you get so bossy?'

'When you buried your head in those damn diaries on Hettie's big day. Now go.'

The Wedding March rang out from the organ pipes and Mia began her slow walk down the aisle. Fred looked handsome and she smiled, trying to forget that this could have been her walking down the aisle as the bride.

And then she saw Jet and she almost stumbled.

She had never seen him in anything other than work clothes or casual clothes – and both consisted of jeans. In his grey morning suit, white shirt and purple waistcoat, he looked like a piece of heaven had beamed down before her eyes. The man was gorgeous casual. Like this, he was divine. His midnight black hair gleamed in the beams of sunlight filtered by the stained-glass windows. His tanned face was clean shaven as usual, but his skin seemed to glow today. And as he watched her – and he definitely was watching her – walk down the aisle towards him, she had to remind herself again that this was not *her* wedding. And she was *definitely not* walking down the aisle to Jet. As his bride to be. But the image was making it difficult for her to breathe.

A smile spread across his face and reached his eyes. And for a second, she thought he was seeing her as she was seeing him and then his smile faded and was replaced by a frown and he turned away, although it looked as if it took great effort because she could see his eyes and head keep twisting back in her direction.

She reached her spot and stepped aside to let Hettie, and Hector's ghost, pass and Jet suddenly looked at her and mouthed the words. 'You look beautiful.'

Or was he saying that to Hettie?

No, he was definitely not looking at Hettie.

'So do you,' she mouthed back, and she saw the twitch take hold again and bloom into a full-blown, sexy, loving smile.

Chapter Eighteen

The ceremony went off without a hitch. The bride shed one or two tears of joy, Fred shed one or two more and Prince Gustav peed on his lavender cushion, but you can't have everything go right when animals are involved.

'That's a good omen!' Hettie declared.

'Of course it is,' said Ella.

Gill offered to take Prince Gustav home to Sunbeam Cottage. 'You can come and say goodbye before you leave for your honeymoon.'

That seemed to please Hettie, so after the photographs were taken, in the sunny garden at the rear of the church, in which Prince Gustav was front and centre with the bride and groom, Gill took Prince Gustav to Sunbeam Cottage and Ella also disappeared. It didn't take much imagination to know what they would be doing for the next half an hour or so. There was a buffet and an open bar at The Frog and Lily, and guests began to make their way from the garden, around to the front of the church and across the lane to the pub.

Jet was standing near the back door, leading to the steeple, deep in conversation with Toby Bywater.

'Are you coming to the pub now, darling,' Lori asked.

'In a minute, Mum. You and Franklin go ahead.'

Lori smiled and left. Mia walked towards Jet; she had something in particular to tell him. The sun was still shining, the sky was the softest blue and a warm breeze lifted the tips of Jet's hair as she looked at him.

The bells were still ringing and Mia wished they would continue for hours; they made such a beautiful sound. Especially one bell. What was that one called. She looked towards the belfry and tried to remember. It was named after the man who paid for it to be made. What was his name? Edward something. Ah yes. Edward Angel, that was it. It was called the Angel Bell. And that's what it sounded like to her.

She saw Jet glance in her direction. She saw the smile reach his eyes. Toby looked at Jet and then at her, and an odd expression crossed his face. He tapped Jet on the arm, nodded towards Mia and walked away.

'The Angel Bell,' she whispered, although she wasn't sure why. 'The Angel Bell. Oh God.' Her eyes shot to the steeple and as she screamed Jet's name, she ran. Faster than she had ever run before. He was only a few feet away and she covered the distance in no time at all, thumping into him, and as solid as he was, she managed to knock him off balance. He stumbled backwards against the church exterior wall, with her landing in his arms, her face thudding against his chest.

The noise was almost like the sound Mattie had described in her diary of the V-1 flying bombs, or doodlebugs as they were commonly known. A buzzing and then silence just before the bomb hit. Mia heard the buzz like whizz of displaced air, or so she thought and then the silence before the carved stone angel shattered on the ground, inches from her and Jet, sending up shards of masonry like shrapnel, one of which she noticed, was a piece of the angel's wing. And it landed on her shoulder before tumbling to the ground.

'Are you all right, Mia?' Jet barked, holding her tight against him.

She burst out laughing, and he eased her away from him to look into her eyes.

'I'm fine,' she said. 'I heard the warning bell, just like the fortune-teller said, and an angel was on my shoulder.'

'Mia!' It was Lori's voice coming ever closer, screaming in fear.

'I think she may've been hit,' Jet yelled. 'She sounds delirious. Where's Bear? For God's sake! Someone find Bear.'

'I'm here,' Bear said, running from the church. 'Are you okay, Jet?'

'Don't worry about me. Take care of Mia.'

'I'm fine. I'm not delirious. Honestly. I'll probably have a couple of bruises where the bits of masonry bounced up and hit me, but there's no blood. Look. No cuts. What about you, Jet?'

He looked deep into her eyes. 'I'm fine, Mia. Thanks to you.'

'What happened?' Franklin said. 'How did the statue fall?'

Tom came running from the church. 'What happened? Oh good heavens. An angel has fallen from its corbel. I've been warning the diocese something like this might happen. The church is in need of repair but I didn't foresee it happening quite so soon. Is anyone hurt?'

'No one's hurt, Tom,' Jet said. 'Mia just saved my life. If she hadn't done what she did, that angel would be on top of me right now.'

'I saw it wobble for a second or two before it fell,' Mia said.

'Then it's a miracle,' said Tom.

'It may be a miracle,' Jet replied, 'but I'm not so sure it was an accident.'

'We should call the police,' Lori said.

'What for?' Tom demanded. 'It was an accident, I can assure you. The police won't find anything but crumbling stone up there. I'll get someone to clear up this mess but I think it would be wise if everyone made their way out of the garden now.'

'Then let's not let it ruin Hettie's wedding,' Mia said. 'And I for one could do with a very large drink. We're okay, Mum.'

'Make that two,' Jet said, glaring at Tom before wrapping his arm around Mia. 'Are you really sure you're okay?'

'Absolutely.'

Lori didn't look convinced and nor did Jet but Mia smiled. 'Honestly, I'm fine. Come on. Let's go and celebrate with Hettie and Fred.'

A little reluctantly, Lori and Franklin walked ahead of Mia and Jet.

Mia glanced up at Jet and whispered: 'Did you mean what you said about it not being an accident?'

Jet looked at her and shook his head. 'I don't know. Perhaps it was. Those stones are centuries old, and Tom's right about the church needing repairs. Mattie paid for the bells to be restored, several years ago and I think Tom was hoping that she had left some money to the church in her will.'

'She did. Originally.'

He stopped and turned her to face him. 'How do you know that?'

Lori and Franklin stopped too.

'It's okay, Mum. You go ahead.'

Lori seemed unsure but Mia beamed at her and winked, trying to convey that she'd like a word alone with Jet, and after a second, Lori nodded and she and Franklin continued towards the pub.

Mia smiled up at Jet. 'I've been reading her diaries. And I can't be sure, because I still haven't finished, but I think there may've been something between her and Grace. Grace Tyburn. I'm not sure if it was romantic, or simply a very close friendship but the way she writes about her, it's clear Grace meant a lot. Mattie said that she was planning to leave Grace "well provided for" although as Grace wasn't that much younger than Mattie, and probably wouldn't be around for many more years, that might not have been a lot. But she would've got it before she did die, and as Tom's her only living relative, and he no doubt, inherited Grace's estate, he would've got Mattie's money too.'

'You said, "Originally". Does that mean she changed her mind? Or do you think that's what's in the codicil?'

'She changed her mind. She hadn't made the codicil at the time. Just a will. But it doesn't say who she left the rest to. She'd been watching me for a while, so possibly me but it doesn't say. Anyway, something happened and she made a new will. She says that Grace is no longer in it but that she's taken steps to make sure Grace will have enough money to last her lifetime. I don't know what that means, because she doesn't elaborate. But Mattie also had other plans. A plan for two people, in fact. And I don't want you to get angry,

351

especially as it feels really nice to have your arm around me again. No. Don't pull away, Jet.'

He grinned. 'I wasn't going to. I was going to put my other arm around you as we're standing face to face.'

'I like the sound of that. Go on then.'

He did and he smiled down at her. 'You were asking me not to get angry.'

'What? Oh yes. The plan.' She took a deep breath and placed her hands on the front of his jacket. 'Mattie didn't mention leaving you anything but you definitely meant a lot to her too. And she says that what you need is to fall in love. To find someone you can really care about.'

He stiffened and the smile faded.

Mia curled her fingers around the edges of his jacket. 'And she says that she feels you and I should meet. Don't be mad.'

He stared at her. 'I'm not. So far. What else does she say?'

'That she's going to have to find a way to make that happen. I know this sounds ridiculous, but I think that's what the condition for me to inherit is all about. She put the term of a year in her will to make me stay here, so that you and I could get to know one another.'

He gave a burst of laughter. 'Did she know how annoying you are?'

Mia nodded. 'She knew. She'd been watching me, remember. She also knew what a stubborn, pig-headed man you are, but she still thought we might get on. She even thought we might like one another.'

'Well, it shows she wasn't always right then, doesn't it?' He grinned.

'I'm amazed just how wrong she could be.' Mia grinned up at him.

'Did she also say that she thought I'd find you almost completely irresistible?'

'Almost? No. She said that you'd constantly walk away and drive me nuts and make me so cross that if I'd known that angel was so loose I'd have pushed it on top of you myself.'

'It's a good thing we've got a year. I suppose there's a slight chance we might like one another by the end of that.'

'I don't know. I think it's touch and go.'

His grin widened. 'I'd like to go and touch right now.'

'Really? Are you saying what I think you're saying?'

'I don't know what I'm saying. When I saw you walk down that aisle towards me, I …' He suddenly became serious. 'I don't know, Mia. I've never had a relationship. A real relationship. I don't know how to. I don't know if I can. I still can't promise you anything. I don't know if what I feel will last. I don't even know what it is I do feel. All I know is that I can't seem to get you out of my head. And that's never happened to me before. Are you honestly willing to take a chance on me? To take that risk? This might end as quickly as it started.'

'It might. But then again …' She shrugged. 'It might not. And yes. I'm willing to take that chance. I've told you more than once I am. You're the one who keeps walking away.'

'Because I can't bear the thought of hurting you. Of doing to you, what my dad did to my mum.'

'Then stop thinking you will. You're not your dad, Jet. You're you.'

They stared into each other's eyes for several minutes until Mia gave a little cough.

'Ahem. For someone with your reputation with women, Jet, I hate to have to say this. But now would be a pretty good time to kiss me, you know. If you want to that is. And if you say you don't, you're dead.'

'I want to,' he said.

And he did.

For some considerable time.

It was only when some other wedding guests walked past and one said, 'Get a room,' and laughed and cheered, that he stopped.

'That's not a bad idea,' Mia said.

'But we've got a wedding reception to go to. There's plenty of time for that.'

She tutted and he laughed.

'Come on then.' She grabbed his hand but he let it go and kept his arm around her instead.

'I'm still feeling dizzy from my brush with death. I need to use you for support.'

'I'm feeling dizzy from that kiss, but once again, it had no effect on you.'

He raised his brows and looked at her. 'You know that's not true, so don't pretend otherwise.'

She grinned at him. 'Then let's go back to my place.'

'That should be my line. I'm sorry, Mia, but I'm not that sort of man.' He laughed.

'Yeah, right. Pillock.'

'Come and dance with me,' he said, pulling her into the pub and onto the dance area where Ella and Gill and Lori and Franklin already were.

And as Mia danced with Jet, she realised that she was having the best time she had ever had. She laughed with Jet. She danced with Jet. Jet held her in his arms in front of everyone in the village.

And later, much, much later, he walked her home to Sunbeam Cottage, with Ella and Gill walking in front of them. He kissed her goodnight on the doorstep. Several times.

But the bloody annoying man would absolutely not come in and spend the night.

'Are you coming in?'

'No, Mia. And not because I don't want to. And not because I think it'll be a mistake. I'm not coming in because that's what I'd normally do with a woman I want to take to bed.'

'And your point is?'

He grinned. 'My point is, I don't want this to be like any other time. I don't want to do what I normally would. I want to take this slowly. To go out on a date with you. A proper date. To take our time. Can you understand that? This is a major step for me and I want to be sure I can handle it before we sleep together.'

'I understand. I think. But I also think there's a very strong possibility I'll die of frustration. I've never wanted anyone as much as I want you.'

'Snap. But I still want to do things differently.'

'Okay. Then you'd better get lost and let me go and take a cold shower right now.'

He laughed. 'I'm going to do the same.'

She leant into him and ran her hand down the front of his shirt, beneath his unbuttoned waistcoat. 'We could shower together. Save water. Be good to the environment, and all that.'

He sucked in his breath. 'I'm going home. Good night.' He eased her away from him and then pulled her back into his arms and kissed her again. 'God, Mia, Mattie Ward has got a lot to answer for. Right. I'm going. Good night.' And this time he stepped away from her and smiled. 'Lock the door behind me. Pleasant dreams.' Then he was gone. She waited for a moment to see if he'd come back, but he didn't. She closed the door, locked it and went upstairs to bed.

Chapter Nineteen

Ella couldn't believe that Jet and Mia had finally got together. But then again, Mia could hardly believe it herself. When she first woke up, she thought it might have been a wonderful dream and nothing more. But when her landline rang at seven-thirty and Jet asked her how she'd slept, she thought her heart would burst with happiness.

'Oh, I didn't sleep. Tom popped round for a night cap and well, you know.'

He didn't laugh. He didn't make a sound. She wasn't even sure he was breathing.

'That was a joke, Jet. A joke. Too soon?'

Jet let out a long sigh before he laughed. 'Much too soon. I'm new to this, I told you. Self-doubt and anxiety are already creeping in.'

'God, Jet. I understand your doubts about having a relationship. But please don't have doubts about how I feel. If Ryan Gosling walked in here right now, I'd tell him I wasn't interested. And that's a big deal, believe me.'

'Duly noted. What are you doing today?'

'Other than reading the diaries, no plans in particular. You?'

'Doing farm stuff. I'd explain but you'd die of boredom. Which is another thing we need to think about if this is going anywhere.'

She sat bolt upright. 'Oh?'

'You're allergic to animals and all things farm.'

'True. But you're allergic to marriage and all things relationships, so we're equal on that front.'

'That's true. Okay. I've got rugby stuff I need to do tonight. We're still trying to find a replacement for Justin and we've missed several training sessions since the season started. If we don't get sorted soon, we won't be playing any matches. Tomorrow is choir practice. Are you going?'

'Sorry. I fell asleep when you mentioned rugby. Only joking. I want to hear about it. Er. I really do want to finish reading these diaries though, so I'm giving choir practice a miss again. And perhaps everyone should unless they want an angel landing on their head.'

'Good point. I'll speak to Tom and see what's happening. Okay. Wednesday's Halloween. You've got to come to that. We all dress up and there's a competition in the pub for the best costume. Let's make that our first date night, shall we?' he said, laughing.

'You really know how to impress a girl, Jet. Casanova could've learnt a lot from you.'

'I'll take you to all the best places.'

'I just want you to take me, Jet. But I know. We're doing things differently. Where do I get a costume for Halloween?'

'There's a hire place in Little Whitingdale. I'll give you the directions.'

'Great. I'll rope in Ella and Mum and Gill too.'

'Gill? Does he play rugby, do you know?'

'Goodbye Jet. Go and do farm stuff.'

He laughed. 'Goodbye, Mia. Find out who gets the dosh if you don't make it to the end of the year.'

'Oh, I'll make it, Jet. You can count on that. I'll still be here long after the bell chimes on that date.'

'I hope so, Mia. I really do. And I never thought I'd hear myself saying that I'd like a girl to stick around.'

'Stick around's a start. But I'm telling you, Jet. I'm in this for the long haul. And don't you dare get all paranoid and panicky and all woe is me and run away, because Mattie had plans for us and I think we owe it to her to try.'

'Of course. I'm only doing this for Mattie.'

Mia laughed. 'You tell yourself that, Jet. But we both know we're doing this for us. Now go and feed those cows and milk those chickens. Or is that the other way around?'

'Nope. Chicken milk and cow's eggs are this farm's specialities. And the occasional slice of human, too, of course. Bye Mia.'

'Bye Jet.'

She fell back on the bed and kicked her legs up in the air and swung her arms around, laughing and screaming. She rolled over and back again, got up and jumped up and down on the bed.

She knew she was right about him. She just knew it. He still might not fully realise it, but Jet Cross was well on his way to being in love. And she was the lucky woman he was falling in love with.

'Ella!' she yelled, leaping off the bed and rushing to Ella's room. 'We need to hire a fancy-dress costume for Halloween. Oh sorry Gill. I forgot you'd be here.'

Gill shot bolt upright but Ella groaned and turned over. 'What?' She glanced at the clock. 'It's just gone seven-thirty, Mia. We didn't get in till one. Go and read a diary or something. Call me in two hours. If this is what you dating Jet Cross is going to be like, I'm moving out.'

'Yeah, yeah. Like that's going to happen.'

Chapter Twenty

Mia read until Ella and Gill got up, and after breakfast they met up with Lori and went to the shop to get their Halloween costumes. When Jet had emailed her the address, he told her he was going as Frankenstein, so Ella said Mia should go as his bride.

'If you're really dating him then you may as well push it to the limits now. If he runs, he probably would've anyway. If he stays, you never know. Miracles do happen. And you don't even have to live together. You can stay at Sunbeam Cottage. He can live at his farm. You can simply be together without actually being together.'

'He is right about that,' Mia said. 'I'm not exactly farmer's wife material, am I?'

'Hey. You overcame your fear of water. You can handle a few chickens and cows. Besides, you won't have to handle them. He will. And he's got Franklin and also Pete. You can stay indoors and bake pies, or whatever farmer's wives do.'

'Okay. Frankenstein's bride it is. What about you?'

'We're going as characters from The Rocky Horror Show. That's always popular with the crowds.'

'And you, Mum?'

'Franklin wants us both to go as Mummies. Don't ask me why. He says he's got a thing about Mummies. And if either of you two, cracks a joke about that's why he likes me so much because he loves ancient Mummies, I'll bring a plague of locust down on you before you can say another word.'

'It's not very flattering or sexy though, is it?' Ella said. 'At least Mia and I can wear low cut dresses or something.'

'Ah, but Franklin says when we get home, we'll slowly unwrap one another. That sounds like fun.'

'It sounds time consuming. He's a big guy. That means lots of bandages. But hey, you go with it, Lori.'

When they got home, Mia went back to reading the diaries.

'You'll never guess why Mattie changed her will,' she said that night as she was about to read the next one to Ella and Gill. 'I told you she was leaving money to provide for Grace. Well, it seems that Grace started being a bit cool towards Mattie. Grace was worried about what people might think of their relationship, apparently. Mattie still doesn't spell out what their relationship was. It seems some things she still won't reveal, not even in her own diary. Anyway, she also says that Grace clearly has a problem, but she doesn't say what. She does say that instead of leaving Grace money in her will, she's making arrangements to ensure Grace has money right away. Enough to last her for the rest of her life. But she also says that they're not telling Tom about this arrangement. She says Tom's now being extra friendly but that she's never really liked him. She paid for the restoration of the bells because she loved the bells, and also because it was what Grace wanted. But Mattie thinks Tom's hiding something. Which is exactly what Hettie says about him, isn't it?'

'She does,' Ella said. 'Does Mattie go on to say what it is?'

'She says she's convinced he's been in the cottage. And listen to this. That he used the key she gave to Grace. That means there might be another key and Tom might have it. And that means, Tom may've been the one who I heard on the stairs.'

'That's a bit of a leap,' Gill said. 'If Mattie and Grace's whatever it was had cooled off, surely Mattie would've asked for her key back.'

'True. But Tom may've already got another one cut. She says things have been moved and at first, she thought Hettie had moved them but it was often on days when Hettie hadn't been round. She thinks he's been looking for her will. She'd told

Grace about the proposed legacy. He might've wanted to see how much. He didn't find it because Mattie had hidden it, but after that he kept saying how much repairs would be for the church and how valued her previous contribution had been. Blah, blah. Basically, he's trying to guilt trip her into paying out more. She decides to make sure Tom won't see a penny of her money. It's for a good cause but she says she thinks he may be skimming money from the church.'

Ella gasped. 'She thinks Tom's a crook?'

'It seems so. And that got me thinking. Tom was the one who saved me at Rainbow's End, but he was also the one who, along with Bear, led me to believe Jet would be there. And he's always lurking, isn't he? And when that stone fell, he came from the church. But so did Bear. Oh I don't know. I just know Mattie didn't trust him. Hettie doesn't and nor do I. And let's not forget all those things he told me about Jet in an attempt to put me off. What if he still thinks he may inherit? That Mattie left him or the church the money in the codicil? He could easily be the one who put the frog and flowers on the doorstep, and the card.'

'Then I think we had all better keep a close eye on the vicar,' Gill said.

By Tuesday, Mia was up to 2016.

'You'll never believe this,' Mia said after dinner that night as she read the last section of the diary. 'Mattie talked a lot about Jet in each diary since she'd met him and his mum. She'd written about how much she liked him. She'd mentioned the loan and his insistence on repaying every penny. She'd given details over the years about his love for his mum and how devastated he was by her death. It was pretty clear Mattie was a little bit in love with Jet herself. But one sentence actually says, "if I were many, many years younger, I'd be head over heels in love with Jet. He reminds me of Will. He reminds me of the power of love." Isn't that amazing? And get this. She also says she's sure there's something going on between Tom and Alexia. Can you believe that? She doesn't say what, as yet, but she says she's going to keep a closer eye on both of them. But Alexia told us she and Tom have never dated.'

'Bloody Nora,' Ella said. 'Now there's got to be a vicar and tart joke somewhere in that.'

By Wednesday, Mia had raced through 2017 and was ready to open 2018; this year's diary and one that would be very short because Mattie died in March. The odd thing was, this diary wasn't just tied in the bundle; this diary had its own ribbon tied around it and up and over the top and when Mia finally unbound the ribbon and let the pages fall open, two envelopes fell out. One was addressed to her and said, "Mia, please read this note first". The other said, "Mia read the other note before this. This is my last will and testament. It also contains my codicil". Mia dropped the diary and ran downstairs, calling for Ella and Gill and telephoning her mum.

'I've got the will and codicil, Mum. I can find out who inherits if I leave. Please come round. I want you to be here when I read it, but hurry because I'm so excited I can't wait long.'

'I'm on my way, darling.'

'What's up?' Ella said, coming in from the garden a few minutes later. 'We could hear you yelling all the way down to the beach. We were walking on the sand, making the most of the first truly sunny day this week. Okay. That's not true. We were already back in the garden but anyway, why the shouting?'

Mia waved the two envelopes. 'Another note to me. And Mattie's will and codicil. I'm waiting for Mum to get here and then I'm going to read it.'

'I'll leave you then,' Gill said.

Mia hesitated for one second. 'No don't. You know as much about Mattie as we do. And I'm pretty sure it won't be you who inherits, so I'm happy for you to hear it. But everyone must promise not to say a word once we find out who it is.'

'Promise,' Ella and Gill both said.

'I'm here, darling.' Lori ran along the hall. 'I think I broke the speed limit getting here but anyway.'

'I'll make coffee,' Ella said. 'Start reading. I'm listening.'

Mia opened the note and read it. 'It says the usual greeting bit then, "I wanted you to live in Little Pondale, you'll know that and you'll know why if you've read my diaries. I hope you have. And I hope in the order I told you to. I'm old and frail now and I'm living on borrowed time. I've had an exciting life. I've known incredible pain both physical and emotional and I've known wondrous love and the power to heal hearts and wounds such love can have. I would only change one thing. And that is, I would have married Will. I should have married him. I don't want you to tell him this but I hope you've told him what I asked in my previous note to you. I have no way of knowing how long you've been in the cottage as you're reading this. I'm hoping it's a few months but it might be longer. What I'm really hoping is that you have fallen in love. And you'll know who with if you've read my diaries. I may be old but I'm still a good judge of character. I know what people really want and I know how to get it for them. You want someone to love with all your heart and soul. I want Jet to be that man. And hopefully, so do you. Because Jet wants a woman who will love him like that. Jet needs a woman to love him like that. And more importantly, Jet will love a woman like that with all his heart and soul and every fibre of his being. He plays the part of a jack-the-lad, but Jet is a prince of men. I know you could be that woman, Mia. I know it in my soul. And if I had the slightest doubt, someone else has told me this is what will happen. You may laugh at this. I don't know. But every year at the village

Fête, a fortune-teller in a crimson tent amazes people with her predictions."'

'The fortune-teller!' Ella exclaimed.

'Good heavens,' Lori said.

Mia nodded. 'She seems to be in all our lives. Anyway, "I visited her several years ago, shortly after I began watching you. I wrote about it in my diary but I erased it because I didn't want you to know of it until you reached this final diary. She told me I was keeping a very close eye on someone, a young woman of my bloodline. That there was a young man with a damaged heart, not physically but emotionally and that I cared deeply for him. That the way to mend his heart and mine, and to make peace with my own past was to bring the woman and the man together. That Fate would take its course, but it needed time. The woman needed an offer she couldn't refuse. The man needed to help her overcome a fear as she would help him overcome his. You will find a way, the fortune-teller told me. You will. Your will. Money is a carrot, she said. That's when I knew. I had to change my will and add a codicil. That's when I started making plans. You may find it hard to believe that a person like me would take notice of a fortune-teller's words, but I have seen her predictions come true, year after year. I believe in Destiny and Fate and the mystical power of things we don't fully understand. I believe what she told me, will come true. Now you can open my will and the codicil. Be happy Mia. Choose Love, no matter how difficult things may seem. True Love can overcome anything." And it's signed the same as before.'

'I may be wrong,' Ella said, grinning, 'but I get the feeling Mattie wants you and Jet to be together.'

Lori and Gill laughed and Mia smiled. 'She's not the only one. Okay. Now let's open the will.'

'Forget the will, darling. You know what that says. You're here in the cottage and you have to stay a year. Read the codicil.'

'You're right, Mum.' Mia opened the envelope and removed the will and then the codicil which was in another envelope inside that one. 'Okay. This is a codicil to the last will, blah, blah. That's all legal stuff. Oh. My. God.' She glanced up at her mum and then Ella before she burst out laughing. 'This you won't believe. It says, "I leave my entire estate..." More legal jargon, then "To Mia Ward, my great-niece, regardless of whether or not she stays the year in Sunbeam Cottage, as stated in my will. She may dispose of Sunbeam Cottage and all my chattels and estate as she sees fit and ..." More legal jargon. So basically, this means that no matter what, I get it all. Every bit of it, whether I stay or whether I go. It seems the will was just a way of getting me to come here, stay, meet Jet and hopefully fall in love. And the codicil was meant to make me think someone else would inherit if I didn't stay. What a bizarre and crazy thing to do!'

'The woman was a nutter,' Ella said, laughing.

Lori laughed too. 'It may be bizarre, darling but it worked, didn't it? You came, you saw, you fell in love, to misquote Julius Caesar. You're going to stay and, unless Jet is a complete idiot, which I don't believe he is, you and he are going to be together. Mattie got what she wanted. And so have you and so has Jet. That doesn't sound crazy to me. It sounds like great-aunt Matilda turned out to be your fairy godmother. And not just yours. Jet's too.'

'Bloody Nora,' Ella said. 'When you put it like that, I suppose you're right. The woman was a genius. And so was that fortune-teller, because she put the idea into Mattie's head.'

Gill smiled. 'It's Destiny. One can't fight Destiny.'

Ella glanced at Mia, grinned and looked at Gill. 'Then perhaps now would be a good time to tell you what that very same fortune-teller told me.'

'Why do I get the feeling that this has something to do with me?' Gill queried.

'Because you're a very clever man,' Ella said. 'Oh, but before I tell you, there's somewhere we women need to go. Come on you two. We've got to get to Rainbow's End.'

'Rainbow's End?' Mia said. 'Oh. The cave. Yes. Come on, Mum.'

'Er? Cave?' Gill asked as Mia, Ella and Lori ran along the hall. 'What cave?'

'See you later,' Ella shouted.

They ran outside, got into Lori's car and drove to the foot of Frog Hill, then ran to Rainbow's End. The tide was out but they had no idea if it was coming in or going out because they'd forgotten to check the tide time tables.

'It doesn't matter,' Lori said. 'We won't be long.'

They found the cave after a few minutes. Inside, it had the same colouration as Rainbow's End and shafts of afternoon sunlight cast a pathway of red, amber and gold before them.

'Let's be quick,' Mia said. 'As beautiful as this cave is, I don't want to get stuck in here and I'm sure the sea is already closer than it was when we arrived. At least it's calm today.'

'I'll go first,' said Ella. She called out Gill's name and a second later, his name came back, reverberating around the cave walls. 'Wow! That was incredible.'

'It's an echo, Ella. It has to come back,' Mia pointed out, laughing.

Lori called out Franklin's name, and again, his name came back.

'There doesn't seem much point,' Mia said, but she called out Jet's name, keeping her fingers crossed behind her back, and thankfully, his name came back.

'Well, this was a wasted journey,' Lori said. 'I suppose we knew it would happen. I'm not sure why we bothered.'

Then Ella shouted out Justin's name, and they were met with stony silence.

'Spooky,' Ella said.

So Mia called out Garrick's name, and again, complete silence, but when she called out Jet's again, right after, his came back, even louder than the first time, as if the cave were reinforcing it.

'I stand corrected,' Lori said. 'Now I think we should get out of here.'

'I'm just going to take a photo of us.' Ella pulled out her phone, clicked the camera and stuffed her phone back in the pocket of her jeans.

As they hurried out of the cave, Ella slipped on a rock and almost fell but she managed to regain her balance by reaching out for the cave wall and steadying herself. They left the beach, got back in the car and drove towards Sunbeam Cottage, all debating how and why some of the names came back and yet some didn't. But they couldn't come up with any answers.

'Stop!' Ella yelled. 'I can't find my phone. It must've fallen from my pocket when I slipped.'

Lori turned the car around and they headed back towards the beach. As they got out and dashed down the beach and across the sand towards the mouth of the cave, they saw Alexia going in.

'Shush,' Ella said. 'Let's creep in and see whose name Alexia calls out.'

'That's not nice,' Mia whispered. 'But okay.'

They quickly and quietly made their way in, but Mia gave a little gasp when she heard the name Alexia called out. It was Jet's. To Mia's relief, the name didn't come back. Then Alexia called out a second name. Tom Tyburn. But that name didn't come back either.

'Stupid bloody cave!' Alexia hissed, storming towards Mia, Ella and Lori and gasping in surprise when she saw them.

'Oh! Hello Alexia,' Ella said. 'Fancy meeting you here. Hettie told us to come and call out the name of someone we like. Have you done it? Does it work?'

'How long have you been here?' Alexia glared at each of them in turn.

'We just arrived one second ago,' Mia lied.

'So you didn't hear anything?' Alexia looked worried.

'Not a thing,' Lori said.

'Well it doesn't work and it never bloody well has. So I wouldn't bother if I were you.' Alexia walked past, almost knocking Mia over in her haste, but Lori and Ella steadied her.

'She was happy to see us,' Ella said, sarcastically. 'I'm glad it didn't work for her. Now where's my phone?'

'But did you hear the names she called?' Mia said. 'First Jet's and then Tom's. What does that mean?'

'That she doesn't stand a chance of getting either. Jet loves you. And so does Tom. Ah! There's my phone.' Ella bent down and grabbed it from beside the rock on which she'd slipped, just as the first gentle wave lapped at the entrance to the cave. 'And it's time we got out of here.'

Chapter Twenty-One

'You're my bride?' Jet said, a look of something close to fear etched across his face when Mia opened the door to him that evening.

She smiled. 'Only for tonight, don't panic. You're a very handsome Frankenstein.'

'And you look beautiful. But then you always do.'

'Thank you. Ella and Gill will catch us up.' She stepped outside and closed the door behind her. 'I've got something to tell you.'

'Oh? Should I be worried?'

Mia laughed. 'No. Quite the contrary.'

'Shall we walk and talk?' He held out his hand and she took it. 'Come on then. Don't keep me in suspense.'

They ambled down the drive.

'I'm up to the very last diary. I haven't read it yet but there's only a couple of months in it so I'll read it tomorrow. But I have read the codicil to Mattie's will. She left it for me with the final diary and another note. That was one of the reasons she wanted me to read the diaries in order. So that I wouldn't find the codicil until I'd got to know her through her diaries.'

He raised his brows and then smiled. 'Wow! And that makes sense. So now you've nearly finished them, what are you going to do? You said at Hettie's reception that you, Ella and Gill are going to write a novel. Is that still the plan?' They left the drive and turned onto Lily Pond Lane.

'Yes. Gill's also writing the biography of his grandad and he's including Mattie's story. I'd like people to know about her life and how brave she was, and so utterly incredible. The novel will also include some aspects of her life, but through a fictional character. It should be fun.'

'And the so-called hero who she and her partner keep rescuing, is he still going to be called Jet?'

'Unless you have any objections, yes. Jet's a lovely name.'

'I've no objections. And you did rescue me the other day, so I suppose that's what they call art imitating life, or the other way around.'

She glanced up at him. 'You haven't asked about the codicil.'

He shrugged. 'Is it important? You're going to stay, aren't you, so it doesn't matter who is named in it. Unless it gives a clue as to who may want you to leave?' He met her look and held it. 'Does it?'

'No. And yes, I'm definitely going to stay. But I don't have to. The whole thing was a ploy to get me here and make me stay. I told you the other day that she thought we might get on. Well, it seems she got the idea from the fortune-teller.'

'The fortune-teller? The one at the Fête?' He grinned at her.

Mia nodded. 'The very same. Mattie was going to change her will anyway but the fortune-teller told her that there was a man whose heart needed to be healed and a woman who was looking for her True Love. And that Mattie could bring the two together and it would help her heal her own past, or something like that. I'll show you the note and you can see exactly what she said.'

'And those two people are you and me?'

'Yes. Mattie was so convinced of it that she put the condition in her will to make me come and make me stay. She was certain we would fall in love. But the thing is. I get it all, whether I stay or not. Are you cross? Do you feel manipulated? I hope you don't because although it was a crazy thing to do, she was doing what she thought was best for us.'

He shook his head and laughed. 'I'm not cross. It seems Mattie knew us both better than we know ourselves.'

'It seems she did. But that's what she was so good at. Mattie could read a person inside out and she rarely got it wrong. And she could manipulate people to get what she wanted. She wanted us to be together.'

He smiled. 'Then it looks as if she's accomplished her final mission, doesn't it?'

Mia nodded and smiled up at him. 'And we don't have to live together or anything. I have the cottage, you have your farm.'

He stopped abruptly. 'Hold on. Are you saying we should live our lives together but apart?'

'It's the perfect compromise. You always said you don't want marriage, or kids, or a woman moving in with you.'

'And you said people can change if they want to. I haven't been able to stop thinking about that angel falling, or that you nearly got sliced up by the harvester. I've been thinking how I would feel if anything happened to you, or to me, and that's made me see the light. I can't make any promises but one thing I do know for sure. I want to change, Mia. I want to be in love. No. I'm already in love, I think. I've never been in love before, but I've never felt like this and I'm pretty sure it's love. I could live without you. But I don't want to live without you. I've never told any woman I loved her. Apart from my mum. But that was different.' He grinned.

'I know, Jet. I understand. Saying the words won't be easy for you.'

'Actually. I think it will.' He became serious as he looked her in the eyes. 'I love you, Mia.' He sighed deeply as if saying that had been a huge relief.

She beamed up at him. 'And I love you, Jet. I have said that to someone else. But this time it's different. This time I know, without a shadow of a doubt, that you're The One, Jet Cross. And there will never be another. So you'd better start getting used to the idea. It's a pity you didn't go into that fortune-teller's tent that day. It would've been interesting to see what predictions she had for you.'

'There's always next year.' He smiled. 'Although I don't think I need to be told what my future has in store.'

'Happiness and joy beyond my wildest dreams is what she told me I'd have. If I chose Love wisely. So as I've chosen you, I'd say you'll have that too.'

'I'm pretty sure I already have.'

The moon was on the wane and a few puffs of clouds drifted across the sky as he bent his head to kiss her in the otherwise silence of the evening, but a second before their lips met, a high-pitched screeching shattered their tranquillity.

'Are those police sirens?' Mia said.

Jet turned. 'Yes. And they're pulling up outside the church.'

'Oh God. Perhaps there's been another accident.'

'I hope not.' He took her hand again and they hurried towards Tom's cottage, the sirens competing with the deafening music emanating from the pub.

'Wait a minute.' Mia couldn't believe her eyes. 'Is that Tom the police are bringing out? Is he in handcuffs or am I imagining it?'

'You're not imagining it. What the hell's happened? There's Bear. Perhaps he'll know. Bear!' Jet called and waved to him a couple of times, and he finally saw them and nodded his head in acknowledgment. 'What's going on?'

Bear scratched his head as they reached his side. 'You're probably not going to believe this, or perhaps you will. Craig, a friend of mine from Little Whitingdale did the video of Hettie's wedding, and caught on camera, that angel that almost fell on you. He hadn't played it all back until today and when he did, part of the video was of the belfry and the steeple. Hettie had asked him to try to film and record the Angel Bell while it was ringing. In one corner of the video, you can see there's someone on the roof, tampering with the carved stone angel. When Craig enlarged it, it was clear that it was Tom. Craig had caught him giving the thing the final shove and then it shows the angel wobbling and smashing to the ground and you and Mia almost being hit by it. I believe that comes under attempted murder or at least intent to do grievous bodily harm.'

'Tom tried to kill me?' Jet looked stunned and Mia gasped. 'Tom? But why?'

Bear shrugged. 'That's the way it seems. Perhaps he thought with you out of the way, he stood a chance with Mia. Oh hold on. Why is Alexia dashing towards the car? What's that about? Is she trying to hit Tom?'

'Oh my God,' Mia said. 'She's trying to kiss him. Look! She's trying to wrap her arms around him.'

'Tom! Tom!' Alexia screamed, as a police officer attempted to hold her at bay. She hit him in the face and attacked the other officer who was trying to get Tom in the car.

Jet let go of Mia's hand. 'Stay here,' he said, and ran with Bear to the officers' aid.

It took all of them to get both Tom and Alexia under control and by this time, Ella and Gill had raced to Mia's side, Gill also going to help the police and Jet and Bear.

'Bloody hell,' Ella said. 'This is just like a Saturday night in London. God, sometimes I miss those days.'

Mia looked at her and blinked. 'Except it's Wednesday and even in London I don't think I've ever seen a vicar being arrested.'

'Or a barmaid coming to his rescue. Hey! This adds a whole new dimension to my vicar and tart jokes!' She grinned.

'It's not funny, Ella. Tom actually tried to kill Jet! He pushed that angel off it's corbel. A friend of Bear's got it all on video. But what I don't understand is why Alexia would risk getting arrested to try to free Tom.'

'You heard her in the cave. She called out his name.'

Mia nodded. 'Yes. But she also called out Jet's.'

'True. But it looked as if she was trying to kiss Tom just now. Perhaps something had been going on between them, just as Mattie thought it had.'

'She *was* trying to kiss him. I saw that. But that's what I don't get. I thought she was dating someone from one of the other villages. That was the last I heard.'

Ella shrugged. 'Perhaps she and Tom have been secretly dating.'

'But why keep it secret? And why pretend to date other people? And does that mean Tom wasn't really in love with me? God. This is making my head hurt.'

'Mine too. I suppose we'll eventually find out. Well, it looks as if they've got things under control.'

Mia and Ella walked forward as another police car roared down the lane towards them and Lori and Franklin, along with several others, came tumbling out of the pub. Lori waved and rushed to Mia, as Alexia was led towards the second car.

Alexia spotted Mia and glowered at her. 'This is your fault,' she hissed. 'Why wouldn't you just bloody well leave? Tom and I should've got at least half of that old bag's money.'

Jet looked furious. 'Ignore her, Mia.'

'And you can drop dead,' Alexia spat at him. 'How could you prefer that silly cow to me? How could Garrick? At least Tom had good taste. He wasn't in love with you, Mia. He was only pretending so that we could find that sodding will and codicil.'

'Get in the car, miss,' the officer said.

Alexia struggled until the officer slammed the door. The other officer she had hit, rubbed his chin.

'She's got a good right hook. I've arrested men who haven't hit me as hard as that.'

He got in the car and after a few minutes more, they drove off.

'Did she say Tom was pretending to be in love with you?' Ella asked. 'He's a bloody good actor, if that's the case. He certainly had me convinced.'

Mia nodded. 'Me too. Although I still don't know what all that was about. Did they think they were named in the codicil?'

'That's what it sounded like,' Lori said, wrapping her arm around Mia until Jet came back and joined them.

'Well. That was a bit of a surprise,' he said, taking her hand and holding it tight. 'Alexia and Tom? Who would've guessed that?'

'Mattie did,' Mia said, as Toby Bywater came towards them, head bowed. The man looked mortified.

'What can I say?' Toby said, shrugging his shoulders and shaking his head. 'Mum, Dad and I had no idea. I swear we didn't. Not until Alexia ran out screaming that the police were taking away the man she loved. Dad tried to stop her and that's when it came out. She's been secretly dating Tom for months, but they both pretended to be interested in other people to divert suspicion from them. She called us stupid and said she had to get out of this dump. And that once they got Mattie's money, they would be off. It seems she was the one who left you those warnings, Mia.'

'And Tom was the one who broke into my cottage, I suspect. He was looking for the will and codicil.'

'And he was the one who pushed the stone angel,' Bear said. 'And I presume, he also tampered with your brakes, Jet.'

'But why? I had nothing to do with the will?'

Toby sighed. 'I suppose because it was pretty clear to everyone except you, that you fell for Mia almost immediately. And it was also pretty obvious that she had fallen for you. I don't know, I'm only guessing, but I do know that Alexia was still bitter at being dumped by you over two years ago, and then, even though she was secretly with Tom, she dated Garrick and he dumped her for Mia. Tom wanted you out of the way, Jet, because he knew Mia would stay if you asked her to. I think they were both starting to get desperate and things took a more serious turn.'

'Then why not simply do away with me?' Mia queried.

'They're both unhinged,' Ella said. 'Nutters do nutty things. There doesn't need to be a reason and it doesn't have to make sense. Perhaps killing you off would bring too much suspicion on Tom, if he had been named in the codicil, as he obviously assumed he had.'

'And I thought Alexia was nice.' Mia shook her head. 'I thought we could be friends.'

'Imagine how we feel,' Toby said. 'We had no idea my sister was like this and we've lived with her all her life. We knew she had a temper, and reacted badly if things didn't go her way, but we never, for even a second, suspected anything like this. We're really sorry, Mia. And you, Jet. We hope you won't tar us with the same brush. Mum's in a right state and Dad's trying to put on a brave face, but this is the worst thing to happen in our family, ever. I'm not sure what we'll do. Mum thought the sun shone out of Alexia. And I can't believe I didn't know my own sister. It's so unreal. We're all in a state of shock. But I felt I had to come and talk to you about it. To apologise for all of us.'

Mia sighed softly. 'It's true what you said, Mum. You can be with someone all your life and never really know them. And you can be with someone for a day and know them inside out and up and down and backwards. I won't hold any of this against you, Freda and Alec, Toby. It's not your fault. But I think I need a drink.'

'Under the circumstances,' Toby said. 'The drinks are on the house for all of you tonight. It won't make up for what Alexia did, but at least it'll help with the shock.'

'And all for nothing,' Mia said. 'I found the codicil and I get everything whether I stay or go. Tom wasn't left a penny.'

Toby blinked. 'Wow! That's great. You deserve it after this. Um. Did you know that Mattie also owned Grace's cottage?'

'What?' Mia blinked in disbelief. 'Grace Tyburn? Tom's gran?' She looked at Jet, who shook his head, and then at her mum and Ella. 'I had no idea. The solicitor told me she owned other assets, but he wouldn't say what until I inherit at the end of the year. Although, of course, once I show him the codicil and he opens his copy, I'll get it all now, I suppose. But no. I didn't know. Are you sure?'

Toby nodded. 'That's what made Tom even more angry, I suppose. And Alexia. They obviously thought Tom would inherit Corner Cottage after Grace died, but when she did, that's when Tom found out that Mattie had bought the cottage from Grace several years ago so that Grace would have plenty of cash to live on. There was hardly anything left by the time Grace died.' He shook his head. 'It seems Grace had an addiction for online gambling and blew almost all her money on that.'

'Wow!' Mia said. 'So that's what Mattie meant. She said she was making sure Grace had money. She didn't say she was buying the cottage.'

Toby shrugged. 'Come on. I'll get you those drinks.'

'Hold on,' Jet whispered, squeezing Mia's hand. 'I'd like a word.'

Ella, Lori and the others smiled and left them to it when Mia nodded.

'Please don't tell me you're having second thoughts,' Mia said.

He grinned. 'Absolutely not. I just don't understand how everyone could see how we felt about each other but we couldn't.'

'I could, Jet. You were the only one who couldn't. But only because you didn't want to.'

'Well, I want to now. And I want to ask you something.'

'Go on.'

'You keep saying that people can change. You, your mum, Fiona, me. Well, if that's true, and even I now believe it is, does that mean you might be able to change the way you feel about animals and farms?'

She smiled up at him. 'With some time and effort, yes. And a bit of one to one training and hands-on experience. I would say I'll have it cracked in a year or two.'

He swallowed. 'A year or two? As long as that?'

'Says the man who doesn't believe in relationships, or a woman moving in, or marriage, or anything else like that.'

'Says the woman who can't wait to get me into bed and says she's sure that I'm The One.'

'Oh I am sure, Jet. I told you that and I meant it. But that's why there's no rush. I'm not going anywhere and neither are you, I think. I also think you're right to want to take things slow. And I think you're right to—'

He cut her short by kissing her and when he finally eased away, he smiled and looked into her eyes.

'And I've told you, you think too much. And this time, I'm not going to walk away. I'll never walk away from you again.'

She grinned at him. 'You won't? Is that a promise?'

'I won't. I promise.'

She ran her hands down the front of his torn and tattered Frankenstein shirt. 'Jet?'

'Yes, Mia?'

'Will you sleep with me tonight?'

He sighed. 'It's always about sex with you, isn't it?'

'Does that mean no?' She gave him a disappointed look.

His lips twitched before blossoming into a huge smile. 'No, Mia. That means yes. Most definitely, yes. Although I think I can guarantee we won't get much sleep.'

'I certainly hope we won't.'

'Do you still want that drink?'

She shook her head. 'There's plenty of wine and beer at home.'

'There's brandy at my home. Do you want to come home with me?'

'Jet Cross. I thought you'd never ask.'

She grabbed his shirt collars, pulled him to her and kissed him. As he returned her kiss, he picked her up, lifted her legs so that they wrapped around him and he carried her towards his new car, parked in the drive of Sunbeam Cottage.

A group of laughing children rushed from door to door, yelling, 'Trick or treat?'

Jet stopped kissing her for long enough to open the car door.

'Treat,' she said, smiling into his eyes. 'Without a doubt, if that kiss was anything to go by.'

He smiled at her and winked. 'I know a few tricks,' he said, his voice crackling with excitement and laughter.

'I know a few tricks of my own,' she replied. 'And I'm telling you now, Jet Cross. You're in for one hell of a treat. I think we both are.'

He kissed her again as he sat her in the passenger seat before dashing to his side of the car and jumping in.

'I know we are,' he said, beaming at her as he turned on the ignition.

She matched his smile, leant across and kissed him on the cheek. 'And all because of a fortune-teller and a great-aunt I never even knew I had.'

Coming soon

Christmas on Lily Pond Lane

A Note from Emily

Thank you for reading this book. A little piece of my heart goes into all of my books and when I send them on their way, I really hope they bring a smile to someone's face. If this book made you smile, or gave you a few pleasant hours of relaxation, I'd love it if you would tell your friends.

I'd be really happy if you have a minute or two to post a review. Just a line will do, and a kind review makes such a difference to my day – to any author's day. Huge thanks to those of you who do so, and for your lovely comments and support on social media. Thank you.

A writer's life can be lonely at times. Sharing a virtual cup of coffee or a glass of wine, or exchanging a few friendly words on Facebook, Twitter or Instagram is so much fun.

You might like to join my Readers' Club by signing up for my newsletter. It's absolutely free, your email address is safe and won't be shared and I won't bombard you, I promise. You can enter competitions and enjoy some giveaways. In addition to that, there's my author page on Facebook and there's also a new Facebook group. You can chat with me and with other fans and get access to my book news, snippets from my daily life, early extracts from my books and lots more besides. Details are on the 'For You' page of my website. You'll find all my contact links in the Contact section following this.

I'm working on my next book right now. Let's see where my characters take us this time. Hope to chat with you soon.

To see details of my other books, please go to the books page on my website, or scan the QR code below to see all my books on Amazon.

Contact

If you want to be the first to hear Emily's news, find out about book releases, enter competitions and gain automatic entry into her Readers' Club, go to: https://www.emilyharvale.com and subscribe to her newsletter via the 'Sign me up' box. If you love Emily's books and want to chat with her and other fans, ask to join the exclusive Emily Harvale's Readers' Club Facebook group.

Or come and say 'Hello' on Facebook, Twitter and Instagram.

Contact Emily via social media:
www.twitter.com/emilyharvale
www.facebook.com/emilyharvalewriter
www.facebook.com/emilyharvale
www.instagram.com/emilyharvale

Or by email via the website:
www.emilyharvale.com

34852208R00234

Printed in Great Britain
by Amazon